DRACO SANG BOOK 3

HUMAN HEARTS

MARY BEESLEY

MONSTER IVY
PUBLISHING

S
GRISTLECOVE
Volkar
Lake
NANSUT
ELYSIU
Vasti River
Sahara River
MITE
NE
BRANMAR
SICCUM
N
W
E
S

DRAGON'S GATE
NOGARD'S PASS
Azure Lake
SHI CASTLE
DANBE CANYON
DRACO SANG CAMP
LION'S CAMP
KIPTOS
ABADDON
EPHA
High Sea
Scorpion Sea

ONE - FOREVER A PRINCE, NEVER A KING

NOGARD

Nogard wanted rest, but the distant clash of blades, tang of blood, and cries of fear disturbed his peace.

His joints ached. His wings lay like iron sheets on his back. With effort, he peeled open a scaled eyelid on a world of ice and darkness. Hunger stirred, but he continued to ignore it.

Why must his children be so loud with their quarrels? He huffed out a long breath of annoyance, smoke swirling around him like mist.

His poisonous wind drifted south.

TWO - MISSION FAILURE

JADE

Jade tugged at her leather helmet, checking that it hid her furry, pointy ears as she slunk around the western edge of battle. She unbuckled her blood-splattered Draco Sang breastplate. The royal insignia, the top of a dragon head and a sword melded together, was painted on it in a deep purple. Her weary spine straightened as the weight lifted. As she hid the armor in the bushes, a welcome breeze cooled the sweat on her tunic.

Sword in hand, she stalked away from the battle raging on the banks of the Rugit River. The humans had fought more valiantly than she'd expected, holding the border all summer. But they would fall today. Queen Mavras's Draco Sang army was mere hours from victory.

Jade had a job to do before her war chief, Laconius, claimed this land for their queen. She jogged southeast across empty training fields toward the tents and squat buildings of the humans' war camp.

Ahead of her, two soldiers guarded the path leading toward the neat rows of tents. They squinted, studying her as she approached. Her face was *nearly* human. Dark skin ringed her eyes like heavy kohl. Her lips were purple above a pointy chin. She kept her mouth closed over sharp canine teeth. She was a jackal Draco Sang, but her face had not completed the transformation as she'd expected. No elongated nose and no fur on her cheeks. Her delicate features remained a sore spot in her pride but a boon when infiltrating Elysium. When she'd attended the enemy's party in Mitera in her silky dress and make-up, no one had questioned her. Today, it seemed, she hadn't done enough to hide her deadly aura or feral features as the two guards' expressions turned wary. Gloves covered her furry hands, and she'd buttoned her tunic up her amber neck. There was nothing she could do about the coating of gore or stink of battle. She was small for a Draco, which helped with her deception.

She strode toward the humans, exuding confidence, acting as if she belonged on this side of the line. "The Dracos are breaking through on the west side."

One of the guard's eyes widened, and his hand went white on the hilt of his sheathed sword.

"Where is Captain Titus? I'm to report to him." Her mission was to kill him.

The men's moment of uncertainly cost them everything. If they'd answered and let her pass, Jade could have continued without the burden of their lives weighing on her tired shoulders. Instead, she plunged her short sword through the leather vest covering the man's large belly and thrust upward. The second guard drew his blade, but Jade had already sent a knife at his throat. They both dropped. She held her breath as she yanked her small Dracosteel blade from the ruined neck. Again, she regretted leaving her favorite knife in Elysium. She should have retrieved it from Thirro's chest, but Ferth had left her feeling distracted and emotional. It was un-Draco-like to abandon a quality weapon. Or leave a mark alive.

Jade banished the nagging thoughts and held her breath until she was four paces away. Still, she could smell death—acid, copper, pain, and regret. She couldn't get away from the stench. These last months of battle, the rot had clung to her nostrils, clawed at her mind, and hacked at any softness in her heart. As the stink grew stronger, Jade realized she'd found the healers' building.

The humans' leader, Titus, hadn't been seen yet this morning by the Draco scouts. His lion was fighting on the front line with the other abominations, but where was the army's captain? He'd broken a leg in the last battle. Maybe he was inside with the other wounded. Jade skirted around the front, staying in the shadows as she watched a woman help a man without an arm through the open doors. His face was white as bone, his shirt red as poppies.

Jade sheathed her dirty sword. Dagger warming her palm, she slipped into the low building behind them. She hugged the wall. No one looked her way. Every cot held a groaning body, sometimes two. Healers ran from bed to bed, their faces as strained as the injured. Jade scanned the humans. She'd never seen Laconius's archenemy, but she was to look for a man with two long scars cutting through pale blue eyes. She picked up linens from a nearby cart to hide her knife as she moved toward the back. Still no Captain Titus. Or Ferth. She couldn't help but search for his face in every human she saw—and killed. She'd left him in Mitera two weeks ago. Alive and whole. And she'd left a piece of her weak heart with him.

She shook her head, trying to dislodge the vision of Ferth that night. His hair was short, accentuating his hard jawline, strong nose, and full lips. His amber eyes glowed. He'd looked at her without judgment or disgust, as he always had. As if he still lov— She cut the thought off before it could do more damage. But he'd made it clear she was still important to him.

He'd saved her life.

When she'd attacked him, he'd fought defensively, never striking to kill. Her army called him a traitor, but she'd seen the steadiness in his stance, felt the power in his words. Those words twisted through her now. *I still care about you. You will never be my enemy. I'm still me, but free.* She couldn't get his voice or his glorious human form out of her head. His hideous pink shirt had hung open in front, revealing corded muscles and stark scars. He did not hide his Draco brand or furless skin. He'd shone like the blasted moon on a clear night—the most beautiful creature she'd ever seen.

She hated herself for thinking it.

She passed a woman writhing on a cot, her torso torn open. Jade ground her teeth, forcing herself not to look away from the pain and destruction her army had caused. Jade tried not to leave the humans to suffer. She preferred to kill them quickly—the only mercy that was hers to extend.

Three paces ahead, a healer rushed away from a soldier she'd been tending to. She wore a blue scarf over wavy brown hair—hair like Jade's before her ma had shaved it last year when she'd joined the underlings. Now, she had short amber-gray fur on her scalp. She hadn't realized how much she missed her beautiful hair until this moment. Seeing how it framed the healer's delicate face in rich browns sent envy twisting through her belly. Her nostrils flared as she tried to dislodge the pathetic thoughts. She was here to kill.

Normally, she had no trouble blocking out unwelcome thoughts and emotions. Follow orders. Show no weakness. Strike first. Feel nothing. Maybe it was the exhaustion or the smell of sorrow all around her. Maybe it was nothing more than the familiar head of lovely hair, but the jackal Draco slowed her search. She shrank against the wall as she watched these pitiable people try so hard. Impressive, especially in the face of certain doom.

The healer's eyes turned glassy as she brought a hand up to her green-tinged face. Scarf-wrapped head tilted toward the floor, she stumbled straight toward Jade. Jade dropped into a corner, crouching behind the cot of an unconscious man. The healer fell to her knees on the dirty floor, grabbed a bedpan, and vomited. From the shadows on the other side of the same cot, Jade could see her well. If the healer bothered to look up, she'd see Jade too. The healer was younger than Jade first guessed and familiar, but she'd never met her before; she was sure of it. The woman ran a hand over her belly, pulling her apron tight. There was no swell of note, except the way she cradled her gut was significant. Jade stifled a gasp. Pregnant.

The woman sighed the sigh of the bone-weary, her smattering of freckles stark against her blanched face. She glanced left and right, never up, before her shoulders hunched and she pulled off the scarf.

Jade bit her tongue so hard she tasted metal.

Scarred into the healer's forehead was the royal brand of Skotar, the top of the dragon icon brushing her hairline. Only the royal family had the right to that brand—inked over their hearts in purple dye. And every last Regium who had the right to bear it had been killed by Queen Mavras fifteen years ago.

Well, almost every one.

"Imanna!"

Jade flinched at the name yelled from the other side of the tent. The healer jolted. Still caved in on herself, the woman wiped the sweat off her face with her scarf and retied it over her brow. Only the tiniest tip of the sword-shaped scar was now visible.

Imanna closed her eyes, inhaling as if she could suck all

the air in the world into her body. She turned away as she stood. "I'm coming."

Jade fell back on her heels and grabbed the legs of the cot to steady herself. Sacora *Imanna* Regium. She'd be eighteen now.

The princess was alive.

Jade wouldn't have believed if she hadn't seen it with her own eyes. The true heir of Skotar. Here in the humans' losing army.

Jade peeked over the dying man's cot, her thoughts a tornado. How? How? How?

"Uriah!" Pain laced Imanna's cry, the sound slicing through Jade like a knife. Imanna dashed to the injured soldier teetering near the doors. His breastplate was gone, his tunic slashed open by a Dracosteel blade. A nasty cut gaped below his right nipple. Blood soaked his shirt, pants, and arms.

There were no empty cots, and the man was too big to share. Healers transferred a woman with a bandaged arm onto another bed. Uriah's eyes rolled back as he fell over, barely making it halfway onto the dirty cot. Sacora—no, Jade shouldn't think of the princess by that name. Too dangerous. *Imanna* whimpered like a dying kitten. Two strong assistants rolled the warrior over and centered him on the cot.

Imanna frantically pulled tools from a nearby tray, her jaw hard as granite. Her pale eyes gleamed as she cleaned his deep wound and accepted needle and thread from an assistant. Her lips quivered, but her fingers held steady as she pulled stitch after stitch through bloody skin.

Jade knew she should move. Search for Captain Titus. Chief Laconius would kill all the enemy soldiers, wounded or not, when they took this camp as their own. It would happen before the day was out. So much wasted effort. But Jade was paralyzed by the scene of devotion and despair. Her heart thrashed against her ribs, straining toward her Draco sister. *Sister.* Her heart snagged on the word, and her thoughts tangled like a spider's web.

A man cut off Uriah's shirt, revealing a muscled chest peppered with scars. And a Draco Sang brand over his heart.

Jade's jackal-sharp eyes squinted. That soldier was born in Skotar. Another like Ferth. How many fallen Dracos were there in Elysium? Confusion swept over Jade. These people were supposed to be abominations. She should feel anger and disgust, but she thought of her ma and couldn't. By example and by word, Ma had taught Jade that true strength came from the heart.

The same turmoil she'd felt since she'd seen Ferth in Mitera came rushing back. He'd been her Draco captain, her whole world. Then he'd betrayed both country and blood. Abandoned her without a goodbye. She wanted to hate him, to despise all these humans not worthy of their heritage, as Laconius did. But when she'd seen the fallen Ferth across that ballroom, at the end of her arrow, his handsome figure and fiery gaze had struck her heart. She hadn't been able to kill him. Or his beautiful wolves. And she didn't regret it.

Regret and remorse had no place in a Draco Sang breast.

Across the room, Imanna stanched the soldier's bleeding chest with a linen compress, her hands coated crimson. "Stay with me, Uriah." A servant handed her another needle and thread. "It's going to be okay, my bravest bear." He didn't wake when she continued to pierce his flesh. "Don't you dare die on me." Her voice had turned hard and commanding. Yes, she sounded like a Regium.

A Regium was still alive. *Another* Regium. The rightful heir. But Imanna was unworthy of her dragon blood. No human would take the Draco Sang throne. Queen Mavras had nothing to fear. *Jade* had nothing to fear. Imanna didn't need to die. She was already dead to the Draco Sang. No one needed to know otherwise.

But how could Jade walk away from… from… She rubbed at her own Draco brand. The lie. A common marking when she should have the same royal scar that marked Imanna's brow.

Her *sister.* The word swirled around her head like strong wine. The truth of it burned through her soul. She gasped for breath.

Imanna's mother was Queen Sacor. Jade's mother was a slave. But they shared King Icor as a father. Jade's claws dug into the scars on her chest. *IJ06289.* But she wasn't born in 289. She was sixteen and born in 286, the year before Mavras had killed the Regiums. She was born in secret and kept secret. King Icor hadn't liked the greed he saw growing within his sister, Mavras. He'd had the foresight and care to protect Jade. She couldn't remember meeting him, but she held the knowledge of his devotion and love tight within her. He'd created the lies that shielded her, preserved her.

As Jade watched the young healer from across the room, warm, sticky feelings bloomed in her chest. She wanted to tell Imanna the truth. She wanted to know her sister.

Imanna spread a brownish-green cream over the long laceration, then a man lifted Uriah enough for her to wrap linens around his torso. Still, he didn't wake. The assistants left to help other healers. Imanna stayed. She rested a small hand over his heart as if she needed to feel the reassurance of his pulse. She lifted her other hand to his head and raked back thick, brown hair.

She kissed his sweaty cheek, his eyelids, his brow. Her lips brushed his. Jade couldn't hear the words Imanna whispered, but she could see the overwhelming love. It shot across the space and lashed at her heart. Never in Jade's sixteen years had she seen such a display of devotion. Heat built behind her eyes. She scowled at herself, confused and embarrassed.

Hardening her jaw, she stood. She ignored the unwelcome yearning of her heart as she fled. Outside, she passed a dog going the other way on the path. The sleek black and tan animal carried a letter in its mouth, which dropped when it whirled around and sniffed madly in Jade's wake. Her hand curled instinctively on her throwing knife, but she didn't unsheathe it. She ran. She needed to escape. Back to the killing field, where she could join her Draco Sang brothers and sisters and fight. Destroy every unwelcome, unworthy feeling.

THREE - HOPELESS

SUZA

Suza was too tired and thirsty to cry. They'd carried Uriah away a lifetime ago. She hoped he'd been able to say goodbye to Imanna before he died—before they all died. She hacked at the white, scaly Draco in front of her. Their blades clanged, sending pain up Suza's sore arm. How was it so unfair? She'd finally made it to freedom, to her brother. Only to die.

And Ferth, where was he? Where was the army he'd promised? It had been weeks since he'd left.

Ferth had abandoned her.

No hope remained in her heart. No energy in her limbs. No family at her side.

Across the battlefield and up the slope, the Draco's human slaves had rebelled mid-battle. They now fought the backside of the Draco lines. Untrained and undernourished, the slaves' numbers continued to dwindle. Suza couldn't stop herself from looking every time there was a gap in the killing. Pearl and Kenji still stood, though she couldn't see Pelussa or Ipsum, her raven hewan.

Suza's blade locked with a Draco's. Her strength faltered,

but the human soldier at her side attacked underneath, his huge sword spearing the Draco's belly. Suza then slashed the enemy's throat, ending the dance. The Draco landed on his side, partially on top of a decapitated human. Blood swirled through the dirt, making patterns that would swim through her nightmares. Would she remember this when eternal sleep claimed her? One of the Draco's eyes snapped open, rolling back as if searching for her. Cursing her.

"Don't look down, Suza. Keep your chin up."

She obeyed the gentle voice. A tear fell when she looked at Guap, his brave face replacing the gore. She didn't know him well, but she knew his name, and that felt like a lifeline. He'd carried her to the healer's tent when her shoulder was cut during a previous battle. He was one of the humans' best swordsmen and her commander now that Uriah was down.

And he was here, fighting and dying with her.

He sent her a grim smile. There was warmth in the depths of his eyes, even though he had blood smeared in his brow, and his eyes looked bruised. Kindness amidst violence. She let out an exhausted sob. Guap called on some other soldiers to fill the space between Suza and the front line, giving her a reprieve.

He set his shield in the dirt and leaned it against his leg. With his battle-splattered sword pointed down at his right side, he lifted his left arm in welcome. She melted against his leather breastplate while his hand braced her waist, feeding her warmth. She wanted to dissolve into his human touch, his tenderness. He didn't say anything, didn't lie to her about a bright future. She counted to ten. Then counted again. Then shifted her weight to her sore feet as she sighed and stepped back.

He looked down at her. She was tall, but he still had five inches on her. "We'll fight together."

She nodded, pinching her eyes against the threat of tears.

Guap's lips were soft as he planted a kiss on her sweaty brow. A touch of sweetness to cut the bitterness of the day.

Ferth wasn't here. He hadn't come back for her. He'd left her to die.

And die for this country, she would. She wouldn't run from her duty.

First, a final taste of life. She rolled to the balls of her feet, cupped Guap's neck, and smashed her lips against his. She kissed him with a fierceness that said she knew this was her final pleasure. She pulled his fat lip between her teeth. He angled his head, his mouth shifting over hers, drawing her deeper. For a blissful moment, she accepted his invitation and drowned herself in his strength, affection, and safety. Fire roared in her belly as she tasted salt and male, drank in this last spark of joy.

When she pulled back, Guap blinked wide, brown eyes at her. His skin was a lustrous bronze, no longer ashen.

Lips tingling and heart crackling, she lifted her short swords. "Let's kill us some Dracos."

FOUR - PLANS

FERTH

Ferth and Tobin rested, tucked into the Seraf mountains outside of Gristlecove, on the west side of Skotar. Ferth's wolves, Lyko and Rom, had gone hunting with a promise to stay hidden. Ferth sat against a gnarled tree as sunlight filtered through the sparse autumn leaves. Tobin sharpened the Dracosteel knife Ferth gifted him and had started teaching him to use.

Rom and Lyko padded into the tiny clearing, dragging a deer in their maws.

Tobin's blue-eyed gaze scanned the streak of blood trailing behind the corpse. "I specifically asked for poached pears and wine-glazed fish."

Ferth chuckled.

"*So high-maintenance,*" Lyko said through the mental connection the wolves shared with each other and Ferth.

Ferth did not relay the message to Tobin. It wasn't Tobin's fault he'd grown up as the son of a raja, sitting on velvet and drinking from crystal. The fifteen-year-old was three years younger than Ferth—shorter by a foot and weighing half as much—but he'd proven himself tougher than Keturah's magu jerky these last two weeks of travel. He hadn't complained as his soft feet blistered and calloused. He hadn't complained when they'd slept on rocks, with nothing but their coats to fight off the chill. He hadn't complained about missing his daily bath or fresh bread as they'd hiked miles through the Seraf Mountains.

Lyko, the white wolf, had guided them to the crossing near Volkar Lake that spanned the deep chasm between the two countries. The memory of the narrow bridge came from his time with Ferth's twin brother, Callidon, before he'd died by the horn of their father, Laconius.

"We can't risk a fire. Not this close to a Draco stronghold," Ferth said.

"Great." Tobin's tenor voice dripped with sarcasm.

"Meat is still warm, if that helps," Rom said.

Ferth huffed out a small laugh as he pulled his knife—Cal's knife—from where it hung on his belt. "Rom says the meat's warm—if that helps."

Tobin pinched his eyes shut and shook his head. He swallowed, his Adam's apple bobbing up and down.

Blood oozed out of the deer's puncture wounds and into the dry grass, making Ferth's upper lip curl back. It would be nice to get a fresh meal and more supplies from the Gristlecove stronghold tonight. "What bit do you want?" The least Ferth could do for the kid was save him the butchering.

"I'm not hungry." Tobin eyed the deer's mangled leg, the white of bone visible through torn flesh.

Ferth crouched next to the two feasting wolves. He didn't like raw meat either, but he'd need his strength tonight when they'd sneak into Gristlecove. He'd guided them here, telling Tobin that while they tracked a dragon's ghost, they would do what they could for the slaves. He owed it to Keturah and Suza. He owed it to all the humans who were fighting the war he was forced to abandon to go on this ridiculous hunt.

He hadn't told Tobin the other reason for attacking Gristlecove and putting their lives at risk—Ferth was going to kill Lord Gristlecove, Suza's father. He couldn't be with her, didn't deserve her, but he could do this for her.

Lord Gristlecove had sent five hundred warriors to Queen Mavras's invasion, but the coward didn't go himself. The barracks should be mostly empty. Ferth would soon find out. Tonight was their first infiltration attempt. Hopefully, it would not be their last.

Tobin believed Nogard was still alive. He'd studied the Dragon in-depth and believed the Ancient One had survived the centuries. He opposed attacking Gristlecove because he thought attempting to free the slaves was too great a risk to their mission. But he wasn't in charge here—thank the stars. Though, Tobin was a surprisingly good companion. After voicing his opinions, he'd given in to Ferth's every decision without resentment or pride.

Ferth wedged a knife between the deer's jaws and pried them open. He cut out the tongue and returned to his seat against the curved tree trunk. Tobin looked pointedly away as Ferth ate it.

With a swig from his waterskin, Ferth washed away the taste of iron and muscle. He ran a hand through his short hair and beard. He'd let his mother cut off his long locks when he'd met her in Mitera a few short weeks ago. A world away. It had made her happy to dress him up like a human, like his clean-cut twin, Cal. Even if it was a lie.

Tobin's hair was also too short to pass for a slave. They didn't have slaves' clothing or brands either, so Ferth's original idea to impersonate slaves wouldn't work.

"Walk me through the plan."

Tobin turned, straightening his shoulders. He blinked as if trying to recall Ferth's many lessons on Draco Sang life. Ferth expected the boy to regurgitate the lectures, but Tobin grinned, his crooked smile full of naïve mischief. "We gut the Draco mongrels and free the slaves."

Lyko chuckled a low, grumbling sound.

"Hopefully, his massive ego and blind bravery will make up for his skinny arms and meager fighting skills," Rom said.

Rom knew what they would find behind those walls. He shared Ferth's past and memories as an underling at Shi Castle, a much bigger stronghold than Gristlecove.

"And raid the pantry." Tobin grimaced at the butchered deer. "Not necessarily in that order."

"That about covers it."

FIVE - WAR

SUZA

*D*izziness came in waves now. With every slash or parry, Suza weakened. Half the time, she couldn't see more than blurry shapes. Numbness blotted out all feelings of sorrow or regret as more bodies heaped on the ground.

Separated in life, human and Draco Sang lay together in death.

She no longer checked the sky for Draco flyers. If they hit her with an arrow, so be it. Standing was nearly all she could manage. She didn't fight with a shield, only her twin short swords, the weapons she'd favored as an underling at Gristlecove. She lifted her right arm to block a strike from a rat Draco. She got under it, but she couldn't throw him off. An axe rose in the Draco's free hand, but Suza couldn't get away. She lifted her left sword, but it wouldn't stop the axe. This was it. She welcomed it. She'd given everything she had.

"No!"

The Draco hesitated at Guap's scream. Guap dove, leaving his back exposed to the Draco lizard he'd been fighting. Horror blasted through Suza's numbness as Guap sliced through the rat's neck at the same time a machete crushed his ribs.

Suza couldn't look away from the man who'd died for her. Stupid, noble human. It had happened so fast. She blinked, willing time to go back mere seconds and undo this tragedy. Her hands shook, her nerves frayed beyond control. With a broken cry, she lunged. She didn't bother with form or defenses, which was probably why the wild stab worked. Her sword buried nearly to the hilt in the lizard's chest. He dropped, and so did she. Her knees slammed into the gory ground at Guap's side. The few exhausted human soldiers remaining stepped in front of her.

There was no point in surrendering.

They would all die, but every Draco they took with them was one less menace moving south to Mitera.

"Guap. Guap. Wake up." She felt for his silent heartbeat.

"May the Dragon…" Her voice stopped as she realized she'd started to repeat the Draco Sang death rite. What did the humans say? Something about honor—"I'm so sorry," she whispered in his ear, her body curled over his. Why did she have to be the last one to die?

"Reinforcements." Xandra's hopeful voice barely filtered through the fog that darkened Suza's mind. *"Captain Titus is here with a unit of Draco Sang humans and their hewans. And a quarter mile behind is Raja Darius with more humans than I can count."*

Suza blinked. Was she dreaming Xandra's words?

"Pull back." Xandra's voice was frantic. *"Have the humans retreat. Regroup. Pull in all the lines. Save the survivors. Make room for the replacements."*

Suza didn't move. She couldn't process.

"Get up." Xandra's voice was a hiss.

Suza lifted her head off Guap and squinted at the afternoon sun. May she dissolve into that bright, golden light.

Russet wings blocked her view. Xandra hovered in front of her face and let out a piercing cry. She flapped her feathers across Suza's cheeks in frantic, silky slaps.

"*Get out of here,*" Suza said. "*You're not safe.*"

"*You aren't safe here either.*" Xandra landed on Suza's shoulder and dug in her claws. Suza didn't react to the pain. "*Ferth sent a whole army from Mitera. They're here.*"

It was his name that snapped her out of her stupor. "*Ferth?*"

"*I haven't seen him yet, but Darius is in front. There are thousands.*"

The scene in front of her sharpened. A human died three feet away. "*We need to pull back.*"

"*Make the order.*"

She had to do it because the last two commanders, Uriah and Guap, were dead. Suza opened her mouth to yell, but the humans' drums cut her off. *Retreat fifty yards. Reform the lines.*

She echoed the orders. "Reinforcements are here." Eagerness garbled her words, but the news still spread down the ragged lines faster than wildfire. Suza retrieved her swords. Tripping over corpses, she stumbled south with the survivors.

Captain Titus and his band of Draco humans descended on the battle from the Southwest. Because of his broken leg, he led from atop a giant horse. Eio, his lion hewan, stalked over from where he'd been fighting on the East. With a bloody maw, Eio let out a roar that stirred Suza to lift her blades again. Prickling adrenaline flooded through her body as she strode to join Titus. The captain looked over from his mount and saw her. His sharp gaze turned stricken as he took in what remained of the human army.

"Go," he said, his voice fresh and loud. "Fall back, all of you! Get food and treatment."

An arrow whistled. Titus lifted his shield, and it fell harmlessly to the ground.

"The slaves..." Suza's voice was paper-thin. Gathering breath, she yelled to him over the tearing in her dry throat. "Get to the slaves fighting on the northern side. Save them!"

Titus nodded in understanding but made no promises. He motioned to his new unit and gave the command to engage.

Suza sobbed as dozens of Draco humans turned to fight their blood brothers and sisters. They were farmers and merchants, peaceful citizens of Elysium, but they'd answered Titus's call for help. So many of them had come. They'd barely lifted their assortment of weapons when a flood of humans from Mitera filled in behind.

A new feeling sprouted in Suza's breast, something she hadn't allowed herself to feel since the day Lord Gristlecove had killed her mother three and a half years ago. It spread like warm balm through her blood before she finally recognized it. *Hope.*

Ferth had come back with an army. Her desire to live and love reignited like oiled kindling.

"Come on, soldier." A blood-stained man at her side put a gentle hand on her forearm. "Let's find you a drink...and a place to rest."

Could she? Could she simply walk away from an eternity of battle? Rest.

SIX - IT'S TIME

FERTH

Ferth nudged the dozing Tobin, impressed he could sleep before his first battle. Or maybe his naïveté ran that deep. Ferth still clung to the hope he could do this without killing anyone, but deep down, he knew he was lying to himself.

"It's time."

Tobin nodded. A black silhouette in the weak starlight, Tobin stretched like a cat and stood. He relieved himself, checked his knife, and turned to Ferth expectantly. They hid their packs in the trees.

With their sharp eyesight, the wolves led the way to the western edge of Gristlecove. A gray stone wall appeared before them, unpassable except for the natural mountain of slate it butted up against. While they scaled the steep slope, they would be exposed to any guards stationed along the wall. After long minutes of watching, no Dracos appeared, no sounds filtered over.

Ferth strode out of the safety of the trees to the base of the cliff. He wedged his boot into a narrow foothold and heaved up. It was steeper than it looked. Too steep for the wolves. Lyko's curses rang through his mind. Ferth would have to open the front gate for his wolves to get in.

"It might take a while," Ferth warned the wolves.

"I don't like it," Rom said.

Ferth clenched his jaw and stretched towards a lip in the rock above his head. His sword hilt banged against stone. Wordlessly Tobin followed. With his weightless limbs and lanky fingers, he beat Ferth to the top of the steep slate. They crouched together in the lee of the wall, panting and gathering courage. From the ground, they hadn't been able to tell that the cliff didn't reach the top of the wall. Eight feet of sheer stone stood between them and the top. Tobin couldn't clear the wall without Ferth's help, but Ferth didn't want to send Tobin into enemy territory first.

Ferth cupped his hands and held them out. Tobin slipped his narrow boot into Ferth's palms and leaped, grabbing the top edge and slithering over like a lizard. Coiling his legs, Ferth sprang. He didn't have the same level of strength he'd enjoyed as a transformed Draco Sang, but he still reached the ledge easily. Grunting with exertion, he heaved his body up and flung a leg over. He kept low as he hoisted the rest of the way. Danger prickled down his neck as he rolled onto the wall. Heart thundering, he lifted his face. Six feet in front of him, a Draco Sang cat held a sword against Tobin's neck. The whites of the boy's eyes reflected the wan moonlight. So much for not killing tonight. Ferth shifted his hands next to his ribs, ready to push up.

"Move, and I'll end him."

Ferth wished he could talk in secret to Tobin like he could his wolves. Tobin and the cat were basically cheek to cheek, leaving no room for error. Ferth would have to be precise. Anxiety tore through his chest, leaving him breathless.

"We're underlings here." Ferth stayed on the ground, face

passive, but muscles tensed. "Lord Gristlecove sent us on a mission tonight."

"Then why not use the gate?"

"This was part of the test."

"Someone would have told me." The Draco shifted, holding Tobin farther from her side so she could look him over, considering Ferth's excuse. "You smell pure human."

Panic roared through Ferth. He forced a deep breath. "I'm going to stand and show you my Draco brand."

Ferth slowly rose to his feet, hands away from his weapons. He locked gazes with the Draco and brought his fingers to the buttons on his sternum, while his mind stayed on the knife at his belt.

The cat's paw lashed down, tearing through flesh and fabric on Tobin's chest. Tobin choked on a scream. His shirt gaped open, revealing pale skin, unbranded and smooth except for the fresh claw marks now trickling blood.

The Draco held her knife precious inches away from Tobin's strained neck. Slit eyes lit up with greed as she turned her focus fully on Tobin. "You're mine now, slav—"

The Draco's words cut off when Ferth's throwing knife embedded itself in the side of her neck. She gagged and toppled on her side. Tobin dropped to his knees. Ferth sprinted forward, refusing to worry about what he would have suffered had he missed. He'd aimed true. *Don't think about it again.*

He knelt and ended the Draco's gurgling and gasping. He didn't see any other guards on the wall. With the majority of their soldiers at war, he didn't expect much defense here, which was the only reason he dared attempt this attack.

A smattering of torches lit the empty courtyard. The long squat building directly below was completely dark—the slave quarters after curfew. Steep stairs led down the wall forty paces away. The gates were on the far side of the compound, near the castle. It was nothing as grand as the queen's citadel at Shi Castle but still, plenty intimating. Ferth turned to his partner.

Tobin stared at the corpse, unseeing, fingers trembling. Ferth cursed as he scrambled over and crouched, bringing them face to face. They didn't have time for this.

"You're okay." Ferth dabbed at the wounds with a torn flap of Tobin's shirt. The gouges weren't deep, but the longest could use a couple stitches. Later. He tried to close the shirt. "Can you tie this?"

Tobin glanced down. He fumbled with the fabric a long time before managing a knot that held it closed enough to cover his brandless chest. His fingers came away bloody.

"Deep breath." Ferth inhaled with him. "Put this behind you. We've got to move."

Tobin gritted his square white teeth and nodded.

Ferth took Tobin's cold hand and pulled him to his feet. They darted along the wall and down the stairs. Ferth breathed a sigh of relief when they landed on the ground without incident or blaring alarms. There would be guards at the gates, and a fight with them could alert the entire compound. Better to open that on the way out, after he'd done his business.

"*Sorry,*" he said to the wolves on the other side of the wall.

"*No.*" Lyko's voice was like a hammer hitting his skull. "*Do not engage without us. Get over there and open the gate right now.*"

Ferth could feel Lyko's near-paralyzing fear. The fear that Ferth would die by the hand of a Draco, just like Cal had.

"*It isn't wise for you to go alone.*" Rom's voice was calm and calculating. "*We might need to leave in a hurry. Better to have the escape route cleared.*"

"*Let us in.*" Lyko was in a frenzy, pacing tight circles in the forest, barely holding back his howl.

They were right. Why was Ferth still trying to avoid

killing Dracos? He flinched against the answer—they were still his brothers and sisters. He thought of Jade. Not all Dracos deserved to die, but he couldn't hesitate tonight if he wanted to get out alive. Ferth turned toward the castle and the gate. *"Stay in the cover of the trees until I have it open."*

Lyko's relief was palpable across the connection.

Dark corners and cloaking shadows lessened as Ferth and Tobin crept closer to the gate. Lights in the windows made glowing patterns against the sides of the castle. A heavy beat of music pulsed. Draco silhouettes passed by the tall windows on the bottom floor of the castle.

Ferth led Tobin away from the Draco evening gathering. They rounded a stone building, and the gate came into view. The Dracos had torches lit on either side. One guard. One sleepy guard. The rest must be in the castle, hopefully already well into their cups. Ferth almost laughed at his good fortune. Almost. He still had to kill this unfortunate female. He motioned Tobin to stay hidden in the shadow of a water-spout. Tobin crouched without argument. The red stain on his shirt had widened.

Ferth drew his sword with a whisper of metal. He slunk forward on the balls of his feet. The guard stood leaning against the wall in the archway of the gate, head down on her chest. She looked up when Ferth's shadow flickered close. He flinched at her fox fur and dark eyes, so much like his old friend Dara's face. While he hesitated, she pulled out a jagged knife. But her next move wasn't to strike, instead she reached for the horn. Ferth jerked out of his paralysis and stabbed his sword. She parried. Strike. Parry. She was good. But he needed her silent.

With regret already knotting his belly, he swept his sword up, forcing her to block him in a downward strike. He used his size and strength to lock her blade against his and force her back. Her arms lifted, exposing her chest. He stepped closer. He drew Cal's blade from his belt with his left hand and inserted it between her ribs. Blood burbled over her lips as she grunted. Her eyes filled with tears.

"May the Dragon keep you and bless you with peace," he whispered, his own eyes hot as he lowered her to the ground.

It had been easier to kill in his Draco Sang body. He felt too much now. He inhaled to the count of ten. Maybe they should just walk out right now. But then these two deaths would have been for nothing, or worse, the slaves would be punished for it tomorrow. He stuck his head out of the gate archway and motioned Tobin forward. The boy glanced at the body and then snapped his gaze to the blank, gray wall. Ferth violated his fresh kill by searching her pockets. The jangle of metal drew his attention to where Tobin lifted the keys from a hook in the stone archway.

"Opening the gate now."

Two sets of gleaming, gold eyes appeared behind the rusting bars. Tobin flinched back, then righted his shoulders and unlocked the gate with only a slight tremor in his dexterous fingers. The gate whined when Tobin tugged it. He held it just wide enough for the wolves to slip through. Lyko was a fraction broader, and his shoulder jammed against the sharp lock. Ferth felt a flicker of pain through their connection. Ferth cringed. Lyko didn't. Tobin pocketed the keys and left the gate ajar.

"To the slave house," Ferth whispered. He led the way, conscious now that they wouldn't have a chance to make any excuses if seen. The Dracos would kill them on sight. And his wolf abominations, as the Dracos thought of them, would end up dead too.

They made it to the slave house without incident. The doors were, as expected, unlocked. Ferth opened the first bedroom door. Empty. A chilling dread crawled up his back as they opened the next door and the next—all empty. There was only one place the slaves would be.

At the castle with the Draco Sang.

SEVEN - DEFEATED

JADE

The humans were pushing them back. Jade couldn't believe their sure victory was slipping away like sand through a sieve. She'd returned from the enemy camp to the killing field on the eastern edge, close to the frothing sea. And she'd finally found Captain Titus. Everyone could see him up there on his horse, leading an entire pack of Draco Sang abominations. There were so many. Her sister must be one too, Jade realized with a jolt. Imanna was too old to be waiting on her transformation. She'd failed her blood. But where was her soul-animal-thing? Jade couldn't call anything about her sister an abomination.

Jade didn't pretend to complete her mission and go after Captain Titus. She'd had enough killing for today. Laconius was fighting here too; let him have the satisfaction of his own revenge.

Chief Laconius, his horns visible above the crowd, fought twenty feet from Titus, but he didn't move closer to his old enemy. His wound must be hurting him, humbling him. After hours of laborious slaughtering, even the mighty bull's strength was waning.

Jade fought defensively, her heart still in the healing tent with her sister. In her mind, she replayed the scene with Imanna and Uriah—she would remember those names, those faces, forever. The depth of their love and the pain this war had brought.

The Draco Sangs were tired. They'd been fighting all day. The closeness of victory had fueled them forward, but that was gone now, washed away by the waves of fresh humans. A blanket of resentment seemed to press down on the Draco Sang army. Jade knew how they felt: cheated.

She felt it too, but it had more to do with the girl who shared her freckles, round eyes, and small nose. All these years, she had a sister.

A fierce need to protect Imanna drove down Jade's spine. If the Dracos took the human camp, Imanna would become a slave to the Draco Sang. Or worse.

Jade could never let that happen.

When a human charged at her, she blocked his blade. It dropped from his poor grip. He was no soldier, just a body to block the border. Instead of sliding her sword over his throat, she hit his temple with her hilt, saving him and herself. His eyes rolled back, and he dropped, unconscious. Jade stepped back, inching closer to Skotar.

The next humans didn't attack. They stood in a line, shield to shield, faces stony. Suddenly it all seemed too hard. Too much blasted work. It wasn't supposed to go this way. Was Laconius going to keep pushing? Order his sluggish troops to continue hacking, hacking, hacking? Would it be this much work all the way to Mitera? And after that? Would they always be fighting to keep their power? Was it worth it?

A horn blasted the air, one high, three quick low tones. *Retreat.*

Jade didn't bother hiding her sigh of relief.

EIGHT - GRIEF

SUZA

Suza woke, jerking her head up from the dining table. Her back barked in protest. Battle juice crusted her skin and clothes.

Uriah.

She jumped to her feet, and her legs went loose as every muscle flared in pain. Her hip rammed into the table as she righted herself.

"Are you alright?"

She ignored the concerned voice coming from a few seats down. How could she be alright with her brother dead? She had to see him. How long had she slept? She'd meant only to get a drink. The soldier dragging her away from battle had insisted. She hadn't been strong enough to fight him or her thirst. But she should have gone straight to Uriah. Had she missed her chance to say goodbye? She couldn't live with herself if she did. She couldn't live without him. She'd already suffered too many years apart.

Outside the dining tent, a chill breeze caressed the dried sweat and blood coating her skin. Indiscernible shouting sounded from the battlefield. Ferth must be out there. He'd come back. Her chest swelled. She sent up a silent plea that he would stay alive.

"*Can you see Ferth?*" She asked her hawk perched on top of the command tent.

"*Not from here. I haven't seen the wolves either.*"

"*Let me know as soon as you do but stay out of danger.*"

Suza shuddered at the thought of losing Xandra too. She veered around a couple of soldiers in the path, her body protesting every painful step. She limped into the healers' tent and reeled back at the smell of blood and vinegar. The moaning cries of the dying were agony to her ears. She scanned the beds, her heart a throbbing mass in her chest. What if she was too late? What if they'd already taken him to the growing heap of dead outside?

Tears built behind her eyes and sweat in her armpits, liquid pooling in both places. She walked down a second row, still not seeing his familiar wide shoulders, somber brown eyes, and thick hair. She blinked at the brine blurring her vision and started down the third row. Halfway down, a terrified sob escaped, her ribs shaking. *No. No. No. Please, Uriah. Please.* It was hard to look at the bodies, cut up like dinner steaks. She hated the Draco Sang with a passion that filled her soul with dangerous energy. She turned the corner and started down the last row.

"Uriah," she whispered. "Uriah."

A few heads turned in curiosity.

Panic made her voice quiver. "Uriah. Answer me. Bleeding skies, answer me."

"Suzaena?" A big body two cots down shifted, his gaze finally landing on her.

Her heart threatened to leap out of her body. She made a sound like a squeezed kitten and burst into a raging fit of tears.

He smiled.

She stumbled to his side, her insides melting. A thick bandage was wrapped around his ribs from top to bottom. She could still see him back on the battlefield, that Draco blade slashing at his heart, tearing leather and flesh. She ran her hand over his shoulder, a few nicks there to add to his collection of scars. He lifted his arm and wiped her cheek with the back of his hand.

"I love it when women weep for me."

She tried to scowl, but a chuckle escaped before she managed to frown. "I thought you died."

"I'm sorry."

The sobbing started again. Suza couldn't help it. It was too much emotion for her to handle in her exhausted state. "Don't ever do that again." She waved her hands, directing him to move over.

His brows knit in confusion. She put her hands on his waist and pushed. He hissed in pain and scooted over three inches to the cot's edge. Careful not to touch his chest, Suza climbed onto the bed. He lifted his arm, and she settled under his wing, her head on his shoulder. He rested his cheek on the crown of her head.

"Guap died saving my life."

Uriah's arm tightened around her back, and he kissed her forehead. "It's not your fault, Suzaena."

She forced a nod as her grief watered his skin. They didn't talk for a long time after that. She tried to focus on the sound of his steady pulse and not the cries of the wounded or the looks of stress on the healers' tried faces. She should get up and help. But Uriah's warmth was like a drug, shielding her, lulling her to rest.

She woke when Uriah shook her. She blinked the world into focus. She propped up on her elbow, checking if he was okay. His lips were in a taut line, his face pinched. She was about to ask when he looked past her. She turned her head to see Captain Titus standing at the foot of the bed.

Fear coiled in her gut at the grim look on his face.

She swung over the side of the bed and stood, ignoring the dizzy rush to her head. Her vision blinked in and out as she steadied. Dread iced her body. "Ferth. He's dead." She had to know right now—no more suspense.

Titus looked surprised. "No. He didn't return with the troops from Mitera."

He didn't return? He'd truly abandoned them—*her*—to this war. Uriah's hand slid into hers. She squeezed hard as, all over again, his betrayal washed through her like acid.

"The Draco Sang retreated. We've won the battle, and hopefully, the war. I don't anticipate them attacking with the number of troops we have now."

It was happy news, but Titus wasn't smiling when he looked at her. "But…"

And that's when Suza knew what he was going to say. "The slaves didn't escape," she whispered.

The sorrow in his eyes was answer enough. *Pearl. Kenji.* All now considered traitors and trapped under the cruel hand of Laconius. Her knees gave out.

NINE - ATTACK

FERTH

erth had forgotten how bad it smelled in the slave houses. In truth, he'd never really noticed it before. His few months as a human had changed him. Tobin had his sleeve over his nose and mouth.

"Should we wait here until the slaves return?" Rom asked.

They were hiding in one of the empty rooms. Pressed against the walls were four bunks with dirty sheets. By the time the humans returned, the Dracos should be in a drunken stupor, an optimal time to escape. But likely some slaves would be forced to sleep among the Dracos. Ferth couldn't leave any behind. They had to save them all, or none. It would be morning by the time they waited for the party to end and found all the slaves, especially if humans ended up scattered around the entire keep. Waiting here was not an option anyway. They'd left two corpses already. How long until the Dracos found them, and the hunters became the hunted? He had not thought this through well enough.

"We'll infiltrate the castle," Ferth said reluctantly.

No reply.

"Tobin and I can dress as slaves." He couldn't stop his

cringe as he eyed the open trunks. He didn't want to touch anything. By the paleness of Tobin's face, he felt the same. Ferth moved to the chest and lifted the top item. A thin shift dress. Gristlecove wasn't big enough to have two slave houses. The mens' rooms would be here too.

Ferth led them deeper into the dark building, checking each dismal bedroom until they found a trunk with shirts and pants. It was probably better the room was too dark to see how stained they were. Ferth and Tobin put the clothes on over their own. It wasn't a great costume. Between the bulge of weapons underneath and the short hair, they'd probably only have a few seconds before someone recognized them as intruders. But every second was invaluable.

"What's the plan?" Rom asked, his tone anxious.

Ferth ripped the flimsy fabric of the tunic on the sides so he could easily pull his knives free. His sword dangled below the hem.

"We hope the Dracos are very drunk." He said it out loud for Tobin's benefit.

"That is not a plan," Rom said.

"We don't know until we get in and see what we're facing," Ferth said.

"We have a pretty good idea," Rom said. *"And Tobin's not going to like it."*

Ferth replied only to his wolves. *"And our best chance is to send him in first. He looks the most like a slave."*

"Absolutely not," Rom said.

"He's tough," Lyko said. *"I'm sure he can handle it."*

Lyko, with all his human memories, had no idea.

"I hate when you three talk without me," Tobin said.

"Sorry," Ferth said. "Rom was just saying he thinks you should stay here."

Rom growled.

"Fine," Ferth said. "He didn't say that. I'm saying that.

You'll be in too much danger, and you're not prepared to defend yourself." His gaze flickered to Tobin's bleeding chest as if the injury were the only problem. "And the humans… They get treated *poorly*…"

Tobin jutted out his hairless jaw. "All the more reason for us to help. I knew the risks when I came."

"No, you didn't."

Tobin hissed. "We're wasting time. I'm coming. You fight, and I'll usher the slaves out and through the gates."

"That seems like as good of a plan as any." Ferth strode out of the door and down the hall.

The night had cooled. The wind from the north smelled of impending winter. As Ferth inhaled, a focused calm settled in his bones. He locked his fears out of his mind.

No Dracos guarded the building from the outside. Ferth palmed a throwing knife as he slid inside the heavy front doors. Tobin held the door open for the wolves. Lyko sent a mental whine at the overwhelming smells of animal, sweat, and hallifer berry smoke.

Ferth scanned the entry. In front of them stood another set of huge double doors with short hallways leading off to either side, both dotted with doors. Deep, throbbing music leaked through the closed doors in front. Ferth turned right. He gripped the first door and swung it open. The tall Draco had his back to Ferth. The Draco didn't see his attacker as Ferth's blade severed his neck. Ferth shoved the body aside when he sensed movement behind the fresh corpse. A woman held up her hands in surrender. He scanned the ground for her clothes, hoping to hide what was happening to her from… He glanced over his shoulder at the open door. It was too late. Tobin was already there, framed in the torchlight, horror filling his wide eyes.

He shifted to block the trembling slave from Tobin's view. "Get dressed."

"Yes, sir." She lifted her dress from the chair, careful not to touch the fresh splatter of Draco blood.

"Sorry about that," Ferth said.

"What do you want?" She was bolder with clothes on. And older. Now that he could focus on her, she appeared well into her thirties. Old for a slave, but good for the role he needed her to play.

"We're here to free the slaves."

She blinked, the edges of her lips turning down.

"I don't want a single slave left behind. The front gate is unlocked, and the guard dead." There had been no alarms indicating the Dracos had found the body, so Ferth assumed it was still so. "Are there any slaves outside this main castle keep?"

"I don't know."

"Find out. We'll send slaves out the front doors to you. Direct them to quickly gather coats, weapons, supplies, and whatever else they need."

"Where are we going? What do you want from us?"

Ferth sighed. He didn't have time for this. "I want nothing but your freedom." He stopped talking when she startled, her gaze snapping to the door where two wolves padded through.

"What's taking so long?" Rom asked.

"She's resisting freedom," Ferth said.

"You're Draco Sang?"

Ferth didn't know what he was. "I'm Ferth. These are my wolf hewans. And that's Tobin. We've come from Elysium, where the bulk of the Draco Sang army is attacking. So, what better time to counterattack? No human should be a slave. What's your name?"

"Leelee."

"Will you please help us?"

She nodded slowly, gaze still glued on the wolves. "There

are fourteen of us here at Gristlecove. Most you'll find in the center room, but a few like me…." She swallowed. "Will be in the surrounding rooms. I doubt anyone will be at the Draco Sang barracks at this time. Two slaves will be in the kitchen."

"How many Dracos live here?"

"Twenty-nine full Dracos were left after Gristlecove sent his army."

"Twenty-six now."

She smiled for the first time, revealing stained teeth, then frowned. "But there are nearly sixty underlings in their barracks."

"We must not wake them."

"The nursery has ten Draco children, two human children, and three slave women."

Ferth ground his teeth. He had not planned this well enough. "Are those three slaves included in the fourteen?"

"Yes."

"Is there a guard at the nursery?"

"No."

"Tobin, go with Leelee to the nursery."

She shook her head. "I will go alone. I don't need help, but if you go into that ballroom, you will."

Ferth led the way back into the hall and escorted her to the door. "Move quickly," he whispered. "Gather in the southern forest, under cover of the tree line."

She nodded once and fled on silent, bare feet. He could only hope she'd find shoes and a coat.

"Ten to go." Ferth turned back toward the doors. "Hopefully, the saving will go faster from here."

They checked the outside rooms first, hiding in one when a Draco staggered down the hall and out the front doors. Ferth's pulse rose. With the hallways cleared, they stood before the great doors. Tobin yelped when they opened.

Ferth had his sword out before he saw two slaves. He jumped to the shadows.

"Close the doors." His voice was quiet but hard.

The slaves were slow to react. Ferth darted into the light, getting a glimpse of the party inside. Smoke hung like fog over the room. He closed the doors and grabbed the slaves. They didn't resist. They were out the front doors in seconds.

"Get the slaves from the kitchen."

"That's us," the man said, his eyes narrowing as he looked over Ferth, Tobin, and the wolves.

"Good." Ferth forced his voice to turn more commanding. "Get coats and boots. Then pack as much food as you can carry, cooking tools, and take everything out the front gates. You have four minutes. You'll meet Leelee in the southern forest."

They relaxed at the familiar name.

Ferth took the empty wine decanter from the woman and whirled, leaving them on the front steps. Eight more slaves to go. He handed the pitcher to Tobin and held the door open. Tobin went in first, slightly blocking Ferth. They couldn't hide the wolves.

"Pretend to pour a drink for the one on the left," Ferth whispered to Tobin. But the boy didn't move. His gaze darted over the scene. Dracos lounged on pillows along the side, smoking. A few were up dancing by the drums. Men and women in various stages of undress dotted the room. A girl, Tobin's age, sat on a Draco's lap, feeding him black grapes.

Ferth pressed a knuckle into Tobin's spine, and the boy finally moved. His hands shook as he tried to lower the pitcher toward the glass.

"Did someone give you a hit of berry, boy?" The dog Draco asked, his eyes half-open, gaze sliding from the fumbling decanter to Tobin's face.

"Where did you come from with such a fresh, new face? So expressive. Dance for me."

Tobin dropped the empty pitcher. It sunk against the pillows.

"Lose the clothes."

Tobin went bone white.

Panic swirled through Ferth. He glanced up, but no one else had noticed them through the haze. The sweet, peppery smoke tickled his lungs and took him back to the night at Shi Castle when he became a commander in the Draco army and joined the officers in the citadel. He'd had Pearl on his lap, the pipe between his lips. Ferth shook the memory and the guilt away as he turned to kill the Draco, but Tobin was already there. He'd dropped to his knees straddling the Draco's wiry thighs. At first, a look of sheer anticipation filled the Draco's furry face, but it dissolved when Tobin's knife buried itself in his chest, all the way to the hilt. He gurgled and gasped, making far too much noise before he died. Ferth knelt and helped lower the body deeper into the pillows.

Tobin's hands shook as he pulled his knife free. "Now ask me that again," he hissed to the corpse. A tear spilled down his cheek.

"Alright." Ferth pulled his trembling friend to his feet. "You stay by the doors and help usher the slaves out."

"Are those wolves?" The Draco voice sounded more confused than alarmed.

Blood surged through Ferth. No more sneaking around. *"Do your worst."*

The wolves attacked.

Ferth unsheathed his sword and ran across the room. His first target was Lord Gristlecove, the hyena lounging in the big fur-covered chair at the head of the room. Two slaves attended to him.

He looked nothing like his children—he was too mean and shriveled to be anything but ugly. The Draco saw Ferth coming, shoved the slaves aside, and reached for a curved, serrated blade. Ferth didn't have time for a sword fight, but that's what he got.

A space cleared for them as they shared a dance of steel and muscle. Gristlecove was vicious and aggressive, but Ferth was precise and fast. As they traded strikes and parries, unexpected satisfaction sang through Ferth's veins. He was good at this. He thrilled at the exhibition of skill, the sharp edge of danger.

The room had quieted. Even his wolves had been left alone. The battle was now between two. And to the victor, all the spoils.

Gristlecove feinted left, and Ferth went for it, barely realizing his mistake in time to double back, blocking the sudden knife Gristlecove pulled from his boot. Ferth stumbled, and Gristlecove's blade nicked his left shoulder. A cheer rose from the Dracos; an anxious bark came from the wolves. Liquid soaked Ferth's shirt. He gasped and grimaced from the pain.

But his doubling over was an exaggeration. And it worked. Gristlecove's next strike was reckless and high. Ferth's sword cut the hyena's thigh. The Draco howled, the sound like claws on slate. Ferth pressed the advantage. He slashed with his sword as he freed Cal's knife from his belt. His injury protested, but Ferth ignored the wave of dizziness. They locked blades. Ferth buried his knife in Gristlecove's kidney.

"That is for Suza."

"Suzaena?" Wide-eyed, the hyena dropped to his knees, his sword still swinging. His face tightened. "That shrew was a coward. Weak as her mother. May they both rot in the abyss."

Ferth's nerves screamed as he cut the hyena's waist. "And that is for Uriah."

Blood spurted out of Gristlecove's mouth. "My son is dead."

"No, he's alive and a brave warrior in the human army." Ferth blocked the hyena's wild strike. "And so is your daughter. Both heroes." He sliced Gristlecove's sword arm, and the hyena's weapon dropped. "And this is for their mother." Ferth stabbed the undefended heart.

Gristlecove toppled sideways without retort.

Red sword up, Ferth swung to face the gathered crowd. His wolves came forward and stood at attention on either side of him, ears back, canines showing. "Every slave will leave this room now."

"Right this way." Tobin swept toward the door and swung his arms in an ushering motion.

The slaves leapt to obey. The glassy-eyed Draco Sangs watched with varying levels of emotion.

A flyer with narrow gray wings grabbed a young slave by the arm and held him back. Her beady eyes focused on Ferth with violent intent. She had sobered fast. "You don't order our slaves around. You will pay for killing our leader."

So much for winning all the spoils.

Ferth lunged. Whipping his sword around, he slashed down hard on the Draco's neck. Draco blood squirted over the slave's face and shoulder. Ferth shoved the boy toward the double doors as the flyer dropped. In the moment of shocked silence, Ferth didn't stop moving. He was halfway to the doors before the drunken Dracos fully roused to fight.

Tobin had left three slaves in the room. Ferth and his wolves tore through any Dracos, blocking their path. They clawed, bit, or slashed and then move on before the Draco could counterstrike. Speed was their greatest ally. Pain radiated from Ferth's shoulder, and his vision blackened around the edges.

Ferth held the double doors open as Rom dashed out. He waited for Lyko and one last slave his wolf ushered from the room. Lyko's jaws closed over a Draco's wrist as the raccoon Draco grabbed for the human. The Draco howled as teeth sank into flesh. Metal flashed in the Draco's free hand, and Ferth screamed a panicked warning to his wolf too far away for his sword to protect.

Horror slashed through Ferth. Not Lyko. Time slowed as the blade arched toward his precious hewan, his bond to Cal. *No.*

The knife didn't find its mark in Lyko's chest. It buried in the girl's back as she flung her body as a shield over him. Blood gushed over her back as the Draco's knife pulled free. She hung limply over Lyko's spine as he kept running toward the exit.

"What's happened?" Lyko's voice trembled. *"What's she doing?"* His eyes rolled up as his neck craned back to see, his hurried steps uneven. *"Did he get her?"*

"Come on." Ferth's pleading voice was ragged as old cloth. *"Carry her out. Keep running!"*

Lyko skidded out the double doors, a pack of Dracos following. Ferth ripped off the slave tunic he wore as he slammed the doors closed. He used the long fabric to tie the handles together. Weight slammed into the doors. The makeshift rope held, but Lyko jumped. The woman slipped off his back and onto the floor. Lyko looked down at the prone body, the torn flesh, and the pool of blood.

Ferth checked her pulse. Nothing. Overwhelming emotions flooded the connection from Lyko. Fear, horror, shock, and then all-encompassing gratitude for the woman that brought tears to Ferth's eyes.

"We can't leave her." Lyko moved to stand protectively over the woman who'd saved him.

"We have to." Rom's calm voice was a sharp contrast to Lyko's agitation.

"I don't want to either," Ferth said. *"But I can't carry her. We'll die."* Another round of pounding on the doors emphasized the point.

"She gave her life...for me." Awe permeated Lyko's words.

Brine slipped over Ferth's cheeks. *"Yes. She did."* A human had died for his wolf.

Ferth cradled his left arm as they ran outside and down the front steps.

Tobin was at the outer gates, ushering out a pack of humans carrying bundles. He let out a giant sigh of relief when he saw Ferth. Ferth's chest swelled with a surge of energy. Tobin cared about him.

"One more coming?" Tobin looked over Ferth's shoulder.

"No. We're the last."

Tobin's face fell, then he pumped his arm as if the motion could sweep them through the gate faster.

Ferth was almost to freedom, already thinking about sheathing his heavy sword when a Draco Sang jumped out of the shadows a few paces ahead and grabbed the last slave in line. He held her against his thick chest, a broadsword poised across her neck. Black tiger stripes slashed down his russet face.

"She's not going with you," he said.

Ferth didn't have time for this. If the underlings woke or the Dracos in the castle came after them, it would be a disaster. They needed this precious head start to make it through the difficult mountain terrain to the hidden caves a mile south that Ferth had chosen as a temporary hideout.

Up ahead, the slaves slipped out of sight. Tobin's face pinched with worry, his hand straying to the knife on his belt, his focus calculating on the back of the Draco's head fifteen feet away.

"Go, Tobin. I'll catch up."

The boy hesitated.

"Go." A hissed threat.

Tobin disappeared through the gate.

"Do we attack?" Rom asked.

"No." Lyko's near-death in the castle was a stark fear ruling Ferth's thoughts. He trembled with fatigue as he sheathed his sword. His left arm was no use now. With his right, he pulled a throwing knife up and cocked it back. His target was ten feet away, a routine shot for Ferth—when he was at his best. But his fingers shook on the knife handle. He blinked at his blurry vision with no success.

The tiger Draco moved the girl directly in front of his face. "I'll kill her."

"No, Marko," the girl whispered.

She said it with familiarity. Ferth didn't have time to interpret what that meant. "If you kill her, I will kill you. If you don't let her go now, I will kill her and then you." His tone was cold with truth. No negotiating. He'd run out of time. He should have known he couldn't save them all. "You're blocking my exit."

A stunned silence.

"Three… two…"

"Wait." Marko shoved the slave to the side, out of the line of fire. He dropped his sword in surrender. "Allie doesn't deserve to die."

Shock slapped Ferth in the face. In a snap, the scene rearranged in his mind. He'd misunderstood. "And now, neither do you." The words popped out, strung together by pure instinct. Ferth lowered the knife. His gut told him that this Draco was not his enemy. He didn't have time to ruminate. He chose mercy over murder and hoped it was worth the risk. Marko stretched out his furry hand to the female sprawled on the ground. It was the look of trust and adoration on her face as she took it that had Ferth offering the unthinkable to the Draco. "You can come with us."

"*What?*" Lyko's displeasure was punctuated with a bark.

"*Quiet. You'll wake the underlings.*" Ferth strode toward the gate, body buzzing from stress. The human and Draco followed close behind.

"*Not all Dracos are monsters,*" Rom said. "*She loves him, and he will protect her.*"

The Dracos' need to protect their own ran deep, a trait that one could count on. Ferth had to trust it. He invited the tiger Draco at great risk, but the alternative was riskier: leaving the Draco to hunt them or fight now.

Despite Ferth's bravado, he was flagging. This was another of too many impossible choices he'd had to make tonight. His mind felt warped and fuzzy.

Ferth stopped at the edge of the gate. Tobin had left the key in the lock. Smart. Ferth, the last out of Gristlecove, slid the bolt into place and pocketed the key, hoping those two inches of iron would buy them the precious time they needed to escape. Marko had Allie tucked under the protection of his arm as they followed the trail of slaves fleeing south into the forest.

TEN - DISASTER

JADE

Losing the battle was a nightmare. Unhappy Dracos dragged north across the Rugit River, adding dirty water to the liquids soaking their clothes and weapons. Camp was a mess. No one had expected to return, and it looked like they'd abandoned it for far longer than a day. No hot meal greeted them. No slaves assisted in the healers' tent. The slaves had revolted, wielding weapons against the Draco Sang—a crime punishable by death. In the Draco's retreat, the army had cut off the fighting slaves' attempt to reach Elysium and freedom. But they couldn't kill the slaves. They needed the few that had survived the battle to run this disaster of a war camp.

Jade and the other Draco officers joined Laconius in front of the command tent. The bull chief's eyes were as bloodshot as a bright ruby, and his hair was a black storm around his head. He'd removed his leather vest and shirt, revealing arms the size of tree limbs. The bandage wrapping the knife wound on his chest seeped blood.

The slaves that had not stupidly gotten killed during

battle stood before him, stripped of their weapons, and looking worn to the bone, their eyes empty and hopeless. There were precious few left and so much work to be done.

Dracos gathered, filling the empty spaces in the clearing and between tents. The sun dropped to the western horizon.

Laconius's voice boomed. "Our father Nogard cursed us today. If we cannot control our slaves, how can we expect to be blessed with more?" The curling horns on his head shook. He paced in front of the two dozen cowering slaves. "Each of you pitiful creatures deserves a slow death, and you're going to get it."

Jade's stomach curdled against the thought of more death and violence. She knew these slaves well. They didn't deserve this. They deserved the freedom that taunted them from across the river.

"It won't come today. Or tomorrow. It will come when you finish the work." Laconius looked over the camp and the gathered Dracos. "We leave in the morning for Shi Castle."

A few Dracos groaned.

"There are too many humans at the border now. Winter is coming, and we do not have the resources to maintain camp. But the Lion can't maintain that defense. We will return next spring, and when we do, it will be a swift strike to the heart."

More groans this time. Jade bit her tongue to keep from voicing her dissent. She had no desire to attack the humans again. With each soul she'd collected, her blood lust drained a little more.

"We've learned not to give them time to rally their numbers. We will not fail again." Laconius scratched at thick abdominal muscles and turned his focus to the slaves. He took a step toward the older woman standing in the front. She straightened her spine as if she could see him with her ruined eyes. "Pelussa, Pelussa. The Pitiful Poisoner."

Jade stared at the old woman. That was the slave who'd invented Lussa and used the poison to kill dozens of Dracos? It had happened before Jade was born, but the story still circulated, a cautionary tale showing the vindictive and ungrateful nature of slaves. She did look pitiful, with a wrinkled face and thin limbs, but below her milky eyes, her jaw was as hard and unyielding as Dracosteel.

"Laconius the Loser." Pelussa's voice was scratchy and low.

Wide nostrils flared, revealing the dark caverns that resided inside the chief. "When will I learn to wait for proof before believing a body dead?"

Jade swallowed the sudden lump in her throat. She dared a glance at Dara at the same time Dara looked at her, their shared secret flashing in her eyes. They'd been lucky Ferth and his wolves hadn't shown for battle, revealing their deception, their failure. Jade looked away first, scanning for Gavriel. She couldn't see the raven Draco she was becoming increasingly attached to. He should have found her by now. Worry coiled in her belly.

"You're blind to far more than that." Pelussa's voice was calm, but it seemed to cut through the crowd.

Jade leaned back as a large raven dropped from the sky and landed on the woman's hunched shoulder.

Laconius's lips curled in disgust. "You are an abomination to your blood."

"Blah de blah," Pelussa said. "I've heard it all, and it's just petty lies."

"Nogard—"

"You know nothing of our toxic father." Her grating voice carried through the air. "You know nothing of the blood you inherited. *You* are the abomination, with your twisted features and your mutant heart."

A shock wave rocked the gathering.

"You squandered your birthright and your potential. You are all a disgrace to your great mother, Ima."

The words sank deep into Jade's heart like a two-edged sword, both sour and sweet. The crack in her heart widened, and her doubts grew. Clearly, Pelussa was not weak-willed. She was powerful in her own way, like Ferth, Imanna, and Uriah.

"You forget your mother's sacrifice. You are too feeble to claim her gift." Pelussa spat. Her disdain landed on Laconius's belly, and the mucus dripped down.

His jaw rippled. "Traitor's Bane!" He yelled out the title Jade had earned by killing his son, Ferth.

The title was a lie. And so was the proud face Jade donned as she stepped forward, dread chilling her bones, her thoughts whirling. She had so many questions for this fallen Draco Sang slave. "Yes, my chief."

"Kill her."

Jade bit down so hard on her refusal that she tasted blood. She bowed her head in submission and turned to do the unavoidable. Pelussa dug a hand into her pocket. Jade tensed to deflect a weapon, but the woman pulled out a scrolled parchment and handed it to the raven. The bird's talons clutched the paper. The bird rubbed its head against her cheek and took off with a sorrowing caw.

"Shoot that down," Laconius said.

Shuffling and cursing rang out, but by the time the few archers in the group had restrung their bows, the bird was out of sight.

Pelussa smiled in Jade's direction, and Jade cringed. The woman reminded her too much of her mother. Neither were as old as they looked, but life had worn them down, given them deep wrinkles, gray hair, and thin shoulders. And Jade, with all her strength and skills, could no more protect this woman than she could her mother. The realization stoked the growing fire of resentment in Jade's heart.

Every part of her rebelled against harming this woman. But Jade followed orders. Same as that hard-jawed slave, Kenji, standing as a mindless statue. Jade was no better than the slaves.

They all did their queen's bidding.

Feeling as powerless as her first time in the hunger pits as an underling, Jade took another step forward. She'd stalled too much already. She pulled a knife from her belt and held it loose at her side. She put her left arm around the woman's bony shoulders and brought them cheek to cheek.

"May the Dragon keep you," Jade whispered in Pelussa's ear.

"Nogard can rot in the darkness where he belongs. I go to our Mother's peace."

Jade closed her eyes against the longing that welled up inside her—a feeling she'd determined to never feel.

"You didn't kill Ferth." Pelussa's voice was as quiet as a drifting feather, but still, Jade tensed. "You are brave, and Keturah is proud of you."

That couldn't be true. "How do you know my mother?"

"We shared a bunk at Shi Castle. She was my greatest friend. I was there when you were born."

Questions clogged up Jade's throat, so many she couldn't speak.

"Mavras has defiled the crown," Pelussa said. "You must take it back, *princess*."

Heat filled Jade's eyes. Regret was a cold pit in her belly as she cradled the old woman close, careless of how it might look to the gathered Dracos. "I'm sorry." Her lips brushed the human's ear. With a force of sheer will, like a good soldier, Jade brought her right hand forward. Six inches of razor-sharp Dracosteel slipped between Pelussa's ribs, but Jade felt the pain in her breast, a cutting torture she would never escape.

She wished the woman peace; a gift Jade would never receive. She lowered the limp slave to the ground, any chance of getting answers to her questions gone. But had Pelussa kept Jade's secrets safe?

Secrets were never safe.

ELEVEN - CAMP

FERTH

obin led the slaves south through the forest. Ferth, falling farther behind the string of runaways, hobbled to where he'd hidden his pack. It wasn't there. Tobin must have thought he was helping by taking both packs, but he wasn't. Ferth needed the medkit. He needed water and food. He sank to the dirt floor, his eyes closing and breath shallow.

"Not the place I would pick to lie down and die," Rom said. *"No view."*

"Get up." Lyko's tone had none of Rom's humor.

Ferth peeled an eye open. Leelee, at the rear of the group, glanced over her shoulder. She circled back and came to kneel at his side.

"I knew I liked her." Rom came up close, and she flinched.

"The feeling is not mutual," Lyko said.

Ferth gazed up at her tired face, her concerned eyes. "Go." His voice was papery and low. "Catch up to the others. Hurry."

She reached for his shirt. "I'm going to rip this to wrap your shoulder."

He nodded gratefully and gritted his teeth as she yanked, sending a flare through his wound. The shirt remained intact.

She forced a chuckle. "Stronger fabric than I thought."

Between labored breaths, Ferth said, "Use the knife on my belt." He exhaled the pain as she rummaged around his waist. His right hand tensed as she pulled the blade free. But she didn't aim for his throat; she cut the shirt. She pulled him to sit with his back lifted off the tree. With deft movements, she wrapped his shoulder.

"Tighter," Ferth said. His blood stained the strips of cloth.

Her tongue snaked between her teeth as she concentrated, leaning over him to pull the knots. She still smelled of hallifer berry smoke, and the rankness made him nauseous. The pain and bloodshed were worth it to free this woman. He didn't complain when she helped him to his feet and put his right arm over her shoulders. Together they followed the path of crumpled grass. The slaves had left a too obvious trail. But after another fifty feet, the trail disappeared. Well done, Tobin.

The wolves split off to carry their scent in another direction. Ferth was dismayed at how much weight he put on Leelee. His thoughts were muddy and his eyelids heavy. After another hundred paces, they stood facing twin birch trees. He was supposed to do something here, but he couldn't remember. The darkness seemed to lull him into a dream. He blinked awake, but the answer didn't come.

"Go through them."

Yes, that was it.

Leelee turned, and Ferth realized the voice wasn't in his head. Tobin's brows were tight with concern as he looked over Ferth's naked torso and bloody bandage. He motioned Leelee to move and lifted Ferth's arm over his shoulders. He smelled much better.

"Go ahead," Tobin said to her. "Careful not to snap any branches."

It was easier going with Tobin guiding and lending his strength. After stumbling across a stream, the caves came into view. Outside the dark caverns, by the light of a small fire, the Draco Sang tiger was held at knifepoint, several knife points, as four slaves had him pushed up against the rocks. Most impressively, Marko had not drawn his sword. The female slave had positioned her body in front of his like a shield—a standoff.

Ferth cursed loud enough that all attention turned on him. He was too tired for this, and his shoulder hurt. "Put the knives down."

No one did.

So, he was going to have to do this now. He stood on the flat rock outside the cave entrance, the fire a welcome heat up his legs. "Listen up. My name is Ferth. I am the son of the Draco Sang chief, Laconius." He ignored the murmurs. Their gazes dropped to the brand on his chest, to the scars peppering his skin, and to the hard muscles of his torso, visible for all to see the story they told. "And the human woman, Mira." His wolves padded up to his sides. "These are my hewans, Rom and Lyko. They will not harm you unless you attack them or initiate violence in my camp. You are now free." He paused to let those words sink in. "You are not my slaves. You are free. I will not be telling you what to do. Get used to making your own decisions." He chuckled. "It is not as easy as it looks."

The knives pointed at the Draco had lowered slightly as Ferth spoke. A baby's cry came from the shadows of the cave. "In the morning, Lyko will lead a group to the bridge that crosses into Elysium. It's four miles through the mountains to the crossing and many miles on the human side before you will reach any towns. Nansut is the closest one that I know of. Lyko will leave you at the border to make your way, but Tobin can explain directions to Nansut if you're inclined to ask him. This cave should give protection to all if you keep a certain degree of quiet and limit fire smoke. Tobin and I will leave here tomorrow at nightfall. You may *not* come with us."

"You would leave us here to die?" a man asked. "Why'd you rescue us then? At least back at Gristlecove we had food and shelter."

"Just because you weren't a favorite toy of the Dracos," a woman said.

"He gave us our freedom, don't complain," another voice said.

Ferth held up his right hand. "I am sure you have much to discuss. What I have done is done, and I will not apologize. You know the way back to slavery if you wish it."

There was no arguing that.

A small child waddled out of the cave and looked up at Ferth.

"I give you no commands but a warning. If you fight or draw blood in my camp, you will fight me." Ferth grimaced. "In the morning."

A few had the courage to chuckle.

"Marko is included in my protection. Not all Draco Sang are bad, and not all humans are good. Most of us are closer to the middle of that spectrum than we care to admit."

The tiger Draco padded forward and dropped to his knees at Ferth's feet. "Son of Laconius."

"Don't call me that. I'm Ferth. I'm a traitor to the crown. Laconius wants me dead… and he's a brute."

Marko leaned back slightly. "Er. Ferth."

"Yes, Marko, what is it already?" He didn't mean to snap, but it was hard to stay standing. Tobin groaned as Ferth shifted over more of his weight.

"I am yours to command."

"What did I just say about commanding?"

"You saved my Allie and my life. You saw past my fur. I owe you two life debts."

"Fine. Just get out of my way."

Marko's cat eyes went wide as Ferth limped past. He dropped flat on his back by the fire and closed his eyes, intending not to open them for a long, long time. Rom and Lyko lay next to him, their warmth leeching into his frayed emotions. Lyko immediately started to snore.

Tobin knelt at Ferth's side. "You're injured, and we didn't make it to the pantry for the feasting portion of the plan, but I'm glad you had us stop at Gristlecove." His voice was soft and sad. "I had no idea."

"I'm sorry you had to see that. I'm sorry you had to kill."

Tobin dug into Ferth's pack. The rummaging suddenly stopped. "Ferth."

At the tremor in Tobin's tone, Ferth's eyes popped open, and his muscles coiled with a surge of adrenaline. He'd expected a Draco attack. Instead, a familiar raven had landed on the rock in front of his face. Firelight cast orange ripples over its glossy feathers.

"Hello, Ipsum," Ferth said.

The raven held out a piece of parchment.

TWELVE - ASHES

SUZA

Suza walked with Imanna to the funeral fires, while Uriah stayed in the healers' tent with the injured. Imanna walked with a hand clutched to her belly and the tiny baby growing in there. Hope in this terrible time. Suza couldn't see the swell, but she knew new life grew within, waiting to emerge. May it be the same for her in Elysium. Out of these ashes, rebirth.

Suza steered them past the dining tent and picked up a roll stuffed with mushrooms and chicken. She handed it to Imanna.

"Thank you." Imanna took a large, unqueenly bite. Sweat soaked her headscarf, and though she'd taken off her apron, bits of blood and medicine coated her arms and legs. She'd fought as hard for life these last weeks as Suza had.

As they marched toward the smell of burning flesh and smoking wood, Suza couldn't help feeling that despite their victory, she'd failed. Her steps shifted to sync with the rhythm of the death drums. Tomorrow was for celebrating their survival; today was for grief. Fires lit up the night, burning her eyes and soul. She could hear singing as she got closer, the sad song becoming much too familiar. After only a few short months with the humans, she knew the warrior's rite too well. She joined in, singing it for Guap. For all the fallen.

> *When we fall into the pit and darkness swallows us whole,*
> *There we find that the Great Ones descend below.*
> *They rise up and carry us on.*
> *Though the road is grim and bleak,*
> *They go before our feet.*
> *Carry him home.*
> *Raise me up.*
> *If they leave us on the brink, for them we will not sink.*
> *Let us carry the sacrifice on. Carry it on.*
> *Grant us their mantel of honor that we might carry it ever onward.*
> *Ever forever onward.*

When Suza's voice faded away, Imanna turned from the crackle of devouring flames, her pale eyes glowing. She drew Suza into her arms.

Suza let out a breath she didn't know she'd been holding and relaxed into her sister's embrace.

THIRTEEN - RAVEN

FERTH

Ferth read the note delivered by the raven and passed the message on to his wolves. The words were scrawled out in haste, partially illegible, but he figured out their meaning well enough. He didn't want Tobin to read it. The boy already insisted the three-hundred-year-old dragon was somehow still alive.

"What does it say?" Tobin asked. As he studied the cunning bird, the needle he'd been threading lowered. His whole focus shifted to Ipsum.

Ferth clenched his jaw to stop himself from snapping at Tobin to get to work. Tobin was not his slave, and it took all his attention to remember that sometimes. The pain wasn't helping the issue tonight.

Tobin reached out his fingers in invitation to the bird. "My, you are beautiful," he whispered in awe.

Ipsum cocked his head, his glossy eye trained on Tobin.

"You do understand me." Tobin chuckled in delight as Ipsum nodded. With obvious regret, he withdrew the outstretched hand the bird had ignored. "Your human is a lucky one."

Ipsum's head drooped to rest on his downy chest, and realization struck Ferth like a punch. "Pelussa is dead?"

The raven's face sank deeper into his feathers. A wing came forward to cover its eyes.

"In battle?" Ferth asked.

"I'm so sorry," Tobin said.

Ipsum slid the wing back enough that Ferth could see his head. He shook it once.

"Not in battle. Then what happened?"

Ipsum just stared.

Ferth sighed in frustration, what he wouldn't give to talk with this hewan too. But no connection formed with the sorrowing raven.

Tobin pulled his coat from his pack and made a nest on the ground with it. "Please, rest here as long as you like."

Ipsum looked him over with intensity before curling up in the coat. He used his beak to coax a sleeve over his back.

Tobin returned his focus to the needle and thread. "Who is the letter from?"

So, Tobin wasn't going to just forget about the message. A shame. "Ipsum's human was a woman named Pelussa. She must have written it, anticipating she was going to die…or be killed." Pain that had nothing to do with the injury to his shoulder pierced Ferth's heart. "They must have defeated the humans at the border." Tears filled his eyes. "And I left them to die alone." He thought of Suza, and the tears fell.

Rom whined, his sorrow as palpable as Ferth's.

"Ipsum?" Tobin said.

The bird lifted a heavy beak.

"Were the humans defeated at the border?"

The bird shook his head.

Hope roared to life as Ferth's eyes dried.

"There," Tobin said to Ferth as if he hadn't just righted the entire world with a simple, albeit smart, question. "All is not lost, but we must find the Dragon and kill him before it's too late." He reached out a hand, and Ferth surrendered the scroll. Tobin checked no one was near before he read out loud. "Follow the tug in your heart. It will lead you true. It is not a link to your mother but a leash to your father. Break the chain. Break the chain and free us all." He looked up. "What does this mean?"

"It means we have a real hunt on our hands," Rom said with interest.

He and Lyko felt the connection stronger than Ferth did. Rom had always wanted to find out where it led. His curiosity couldn't stand not to know. When growing up, all the underlings were taught, in no uncertain terms, that Draco Sang who followed the pull into the mountains, didn't come back. It was a death trap laid for the dimwitted and unworthy.

"It's the insane ramblings of a dying woman." Ferth was beginning to doubt his sure knowledge of Nogard's death, but he didn't want to feed Tobin's resolve anymore.

Ipsum lifted his head and cawed at Ferth. Black feathers fluffed in anger.

"I'm sorry." Ferth lifted a hand in surrender. "I didn't mean it."

Ipsum turned his back on Ferth and resentfully sank into the coat.

"I am sorry, Ipsum." Ferth sighed. "I know what it means. But just because I understand what she's saying doesn't make her words true."

They went quiet as Leelee approached and handed Ferth and Tobin drinks. "We smuggled out a few bottles."

Ferth inhaled the scent of strong, earthy wine. "Thank you." He drank deeply as Leelee slipped away. He handed his empty ceramic cup to Tobin, who poured Ferth another portion from his own. Ferth reached for it, but Tobin poured the alcohol over Ferth's gaping wound instead.

Ferth hissed out a string of colorful curses as a wave of nausea rolled through his body. He panted like a running boar, trying to decide whether to punch Tobin in the face or somewhere lower.

Tobin, composed and calm, set the letter down and crouched at Ferth's side. "Ready?"

"No." Ferth groaned through gritted teeth as the needle pierced his flesh.

"Toughen up." Rom's voice cut into his thoughts. *"You're ruining my sleep."*

"Start talking," Tobin said. "It helps me work faster."

Ferth sucked in and out sharp breaths. Everything hurt. He pressed the back of his head into the cold rock and closed his eyes. *Let it all go, float away.* "Most Draco Sang feel a constant tug northward."

"Really?" Tobin leaned back, bloody needle poised.

"Sew."

"Right." Fingers prodded at flesh. The needle sank deep.

Ferth went to that place in his chest that he'd learned to ignore. At Shi Castle, the quiet invitation had come from due north. But to his horror and surprise, as he was currently west of Shi Castle, now the call tugged him north and to the east. He cursed inwardly. Could this annoyance lead him to an exact place? "Pelussa is saying that this internal compass will lead me to Nogard." He opened his eyes long enough to see the utter glee on Tobin's face. "It doesn't make her right."

"But she believes the Dragon is alive and that our mission is important. Nogard has a connection to all the Draco. We must sever that line. We must go right away. No more detours."

Ferth wasn't in the mood for making additional stops to pick up more wounds anyway—the one in his shoulder was one too many. "Fine."

FOURTEEN - CULLING LIVES

JADE

Jade found Gavriel's body in the healers' tent. She hadn't come soon enough to say goodbye. She ran her fingers over his soft black feathers. Blood crusted his lips. She lay a kiss on his downy brow. Two Draco Sang, an elephant and a bear, didn't acknowledge her sorrowful vigil before they scooped up his corpse and hefted it out. Jade should follow, watch him burn. He'd hid it from the Draco Sang, but she'd seen his kind and gentle heart. Now that heart was silent. Her legs gave out, and she dropped onto the now-empty cot. It was cold.

She wanted someone to hold her. She wanted Ferth. But he wasn't here. He'd left her as assuredly as Gavriel had. She needed to get out of this tent and escape the smell of acid, metal, and vomit. She should get dinner and find her bed.

Overwhelming exhaustion pressed an avalanche of weight down on her. She couldn't move, could hardly breathe. She'd been fighting her whole life. And for what? So she could live while her friends died? She closed her eyes as waves of unhappiness washed over her.

She woke to the sound of whispered voices near the front

of the tent. Jade opened her eyes but didn't move. It was dark outside the windows, the fires in the braziers turned down to a dim glow. How long had she slept? Chief Laconius talked with Captain Mina and a Draco Sang healer. They argued in hushed tones above a body. Jade flinched when Mina's blade sliced across the injured Draco's neck. They moved to the next cot, and their voices became clearer.

"What are her injuries?" Laconius asked.

"Broken arm," the healer said. "It's set. She won't be able to use the arm for weeks, but she'll be fine."

"Can she walk out of here tomorrow?" Laconius asked.

The healer nodded, face pale and eyes wide.

They stepped to the next cot. "His injuries?"

"He took a sword across the chest. He's lost a lot of blood. If there isn't an infection, he should heal, but I can't guarantee it." The healer didn't look hopeful.

"Is he strong enough to walk tomorrow?"

The healer looked down. "I don't expect him to wake for a few more days."

Laconius nodded to Mina, and she severed his throat. They moved to the next bed.

Horror filled Jade's belly. She gagged and rolled off the cot. Shaking, she crawled toward the door. She couldn't let anyone see her. Not because she was afraid Laconius would be angry. No, she was afraid he would make her help with the culling.

She peeked her head above a bed, and when Laconius's back was toward the door, she slipped out. Standing mostly upright and walking mostly in a straight line, she gulped down the cool, fresh air. Slaves, looking worse than the bodies in the healers' tent, were packing carts by torchlight. Was Laconius worried the humans would cross the river and attack, or was he just anxious to flee the scene of his humiliation?

Exhausted, heartsick, and sore, Jade dragged herself to her tent. As a commander, she'd had her own until Dara moved in without asking. Jade hadn't kicked her out. She had to tread carefully around the fox Draco. Now that Gavriel was dead, Dara was the only Draco who knew the truth: on their trip to Mitera, Jade had not killed Laconius's treasonous son as ordered. She'd killed her mission leader, Thirro, instead.

Jade was a traitor.

FIFTEEN - REPORTS

SUZA

*W*hen Xandra flew into the tent with her morning report, Suza woke to her body in revolt. Everything hurt, even the pads of her fingertips. Sun leaked through the seams in the canvas roof. With a guttural cry, she swung her body to a sitting position. She cursed for a while before asking Xandra what she'd seen of the Draco Sang camp.

"They killed Pelussa but haven't touched the rest of the slaves, not even with the whip. They just put them back to work."

"Should I thank the Mother for that or not?"

"They can barely stand, and they won't escape greater punishment in the end."

Seeing freedom across the water and being pushed back into slavery was punishment enough. *"What is Laconius doing?"*

"Leaving."

Suza blinked in surprise.

"This morning. The Draco Sang will be on their way back to Shi Castle within hours. Everyone that can walk, that is. If they

couldn't march, Laconius had them killed. He put down *half of the wounded."*

Suza shuddered and forced herself to her feet. Her body felt like a piece of rope knotted up by a giant child and used as a chew toy. She eyed her fighting pants. All she'd managed to do last night after her bath was put on clean underthings and drop into bed. Yesterday's clothes were still filthy from battle, and she wouldn't have been able to get on the tight uniform in her stiff state anyway. She stumbled to the trunk and pulled out a shift dress. Humans here wore them as a base layer under gowns. Humans in Skotar wore them as slave uniforms. Even with Xandra helping by flying the fabric over her head, she barely managed to get the loose garment on.

The fabric was thin, draping over her curves, a different kind of exposure than the empowering feeling of her skin-tight fighting pants. She'd sworn to never dress as a vulnerable slave again, but there was nothing for it this morning. She was not lifting her arms again. Ever. But she did manage to strap her short swords around her waist.

"No one will confuse you for a slave now," Xandra said.

"They don't have slaves here anyway." A sob rose in her throat as she thought about her exhausted friends loading up carts and hauling them back to their prison far to the north.

She looked up at the knock on the doorframe. "Yes, come in."

A young man entered. "You're invited to join Captain Titus in his tent. You will find breakfast there."

"Thank you."

"And are these the items for the laundry?" He pointed to the stinking pile as he strode over.

"I'm so sorry they are disgusting." She knew what it was like to launder someone else's soiled clothes.

He stopped and faced her again. He bowed. "It is an honor

for me to serve where I am needed. I must thank you for risking your life to save my freedom and my country."

She blinked at him. He was serious. She let his words wash over her and heal a touch of her sorrow. It had been worth it, every strain and stroke of her swords. For this freedom. "Thank you." It came out as a whisper. She turned to her table to hide her emotion and lifted her hairbrush. Fire lanced her muscles when she brought it to her tangled dark mane. She hissed, lowering her hand. She scowled at the reflecting glass. Her hair was short as her shoulders. She'd gone to bed with it wet, and now curls stuck out in every direction. It looked like Xandra had made a nest on the left side. Suza could not go to Captain Titus looking wilder than Eio. She turned her neck to the servant then regretted the movement.

"Please, sir. Could you help me with something?"

He turned from reaching down for the laundry.

A flush of embarrassment heated her cheeks. "I can't seem to manage my hair this morning."

He smiled, showing a dimple on his hairless face. He glided over and lifted the brush from her limp fingers. "I used to have my hair longer than yours."

His hands were soft and dexterous. Suza tried not to let it show how much pleasure she took in the tender touch, in being taken care of, but her eyes closed on their own, and her shoulders lowered. He was patient with the tangles, and she was in no hurry for him to finish. Even with all the time he'd spent ogling Xandra, who was preening herself on the table, within minutes, he'd brushed out the storm and applied a drop of her hair oil.

"Thank you."

His cheeks pinked. "It was fun."

Her mouth curved up, something she had never expected her lips to do again. She was more grateful to the young man for giving her a moment of simple joy than for the smooth hair or clean laundry.

Walking as if made of tin, Suza went to Titus's tent. Xandra flew off to nap in a tall tree.

Titus sat behind a desk, his broken leg elevated on a chair to the side. Uriah was lying in the captain's bed with Imanna perched at his side. A handful of other humans sat around the table. She ignored the buffet of food and went straight to her brother. She took his hand, glad to see his skin a richer color than last night. He'd survived. He'd heal, and together with Imanna, he would thrive. Suza could only hope she might someday too. She pushed Ferth from her mind.

"How are you?"

"It hurts." Uriah's bottom lip stuck out like a toddler.

Imanna leaned over and kissed it. "I told you not to try and move this morning." A wash and rest had done wonders for the secret princess. Her curls had regained their bounce, the shadows under her eyes weren't so deep, and her cheeks not so pale.

"It hurt before that too."

"Be glad you're not in Laconius's army," Suza said.

"I'm always glad about that," Uriah said.

She angled toward Titus and spoke louder. "He killed every injured soldier not strong enough to walk. They're pulling out this morning and marching back to Shi Castle."

The others in the tent cheered.

Uriah swore, and then he smiled too.

She didn't let go of her brother's hand, needing to feel his rough skin and living warmth. She turned her gaze to Titus. "Good morning, Captain."

"Yes, I think it is." He grinned, but it didn't reach his blue eyes. The scars across his face seemed especially stark this morning. Suza could almost see the weight of responsibility and sorrow pressing down on the captain's strong frame.

She couldn't help but think of the cost of victory. Of course, it had been worth it, and more, to save this land from tyranny. But every time she closed her eyes, she saw the funeral fires, as big as mountains: Callidon, Zemira, Guap, Pelussa, and thousands of other nameless heroes, all gone. At least there was one who'd avoided the sword. "Ferth stayed in Mitera?" Her resentment came out in her tone.

"No." Titus seemed to age before her eyes. He ran a hand through his graying hair. It was longer than his ears and in need of a cut. "He's in Skotar."

Her heart sank to her shoes at the same time she clung to the implication he hadn't abandoned her by choice. "He's been captured." Her hand went limp in Uriah's. He didn't let her go.

"No."

Cold dread crawled over her skin. Why would Ferth return to Draco country, a place he'd be enslaved or slaughtered?

Titus rubbed the thigh of his broken leg. "He's gone on a mission to hunt down the Dragon, Prince Nogard."

Suza had no words for that ridiculous, dangerous notion. No words, only a puff of air.

The door opened, and Raja Darius walked in with his bandaged left arm in a sling, his face a sickly gray.

Titus nodded at Darius before he looked back at Suza. "King Darius has the details."

"King?" Suza repeated in surprise. He didn't exactly carry himself as if he owned the country. Probably a good thing he didn't remind her of Queen Mavras. He seemed like a fine choice for Elysium: brave, intelligent, and just.

"At your service." Darius dipped his head to her.

She didn't know how to respond to his graceful civility, so she stared in silence until Titus said, "I'll let him explain what happened in Mitera two weeks ago when the Dracos assassinated King Abner and tried to kill Ferth."

Suza sat abruptly on the chair next to Titus's bed, hardly feeling the pain that surged through her muscles. It was nothing compared to the agony that clutched her heart. *Ferth.* His name clanged against her ribs.

King Darius sat by Titus, resting his right arm on the desk for support. The officers mingling around the tent quieted. "A small band of Draco Sang attacked the king's Lammas party. Nineteen people died, including King Abner and one of the Draco Sang—a flyer named Thirro."

Suza gasped.

Darius nodded. "You knew him?"

"Did Ferth kill him?" She pitied him having to turn on an old friend, even if Thirro was often cruel and vindictive.

"No." Darius shook his head. "Thirro was killed by a member of his party. A female. Ferth called her by the name of Jade."

Suza was glad she was sitting down. Shock slowed her thoughts. It had only been a couple months since she'd been in Skotar. All these names and faces were still familiar to her. Among the slaves, Jade was considered one of the better Dracos. She wasn't sadistic. She'd been an underling last winter when Suza and Ferth had left Shi Castle for war, but even back then, Suza had seen how infatuated Jade was with Ferth. She couldn't imagine the jackal turning against Ferth. A reminder for Suza to never trust a Draco.

"During the attack, Jade and Thirro and two other Dracos were shooting down at the crowd from an interior balcony. Thirro aimed at Jade first. He was going to shoot his own soldier, but Ferth warned her to dodge. She listened to him instinctively, and it saved her from getting an arrow in the back. When Thirro aimed for Ferth, Jade threw her knife into the flyer's heart. A remarkable shot."

"Yes," Suza muttered. "She's very good."

"She saved Ferth's life but exposed his Draco heritage in the process. He'd stepped forward to try and talk the Dracos down and give the rest of us time to flee. He saved innocent lives, but many people there felt that he was in collusion with the attackers. He obviously knew the Draco assassins well, and they knew him. Jade had trusted Ferth out of habit. They couldn't hide that history. After he talked the three remaining Dracos into leaving, Ferth was viewed with suspicion by many." Darius looked her in the eyes. "I sent to him to hunt Nogard, in part to protect him."

White-hot fury hit with his words. This man had sent Ferth away. When Ferth had finally earned his freedom, Darius had sentenced him to a terrible death. "Sending him to Skotar is the opposite of protecting him." Suza's tone was harsh.

Captain Titus frowned at her lack of respect, but she didn't care that Darius was king. He'd been blind and cruel to rob Ferth of his future and his freedom. Her future. She was too frayed from facing death for days, taking lives—as if she had the right—to lay down and let this human upstart stomp on the parts of her soul she had left. She was sorry she'd thought Ferth capable of abandoning her. Of betrayal. She should have known better. Ferth had been fighting his own impossible battles, and he must have felt even more alone and out of place than she did.

Darius's face softened. "It wasn't an easy choice to make. I bear the heavy responsibility of sending him into enemy territory, but I believe it worth the risk. Killing Nogard is the only chance we have at protecting our border. I am king now." He looked like he was trying to convince himself of the fact. "And I must do all I can for Elysium, and that means finding Nogard and ending his control."

Suza ripped her hand out of Uriah's grip. Her face

prickled with heat. "Nogard cannot possibly be alive. It's a fool's errand. A suicide mission. Ferth will die." Her voice came out like rock chips.

Darius lifted his chin and sat up straighter as if preparing for a fight, but his voice remained calm. "I believe he will succeed."

"Then you're a fool." She spit the words out, not caring that the handful of gathered humans looked at her with reproach. She'd fight them all if it brought Ferth back. Ferth might not feel like he had anyone on his side, but he had her. She'd never doubt him again. She'd prove her loyalty. Somehow.

"Suza. Hold your tongue," Titus's voice was sharp. "That is your king."

She glared at Titus. "I don't care. He sent Ferth, my…" her voice caught, "my Ferth to die."

Titus flinched, the pain in his eyes mirroring hers. She took some solace, knowing he wanted Ferth safe too. Little good wanting did.

Ferth deserved life. He deserved it more than anyone on this continent.

Darius's steady tenor drew Suza's attention away from the shared grief. "I know I can't guarantee his survival, but he is the best chance we have. He is tough and smart. He knows Skotar. He's a survivor like I've never met." The king's eyes shone.

She gave a curt nod of agreement. Ferth was all those things and more. Something weird was happening inside her ribs. She couldn't name it, but it was uncomfortable, like pride mixed with pain—desire and dismay. She scratched her sternum, but the sorrow didn't recede.

"He conquered the Dragon before. I trust he can do it again."

Foolishness. Ignorance. But what could she do? Her gaze

lowered. Helpless. She was utterly helpless. The icy feeling took her back to when she was a new slave at Shi Castle. Fear descended on her like a hungry monster. This morning she wore the slave's shift again like a bad omen. Despair. Loneliness. All was lost.

And then Uriah's hand found her shoulder. His big palm slid down her arm and clasped her hand. He held tight, chasing the darkness away. She looked at him. His jaw was hard, and his gaze steady. She was here in Elysium with her brother, who loved her. The victory won. Free.

But her brave, kind-hearted Ferth was... was... a sob escaped, and she couldn't finish the thought, couldn't imagine what trouble her love was in right now—exiled the moment he'd found freedom. It wasn't right.

"I hope he will succeed in his mission," Darius whispered.

She pinched her eyes shut and inhaled, forcing her fists not to connect with the king's sharp nose. A terrible thought popped into her mind. "Did he want to go?"

He hesitated, and the world seemed to crash around her. "No. He did not want to go, but he accepted the mission of his own free will. I did not force him." He exhaled pure exhaustion.

Suza couldn't bear to hear it, couldn't breathe until she knew everything.

Darius's shoulders slumped. "Ferth is a good man, but I cannot say I expect him to return. I told him he was welcome back in Elysium." He pursed his lips as if fighting the next words, and Suza steeled herself against what pain he might spread next. "He and his wolves..." He rubbed his shaved chin. "They were not comfortable in Mitera. I don't know if it was guilt over his past, the difference of culture, or something else, but he didn't feel like he belonged."

Wild, thoughtful, powerful Ferth. He must have felt like a

wolf among chickens—a pack of wolves. She rubbed at the broken spot on her chest as her heart shattered.

She'd lost him. Ferth was gone.

Imanna brought Suza a cup of tavo. She took a warm sip before whispering her defeat. "He's never coming back." The declaration hit with a solid ring of truth. He'd told her he loved her just weeks ago, kissed her like he couldn't breathe without her. And then he'd given up on his humanity. He'd left her, taking her heart with him.

Darius's voice was heavy. "I'm trying not to put too much hope in seeing him again." A gentle suggestion for her to do the same.

She nodded dumbly. There was nothing more she could say. Her chest swelled with hurt, and her eyes burned.

Darius pulled a letter from his breast pocket and, with sorry eyes, passed it to Imanna to give to Suza. "He left that for you."

Suza couldn't keep back her sorrow any longer. Tears fell as she stood, Uriah reached for her, but she slipped out of range. "Please excuse me, captain, your Majesty." Darius flinched at the title, but no one said a word as she fled the tent, the words from Ferth clutched to her breast.

She ran south, past the southern guard, and into the forest where she followed Xandra to a tall pine. She couldn't see Xandra, but she could sense her napping forty feet up. Suza sat on the mossy ground and held out the letter, knowing it contained a goodbye she wasn't ready to hear.

Suza,

I'm leaving Elysium. Despite my thin skin and fur-less back, I am not human. I am returning to Skotar, but not to join the Draco Sang. I have lost my place among them as well.

I am hunting for Nogard's remains. I don't expect to find anything, but I told King Darius I would look. And so, I shall. I have a young tracker with me named Tobin Forsythson. He will be interesting company. Lyko and Rom are glad to be leaving civilization.

I wish I could come to you, hold you, and love you as I've dreamed. But I must accept that you will always be a future I am unworthy of. I cannot give you the life you deserve. Go to Mitera and enjoy the bounty, beauty, and safety. I wish you all the best this world can offer.

I will love you until the end.

Good-bye.

Ferth Mirasson

"No. No. No. I do not accept this."

Xandra glided down and landed in Suza's lap. The feathered, little animal was nothing like the embrace of a warm, muscled human. The touch of a downy head against her chest did nothing to assuage the pain inside. Suza ran her fingers over Xandra's soft wings, aching for Ferth.

Frustration hummed through her veins. "That stupid brute has no right to decide what's good for me and what I deserve." She huffed, her tirade gaining steam. "That self-deprecating coward might choose misery and a sad life of guilt, but he's not going to choose it for me."

"You tell him."

Suza straightened up, the tears abating. Resolve fed energy to her tired soul. "I will."

SIXTEEN - FORWARD

FERTH

Outside the crowded caves, Ferth slept poorly, waking periodically to the heart-wrenching sound of Ipsum's cries and Tobin's responding coos. Ferth expected the raven to leave in a fit of feral caws at any moment, giving himself up to a wildness that would surely send him to an early death, but when the sun rose, the black bird was tucked against Tobin's chest.

Ferth blinked up at a semi-circle of ragged people staring down at him. He was glad to see the majority, including the children, had packed their meager belongings to move south. Ten of those children were Draco Sang. His wolves could smell it on them. He pointed to each one, including the youngest four Draco children standing close to the nurses' legs. He motioned them forward. The human caretakers looked afraid, reaching to shield the children they had stolen from the Draco Sang.

"There is no one left to properly care for them at Gristle-cove," one of the women said, her voice bold, despite the fear in her eyes.

"It's okay." Ferth motioned them forward again, and this

time a woman walked them closer, her hands on their necks and backs reassuring.

He didn't get up. He wasn't sure what sort of embarrassing, grotesque, profane scene he would make when he moved his shoulder for the first time in hours. His torso was propped up against the rock at a high enough angle that he could talk to the youngest children at nearly eye level. "You are Draco Sang."

The woman flinched.

Ten children stared back at him with big eyes.

"Like me." Ferth smiled, hoping it came off as encouraging and not creepy. These children had a harder road ahead of them than most. "Remember as you grow that you are stronger than your blood. You are capable and intelligent. You can control your dragon instead of becoming a slave to it." Ferth looked up at the adults. "Do not shun them or shame them. They will learn to become what you teach them. Show them love."

One of the nurses wiped tears from her eyes and held the infant at her breast tighter.

"If you need help... *when* you need help, find Captain Titus. He is a Draco Sang like me. Like us. He will help you."

Leelee stepped up and knelt by Ferth's dirty boots. "Thank you."

"You're welcome. Lyko will show you the way to Elysium. Good luck."

"*I do* not *want to go*." Lyko roused himself to his feet, leaving Ferth's right side cold.

Rom rolled over, let out an exaggerated yawn, and closed his eyes. Lyko made sure to step on Rom's tail as he marched past. The white wolf padded straight into the forest, leaving the travelers scrambling to catch up. A weight lifted off Ferth's chest as they disappeared. He scanned the camp. Marko and Allie ate bread and cheese near the low fire. Too bad they hadn't gone too, but what place did a fully trans-formed Draco have in Elysium? Tobin appeared at Ferth's side and held out a steaming cup.

"Help me up," Ferth said. "I need to pee."

"I'm not helping you with *that*."

He held out his good arm. "Just…"

Tobin tugged. It wasn't as helpful as Ferth had hoped, but he managed to get to his feet with minimal grunting. The slice in his shoulder flamed with every shift of his muscles. The not-so-old arrow injury on his side from this spring seemed to have woken from its slumber. He lifted his shirt to see the red scar puckered and bruised but not bleeding. Good enough. After visiting a tree nearby, Ferth sat by the fire, drinking hot spiced cream, and letting Tobin change the dressing on his shoulder. Ferth would give anything for some of Keturah's healing balm this morning. They had bandages but nothing to prevent infection. Except alcohol. Ferth thought it at the same moment he felt the sear of Tobin pouring a portion of that very same acid over the stitches. Ferth hissed and glared but thanked Tobin sincerely when he finished.

Ferth didn't talk to the others. He didn't want to know their plans or get involved with their lives any more deeply. After breakfast, Ferth went back to sleep. He woke near sunset. Lyko was already back, thank the stars. It was easier to stand, and his shoulder had muted to a dull throb.

"Time to go."

Tobin, sitting by cold embers, nodded. He had already packed their bags. To Ferth's surprise, Ipsum sat perched on the log next to Tobin.

Ferth rubbed at his sore fighting arm as he walked over. "Hello, Ipsum."

The bird nodded his head.

"You are welcome to come with us."

Tobin rested his hand on the bird's back. The gesture was protective and territorial, and Ferth realized there was no way Ipsum was not coming.

Ferth glanced around. "Where are the others?"

Tobin shrugged and held out a portion of bread and meat the slaves had brought from Gristlecove. "They left."

"Great." Ferth had been a little worried Marko and Allie might have tried to join them. "We'll need to head due west to avoid any patrols searching from Gristlecove. We must stay off the roads." Not that Tobin would be impressed with the roads. They were packed dirt, flat and even in the nicest areas, rocky and undulating in the worst, nothing like the stone streets Tobin grew up with in Mitera.

Tobin helped Ferth put his pack over his good shoulder, and the five of them, including the raven standing on Tobin's pack, slipped into the forest.

"We're being followed," Rom said an hour later.

Ferth looked over his shoulder but could see nothing but the twisting silhouettes of trees in the darkness.

"Rom says someone's following us. Stay close, and we'll try to catch them out."

Tobin's nervous gaze darted. Ipsum took to the sky, black on black.

Ferth stopped at a clearing, and they hid behind a cluster of boulders. It wasn't long before two figures burst out of the trees. Moonlight revealed a tiger Draco Sang and a human woman. Naked sword up, Ferth and his wolves padded into view. Marko and Allie reeled back, hands up.

"What are you doing?" Ferth's tone rang with the command he'd learned from his father.

Ipsum swooped down and landed in a high branch with a good view.

"We're just traveling this way." Marko had a voice that put Ferth on edge. Even when he spoke softly, it was gruff, with the ghost of a growl lacing each word like a deadly caress.

Ferth's face set in hard lines. "That's a lie."

Allie stepped forward. "Please, Ferth. We cannot go with the others to Elysium. The humans will never accept Marko."

"Then go somewhere else."

"You know there is no safe place for us," Marko said.

That was not a lie. Ferth exhaled in frustration. He had the same problem and didn't particularly want to be reminded of it.

"We can help you," Marko said. "I will protect you until I have paid my debts."

Ferth had more to atone for himself than he'd ever make up for. He looked at their pleading eyes, Marko's deep brown and Allie's hazel. She was lovely, sad, and needy, reminding him too much of his own debts. Of Keturah and Pearl. Shale—Suzaena. He glanced at his wolves. He didn't have to ask them to know that Rom was for and Lyko against.

He sheathed his sword and motioned Tobin to help him put his pack back on. Wordlessly he led out, turning north, answering the call of his blood. Too many muffled footsteps followed.

He didn't like it. Tobin, and then Ipsum. Now these two. He wasn't interested in collecting lost souls. Even if he was one himself.

SEVENTEEN - TWISTING JOURNEY

SUZA

Suza found Uriah in the tent he shared with his wife. He lay in bed scowling while Imanna flitted about packing.

Suza closed the door flap and stood tall at the foot of the bed. Uriah trained his frown on her.

Suza put her hands on her hips. "I'm going back to Skotar."

Imanna whirled from where she folded clothes on the table, the scarf tied around her brow fluttering behind her.

Uriah jerked to a sitting position, clutched his chest with a groan, and flopped back down. Suza flinched against his angry roar then rushed to his side. He panted, his face pale, but when he took her hand, his grip was as strong as Dracosteel. "That. Was." He heaved in painful breathes. "Not. A." Breath. "Funny. Joke."

She didn't answer.

"Suza." Imanna's voice was a warning.

"I am serious. I am going."

Imanna's brows crawled together. "Why?"

"Ferth," Uriah spit the name out like an accusation.

Suza bristled.

He studied her as if trying to read what he should say from her face. "He left you without saying goodbye, so what, now you're going to hunt him down?"

That was not the right thing to say. Suza tried to pull her hand free, but he squeezed.

"I didn't mean it like that. I meant that if Ferth loves you, he will come back. He wouldn't want you putting yourself in danger by traveling as a slave on your own through Draco country."

When Uriah put it like that, it sounded incredibly foolish. No matter, Skotar was the only place she'd ever known, her home. "He's not coming back for me. He thinks I should stop loving him and find someone else."

Uriah's eyes brightened for a flash before he schooled his face into gentle concern.

"You agree!"

"No one is good enough for my sister."

"He's wrong, and so are you. You don't even know him." She ripped her hand free. She would never find better than Ferth. Her heart called for him. She needed to find him. She held in a sob at the thought Ferth could move on from her so easily. She didn't—couldn't believe it.

"I know." Uriah held his hand up in a placating gesture. "And I trust you." He held her gaze as he said it. "But please, Suza. Don't go to Skotar *yet*. We leave for Mitera in the morning with Titus and Darius. Darius is anxious for our help in securing his new throne and settling the country in the aftermath of this war. They expect you to come with us."

"I am free to go where I please."

"I know," he said quickly. "But I'm begging you to come." His eyes watered. "I want to know my sister. I'm desperate for time with you outside of Gristlecove or war." His big brown eyes turned soft and pleading, impossible to deny, and she wondered again what his bear hewan must have been like. She sorrowed that she would never get to meet Poe and realized she did not want to live with the regret of missing out on more time with her brother. It would be better to wait until after the winter to return to Skotar anyway.

"Who would you go with?" Imanna tried to sound casual as she tucked a folded shirt into a trunk. "How would you protect yourself? Where would you travel?"

All questions Suza kept asking herself, thinking they didn't matter because she was going after Ferth. She would find him because their hearts were connected. Her love for him was all she needed. It was a lie.

"You must see the capital," Uriah said. "They have pastries that melt in your mouth and fabric as soft as kittens. You must experience Elysium first. Please wait until then to make your choice."

It was with a measure of relief that she said, "Fine. I will come to Mitera with you in the morning." But she did not intend to stay. This winter, she would make her preparations, and come spring, when Ferth had not returned, she would hunt Skotar for the fragments of her broken heart that had remained in that wild place she'd long called home. She would seek the man who needed love and healing even more than she. She felt sure... she hoped... that together they would find it. Come what may, she couldn't face a future of not knowing. She'd fought for her freedom. She would fight just as hard for her love.

EIGHTEEN - REBEL

JADE

Each morning the traveling army woke up smaller than the day before as Dracos drifted into the forests and hills. Laconius didn't try to stop the defectors. They had lost the war. The food was gone. He wanted them off his hands. He only guarded the precious few slaves they had left. Each day the dwindling army marched until the ragged humans dropped in exhaustion. They slept in blankets on the dirt road.

The storm hit the fourth day. Jade wore a canvas tarp as a shield against the sleet as she marched, but the cold drilled into her bones. The icy rain continued into the afternoon. They stopped early, and Laconius commanded the slaves to set up tents. They were a sorry group, those dozen humans. But they persisted with stunning grit and determination. As Jade sat with the rest of the Dracos under an open-sided tent eating magu stew, she watched them work with begrudging respect. She'd always thought herself tough, but in the face of their display of sheer perseverance, she felt like a tender pellistium blossom.

Pearl's wet braid hung limply down her back as she

carried bedding to the hastily erected tents. She trudged past the dining soldiers, shoulders bowed.

"You there, slave," a pangolin Draco with extended lips and scales pleated over his scalp and shoulders called to Pearl.

She pretended not to hear, picking up her pace.

"Slave with the milky hair, stop."

Pearl halted but didn't look up.

"Go ahead and stay in my bed after you make it up."

The slave slowly blinked. She looked tired and exhausted to the point of death.

"No." Jade was surprised to hear the voice was her own. "That slave is mine for the night." Jade was the highest-ranking Draco here besides Laconius and Mina, and those two were having their meals delivered to their private tents. She ignored the soldier's scowl, focusing on a surprised Pearl. "Quick. Finish your duties. I want you in my tent before I finish this stew."

Pearl trudged away, no faster than before.

Jade refilled her bowl and pocketed a loaf of stale black bread. She took the food to her tent, already feeling less depressed. It was blessedly empty as Dara had taken a liking to a zebra Draco she'd been bunking with the last few nights. Jade set the food on her sleeping cot as they didn't set up other furniture tonight. Then she headed back into the rain. The slaves gathered for the night in a low tent. Jade peeked her head in the door. They shared blankets on the cold floor. The males and females had to share a tent tonight, but they divided themselves down the middle with a canvas partition. She wrinkled her nose against the smell of sweat and desperation.

The humans went quiet, eyes gleaming as they looked at her—waiting for her will.

She couldn't help them all. Not tonight, not without

exposing her sympathies to the Dracos. She couldn't lose the standing she'd gained in this army. Her plans depended on staying in Laconius's good graces.

"Kenji." Jade knew all the slaves by name. She couldn't be the daughter of a slave and see them as nameless. Usually, she pretended not to know, but that was a lie.

He lay on a blanket against the far canvas. His chin tilted a fraction, the only indication he listened.

"You'll come with me." Her voice sounded like law. It was no wonder they were afraid.

He said nothing as he rose from his resting place, his bulk graceful. He towered over Jade, a meek giant in her wake as she led him to her tent.

She peeled back the door. Kenji glanced at her with a flash of resentment before his face turned to emotionless stone, and he strode inside. He stopped short when he saw Pearl standing at the foot of the bed.

Jade tied the tent closed against the sleet. "Share the food, and don't spill it on my blankets." They stared. It was like talking to statues. "Hurry up. It's getting cold."

Kenji sent her a questioning look. Pearl's brows pinched in confusion.

"Share the food." Her voice was hard.

He hesitated a moment longer before stepping up and lifting the bowl. The army was dangerously low on food, and Jade had seen the sad pot of stale porridge the slaves got for dinner tonight. Kenji shielded Pearl from Jade's view with his broad back, but not before she saw him tenderly bring a spoonful to her mouth.

Jade turned away, peeling off her wet boots and coat.

"Your turn." Pearl's voice was hushed.

"Eat."

"Bite for bite," she whispered.

"Two for one." His voice was a low rumble full of concern.

Though Jade tried not to listen, her lips curved up at their selfless arguing. Her heart twisted for them.

The slaves finished the stew and the bread. Kenji set the bowl by the door and then stood like a sentry at Pearl's side. They looked to Jade and waited. They would do as she commanded—anything. The thought always gave her a bit of a thrill. At the same time, it twisted like venom through her belly. She was anxious to return to her mother at Shi Castle. Make sure all is well. Jade's new position as commander gave her more power to protect Keturah.

"I'm tired," Jade said. "Into bed. Kenji, you'll sleep on your side, so your back keeps me warm all night. The bed is small, so I guess you'll have to deal with holding Pearl to keep her from falling off." It took everything she had to conquer the urge to smile when the two slaves realized what she was demanding of them. They couldn't quite repress the look of luck that brightened their sad faces.

Jade climbed into bed, making herself small against the side. A moment later, she held her breath against the stink of unwashed male as Kenji lay next to her, his back as big and warm as she'd hoped.

All was quiet until a few minutes later when Pearl whispered into the darkness. "Good night, Jade."

A tear leaked out the side of the jackal Draco's eye and soaked into her fur. Mortifying. She wasn't supposed to be like this. It seemed, even after all the killing, she was weak, hiding tenderness. But seeing the devotion between these two humans, despite the horrors in their lives, made her want to keep her soft heart and protect them. She enjoyed bringing a touch of sun to their dreary days. She hadn't felt this good since she'd kissed her mother goodbye. She could feel the couple holding tight to each other behind her back, and she yearned for a partner of her own to chase the shadows away. She hated that she thought of Ferth.

Let them have their love and keep it. "Sleep well."

They did. Jade woke early, and the humans didn't react when she slipped off the bed. They slept as hard as naïve newborns. Faces slack and young, breathing slow. Her nightmares would never let her rest that deep. The pair lay together like moss clinging to a damp tree. She'd never seen slaves so relaxed in a Draco tent. Either they had realized she wasn't a threat to them tonight, or they were past caring. She hoped she wouldn't be the one ordered to strip them of the skin on their backs when this mad ordeal was finally over.

The slave Tiberian had died during the night. They left his body under a pine off the side of the road, unburned and unburied. Jade whispered the funeral blessing before she moved on.

They were three days from Shi Castle when Laconius spoke to Jade in private and told her of her part in his plan to kill Queen Mavras.

It was a well-laid plot, even if it put all the danger on Jade. Now, she merely had to decide whether she wanted to go through with it or inform her queen aunt that Laconius was a traitor.

NINETEEN - INFECTED

FERTH

Ferth's wound was infected. The fever had come last night after the storm hit and cold sleet had soaked through to his skin. This morning his clothes were still damp. He mumbled obscenities about the weakness of his human body as he shivered.

Tobin brought him a drink where he lay under a rocky overhang and touched his forehead. "You're burning up."

He felt as if he'd never be warm again. "Thanks." He took the cup with shaking hands.

Despite the concern on Tobin's face, he didn't bother checking the wound. They were out of bandages, and it didn't help anything to see the green puss grow.

Ferth had changed course for Shi Castle three days ago, knowing he needed help. He'd never been sick before. Disease was a rare thing for the Draco-blooded. It had been a very dirty blade that buried into his flesh, and it wouldn't have been beneath Gristlecove to slick it with poison. He shuttered, fighting the urge to vomit. He needed to hold down his drink. He'd lost too much strength already.

"Time to move." Tobin held out a hand to Ferth.

"Who put you in charge?"

"Cute." Tobin gripped Ferth's palm. "On three. One, two, up."

Ferth heaved to his feet. Dizziness clouded his vision. His guts rolled like the High Sea. He failed to shield his wolves from the surge of pain. Lyko whined.

"Walking stick." His voice sounded as bad as he felt, dry and gravelly. Tobin handed him the knotted branch he'd whittled into a smooth twisting staff. "Nothing like a winter walk in the woods." Ferth started off. Marko carried his pack. The wolves stayed close on his heels. He hobbled and panted with every step. It was all very humiliating.

They trekked through the familiar forest to the west of his childhood stronghold. Ferth stopped his dragging death march at a little clearing he knew well. The same place he'd cooked his first kill as a newly transformed Draco Sang wolf. He pursed his lips at the irony as his two huge wolves circled the spot, sniffing at charcoal and old bones. He felt like he'd aged a thousand years since that night a year and a half ago.

Ferth's legs nearly gave out as he sat on a log. "We're within an hour's walk to the gates."

The problem was getting through them.

Allie force-fed Ferth sips of warm, wild herb tea, but he couldn't manage any of the dried meat.

Being sick was really no way to live. He was not okay with it.

They went over their plan of entry once more. Good chance he'd die before the day was out. Ferth plastered on a grimace. "Let's get to it."

Marko hauled Ferth to his feet. He waited for the waves of dizziness to pass before he took a step. Ferth held onto the walking stick in one hand and Rom's fur in the other as they picked their way through the sparse trees. He trusted the wolf to lead them home. Was it home? It still felt like home at the moment. Half the time, Ferth's eyes were closed, his head lulling heavily around his shoulders. When Shi Castle loomed before them, and they reached the end of the tree cover, Rom stopped the group. Tobin helped Ferth into the slaves' clothing they'd taken from Gristlecove.

Ferth didn't even flinch when Marko took Ferth's sword and strapped it to his own waist. If the Draco turned on Ferth now, it'd be a mercy. Marko strapped Thirro's bow to his back.

Three males turned to Allie and the wolves. Ipsum perched in a tree above her head. Marko had insisted Allie stay behind. He wouldn't risk taking her among powerful Dracos ever again. She had been quick to choose to stay with the wolves instead of acting the slave.

Allie darted up to Marko and threw her arms around his shoulders. He lifted her easily off the ground as she kissed him, her hands raking through his furry scalp.

Tobin and Ferth trudged away. Marko caught up a few paces later.

"Don't go too far," Ferth said to his wolves.

"If anything happens..." Rom said.

"I'll be fine."

The three men stepped onto the dirt road leading to the gate from the direction of the planting fields. Tobin tilted his face back and gawked at the towering white stone castle visible above the walls. His gaze latched on the massive copper statue of Nogard the Dragon guarding the gate.

"Keep your head down," Marko whispered behind them.

Tobin's chin snapped to his chest.

A goat Draco appeared at the gate as they approached.

Marko shoved Tobin, causing the boy to stumble forward. "Keep your feet, you little pisser."

Tobin glanced over his shoulder in fear and betrayal at

the unfamiliar tone of cruelty in Marko's gruff voice. The tiger sneered.

Ferth gripped Tobin's elbow, reminding him to face forward and keep walking.

The goat turned away, uninterested, and Ferth let go of a ragged breath. The trio walked through the gate. Nogard's wing blotted out the sun, and a chill ran down Ferth's fevered spine. Shi Castle. Ferth had returned. Not as a war hero but as a traitorous abomination on the verge of death. He couldn't bear to think about it.

The only home he'd ever known looked the same, with various buildings surrounding a white castle. Muddy and smelling of woodsmoke and animals. Only a few Dracos were in the courtyard. He didn't look to the citadel as he silently pleaded Queen Mavras would not appear. The clang of metal sounded from the training fields to the west.

He had no trouble acting the dejected slave as he lugged himself across the clearing, head down, toward the slave quarters. They hadn't been noticed or questioned yet, but his feet moved faster, and his heart quaked with worry as he felt the eyes of the deer Draco near the citadel graze over him. Marko strutted with confidence behind Ferth and Tobin, walking as if driving cattle to the slaughter.

"That door," Ferth whispered, pointing to the low building near the high outer wall. "Open it."

Like a frightened rabbit, Tobin darted forward and pried it open. A slave walked out, looking over Tobin, Ferth, and Marko. His eyes widened for a blink but he continued past without slowing. Ferth scrambled up the three stone steps and, in his rush, bumped his shoulder on the door frame. He gasped at the shock of agony. His vision went black, and his body gave out. Marko caught him by the waist and hauled him inside. The door slammed shut.

"What happened?" Rom demanded.

"We can be through the gates in seconds," Lyko said.

Ferth could sense the anxious wolves pacing to the east. *"I'm fine."* His vision returned, and he gagged at the smell of urine and sweat. He blinked, but the dark walls still seemed to be closing in on him. "Down the stairs at the end of the hall."

Marko on one side, Tobin on the other, they ran/dragged Ferth through the narrow corridor. His shoulder grumbled with every jostle, but he was too far into the abyss to take interest in the pain. The laundry wasn't as busy as he remembered, but that was probably because most of the usual inhabitants of Shi Castle were killing humans at the border. Hopefully, Keturah had a reprieve these last months. The handful of slaves working the vats looked up in surprise as they entered the low basement. Every eye fixed on Marko, the tiger Draco loaded down with weapons.

"Take me into that office there." Ferth pointed to the closed door.

Tobin opened it without knocking, and Marko helped him inside.

"Oh, thank the stars," Ferth said when he saw the familiar woman jump up from her desk. He slumped into the chair she'd vacated, still warm from her body. He'd made it. And he knew that now he was in Keturah's care, he would be okay. She would take care of him. The last of his energy slipped away, and he turned to pudding. "Help me."

Keturah paled as she looked at Marko, then Tobin. She rapidly blinked when she focused on Ferth. She squinted.

"I need the med kit again." His whisper was cracked and low.

Her whole face changed, like sunlight breaking up a storm. She beamed as she stared at Ferth, realization dawning as she soaked in his human features.

He tried to smile but didn't have the strength. When he'd

envisioned this reunion, he'd at least had the use of his arms, but still, seeing the joy on her face filled him with hope and warmth. She looked good, tired and too thin, as always, but her eyes were bright, her shift clean, and her white hair brushed back in a neat braid.

Her delight in seeing the boy she'd raised return in human form descended into concern. She rushed to her cabinet and withdrew the basket. "Of course, it's you who needs the med kit." Her voice quivered with emotion.

Ferth glanced up at the man with the weapons. "Help me out of this."

Marko pulled a knife and cut the shirt and bandages off. Ferth's nostrils tried to cinch closed at the smell of rot that wafted up.

Keturah turned from the cupboard and nearly dropped her supplies when she saw the infection.

"I think I need some of your healing balm." He let out a weak chuckle.

She did not laugh. Her face shifted into serious lines. "Cleaning first."

"That sounds painful."

"You'd know better than I since you have so much experience in this area." Her voice was harsh, afraid.

Worry hollowing her eyes, she set the basket on the floor and leaned close, studying his inflamed wound. She had the same kind eyes, but she'd aged. Her wrinkles had deepened, and more spots dotted her skin.

He'd missed her dearly. His love for her hit like a wash of healing tonic. Tears filled his eyes that had nothing to do with the simple pain of infection. He'd meet his blood mother, and Mira had his whole heart. But Keturah had raised him. She'd braved Skotar. She knew him truly, all the ugly bits. She'd seen him fight to become a Draco, and she'd still loved him. Keturah was worn, wiry, and worked to the bone. And she had his whole soul.

"Are you okay, Ma?" Ferth asked, taking in the darkness below her eyes, her sunken cheeks.

She stilled at the word Ma. He'd never called her that. Never admitted what she was to him. He had two mothers. He'd always had two mothers. But now he'd claimed them. He felt like the richest man in the world. He was going to love and keep them both.

She looked over his face as if seeing him for the first time. She put a hand to his bearded cheek, a welcome cool against his fever. "I have never been better. My plumloch has bloomed." A tear slid down her leathered face. She kissed Ferth below his eye. "My boy has returned to me a man, and I could burst with joy."

"I'm sorry it took me so long." He lowered his gaze.

She kissed him again. "I am not." Her voice turned to business. "Help him to the floor. I need to get saltwater."

Ferth groaned as she slipped out. He could hear her muffled voice talking to the other slaves, but he understood nothing. Hopefully, they would keep their presence a secret. Slaves gossiped, but they usually watched out for each other. Mavras would give a hefty reward to have Laconius's son in her hands, but Ferth was unlikely to have been recognized. Pain flared as Marko jostled him to the ground. The cold stone caused goosebumps to break out over his fur-less skin.

"I'm going for food." Marko left Ferth's sword and bow. Ferth appreciated the gesture, though he didn't have the strength to wield them.

A fierce Draco of Marko's size shouldn't have trouble walking around Shi Castle. If anyone questioned him, he'd tell the truth: he'd come from Gristlecove to report to the queen about the death of his lord and the revolt of the slaves.

Ferth was grateful to have Marko on his side. He was fully aware of how much he depended on the trust and strength of this fully transformed Draco. Not for the first time, he wondered how different the Draco Sang would be if they had people like Titus as their leaders instead of Mavras. Suppose the queen cultivated those like Marko and Jade instead of rewarding the cruel Minas and Thirros of the world.

Tobin sat near Ferth's side and hugged his knees to his chest, rocking back and forth. It looked like a habit. He wondered why the boy had learned how to self-soothe in such a way. Then he remembered his mother, Forsyth. She clearly wasn't one for cradling. It seemed where Ferth had mothers in abundance, Tobin went without. A brutal injustice.

Tobin jumped to help Keturah with a heavy pot when she appeared in the doorway. After some uncomfortable maneuvering, they propped Ferth's shoulder over an empty bowl and washed the wound with hot saltwater. He bit down on his screams and confined himself to heavy breathing and sharing vibrant thoughts with his blameless wolves.

"Come on," Rom said. *"You can do better than common curse words."*

"You want me to wax poetic about pain?" Ferth grit his teeth so hard he thought they would break. Tobin kindly stuffed linen between his jaw after that.

"I want you to toughen up and let me nap." Lyko flopped down next to Allie, hidden among the trees. He put his head in her lap. Ferth could sense behind the wolf's bravado the constant fear that Ferth would be taken from him as Cal had been.

Ferth gasped when Keturah finished the wash of burning water. He was less than thrilled that she refilled the pot three more times before being satisfied. She dabbed the wound—

which already looked better—with clean linen before
smearing her cool herb and loodia pulp concoction over it.

He sighed in sweet relief. "Thank you."

"It was my pleasure." She grinned.

"Now, who's sadistic?"

"Just wait until I make you your drink."

He remembered her bitter healing tea and tried to
grimace, but his smile broke through. He was going to be
okay. He was here with Keturah. She still loved him.

TWENTY - ASSASSIN

SUZA

The triumphant parade snaked through the wide streets like a molasses river, heavy and slow, filling all the cracks. Soldiers peeled off from the horde as they found their places and people. Not Suza. She didn't have anyone watching for her with eager eyes, hoping she'd returned alive.

Mitera was everything Uriah had promised. It sparkled and smelled as sweet as kumberry blossoms in spring. She marveled at the wealth and technology, deeply grateful the Dracos had not taken this and soiled it.

But it was not her home.

She marched at Uriah's side behind Darius, deeper into the heart of the human capital city. The Draco humans who'd come to aid the army, and saved Elysium, had all silently returned to their homes along the march south. As the citizens of Mitera crowded close with their cheers, there was not a hewan in sight. Even the great Eio had slipped away before the army had reached the gates. Would the returning soldiers tell their fellow humans the truth? That Draco humans and their hewans were heroes, deserving praise and acceptance?

The king stopped at a grand swath of trimmed green grass. Around the park, food vendors and musicians were setting up for a victory party. Carts of vibrant fruits and the smell of roasted spice and fat made Suza's mouth water.

Darius waved for the celebrations to begin, and a handful of well-dressed men and women strode forward to meet him.

Uriah leaned down to Suza. "Those are the ruling rajas, wealthy landowners, and advisors to the crown."

"The last one there looks to be wearing the crown." She nodded her head to the sour-faced older woman.

"The rule of succession dictates that the rajas are next in line for the throne, not Darius's wife. Forsyth was regent while Darius was at war, and she wants to be queen."

Forsyth had yet to greet her king, instead she loitered several paces away from Darius. "Clearly, subtlety isn't her strong suit."

Uriah chuckled. "I am thinking of the strength of her suit. It must be an impressive garment to hold up that belly."

Suza elbowed her brother and tried not to laugh. She squinted at the wide raja, the last to come forward. With reluctant steps, Forsyth inched closer to her king. She looked up to her right. A small flicker of focus, but Suza followed the gaze. Her heart stopped at the glint of sunlight hitting metal. The figure hunched on the roofline across the town square was dark and indistinguishable, but the arrow aimed at the king was as clear as the Shi Castle dinner gong.

Suza leaped.

She crashed into Darius, her shoulder ramming into his thighs as her arms went around his waist. He grunted. She tensed against the whistle of an arrow and her brother's shout. Darius went down, and Suza spread her body out over his, her breath turning rapid. She didn't feel any sharp pain except her left forearm and wrist, stuck under the king. He was heavier than he looked. *Please don't be hit.*

"Stay down," Uriah ordered. "Guards! Get me that shooter. Now."

Suza lifted her head to see Uriah standing between her and danger, pointing at the roof. She looked the other way, afraid she would see a fallen body, but instead, an older man held up his plate of dinner. The arrow stuck out of a stuffed bun like a flag while chunky gravy oozed out of the bread's wound. Suza exhaled.

The arrow's fletching was painted bark, nothing she'd seen in Skotar. For a heartbeat, she'd feared Thirro had returned, but no. The attacker was human. They were just as petty and honorless in Elysium as the Draco Sang in Skotar. Had she traded one cruel society for another?

When the assassin fled from the roof, Uriah helped Darius and Suza to stand.

"Are you alright?" He first addressed his sister, a breach of protocol she greatly appreciated.

She nodded.

Darius wasn't hurt or afraid. He was angry. A muscle in his cheek twitched as he ordered more soldiers to sweep the area. All around, oblivious people continued to party. Darius didn't brush the dirt off his uniform as he stared at Forsyth.

"Shall we get you inside, your majesty?" she asked.

He didn't respond. Suza half expected him to chop the woman's head off. Had he seen Forsyth's guilty glance? "I thank you for your service as regent." He held out a hand.

Forsyth's face puckered, but she lifted the crown from her gray hair and reluctantly passed it over.

Darius did not smile as he put it on his head.

Within seconds, four men dragged the cloaked assassin into the clearing. They ripped back her hood, revealing an older woman's wrinkled face.

"Who hired you?" Forsyth's voice was harsh and demanding.

Darius's nostrils flared.

The kneeling criminal glanced from the king to the raja and back again. She had a look that indicated the question was utterly stupid. Her voice was dry and bland. "I was never given a name. I don't know who wants you dead."

Suza looked at Forsyth, but unfortunately, the raja didn't sigh in relief or do anything incriminating.

"You couldn't have expected to get away." Darius indicated the crowded square.

"I didn't. Payment is not for me, but for someone who needs it."

"You won't get paid for a job not done," Forsyth said.

The king raised a brow at the raja. "And how would you know the details of her contract?"

"Obviously, I'm guessing. Since you're not dead."

"Aren't we glad?" Darius's voice was flat.

Forsyth folded her arms over her ampleness. "Of course." She didn't pretend to sound sincere.

Suza's shoulders slumped in disappointment. The humans weren't above power-hungry greed and violence.

A heavyset soldier approached. "Your majesty."

Darius nodded.

"We did not find any more threats. The area appears safe."

The king ordered the attempted assassin taken to the castle for further questioning.

"I will take over the interrogation," Forsyth said. "See what information we can get."

"No."

"This treason will not be tolerated."

"No. It will not." Darius's voice could have cut glass.

Forsyth paled a fraction before swallowing and straightening her spine.

Darius thanked his guards. He turned to Suza and held out a hand. "Suzaena, I owe you a life debt."

She wasn't interested in keeping score. Not after the mess of war. "You're welcome."

"How did you know?"

She chewed on her answer, then decided on the truth. "Raja Forsyth looked up at the roof when she approached you. I followed her gaze, and there was the killer."

Forsyth smiled at Suza, but her gaze held nothing but spite. "Yes. I was as startled by the sight as you, but as I'm not used to all this violence, I didn't realize what I was seeing at first glance. Good thing you're young and quick and could move faster than I when it came to getting our precious king out of harm's way."

Darius's eyes narrowed. "The Dracos took down Abner and his father with lucky shots. I will not be so easily removed."

"And we are so grateful to have such a strong ruler on the throne."

"Yes." Uriah's voice was hard as he glared at Forsyth. "We are."

She bowed. "Enjoy the festivities, your Highness. Welcome home." She turned and disappeared into the crowds.

The king watched her leave before turning to Suza and putting on a brighter face. "How can I repay you?"

She had no reply. There was nothing Darius had that she wanted. She wanted Ferth and a home where she didn't have to keep looking over her shoulder. She wanted to stop fighting. She wanted love and peace.

He seemed to read her desperation because his face softened. "For now, I would be honored if you would stay at my Azure Estate during your time here. However long that might hopefully be."

"I accept your hospitality. Thank you." It seemed the only proper response.

TWENTY-ONE - BEAST AMONG HUMANS

SUZA

The next morning, after a late night of too much food, drinks, and dancing, Suza sat in her plush bedroom at Darius's house. It was a nicer space than she'd ever imagined, and the king had given it to her to use indefinitely. One night in the overly soft bed, and she already wanted to leave.

Uriah had gone with Imanna to her suite at Titus's estate outside the city wall, where Eio had more privacy and freedom. Suza would meet them this morning after breakfast, but they seemed far away now.

She studied herself in the polished mirror—a clearer reflection than she'd seen before. She looked sharper than she'd remembered, older. The haircut Zemira had given her had started to grow out, and her brown hair now brushed her shoulders. Her face had lost some of the strain and stress of war. Luster had returned to her olive skin. She saw her mother in her wide mouth and bushy eyebrows. Her mother had been the most beautiful woman in the world. Sadness leaked from Suza's green eyes. Tears bubbled and spilled over her cheeks. A dribble rolled over her lips, and she licked it away. She should not have come to Mitera. She felt like a fragile egg set on a silk pillow.

She needed to break out and learn to fly before she got crushed.

"Oh, Ferth, why did you leave me?" Pain prickled through her chest. "We were supposed to figure this out together."

She jolted at the knock on her door. Quickly she blotted off the tears with an embroidered linen from the table. After a steadying breath, she padded to the door. Hopefully, it was her laundry. They'd told her she'd have her clothes back this morning. Currently, she wore a man's shirt and trousers that were too big. She'd found them in the closet behind some fancy dresses she didn't even consider putting on.

She opened the bedroom door to a woman carrying a tray of food. Suza moved out of the way. Breakfast was always welcome.

The woman looked over Suza's baggy clothes. "Your laundry will be here shortly." The woman was willowy, with narrow curves. Beautiful in a simple and understated way. She walked with graceful lines. Her blond hair was pulled back behind her head, accentuating the angles of her face. But there was something else about her that had Suza staring. The woman set the tray on the table and arranged the plate and drink.

"That looks delightful." Suza's stomach lurched at the smell of fresh bread and roasted vegetables. "Would you please join me? I see there is enough for two."

The woman looked around as if searching for something. "I thought you might have a hungry companion."

Suza twitched in surprise. Did she know of her hewan? How? Xandra had left Mitera last night, unable to get comfortable among the buildings and crowds. She was currently miles away in the forest. No one could have known by looking at her that Suza was Draco Sang. She was sure

Darius wouldn't have mentioned it to his servants. The woman must have thought Suza had a human companion. Though, that was an odd way to state it.

"I'm sorry to disappoint you. It's just me staying here from our traveling party. My brother recently married and is with his wife." That was the verbiage Uriah had used to describe his relationship with Imanna. The idea of marriage was new to Suza, but she already wanted to make her promises to Ferth. If he would stop running away long enough for her to do so. "They live with Captain Titus." She didn't know why she kept talking, but she hadn't figured out what had intrigued her about this woman, and she didn't want her to leave.

She looked at Suza, and Suza reeled back. Those eyes. Like glittering orbs. Amber with shots of gold fanning through them. She knew those eyes; they haunted her dreams and claimed her heart.

"Mira."

The woman went still. "Yes. Have we met?"

"No. But I see your sons in you."

Mira gripped the back of the chair she'd pulled out for Suza and jolted down to sit abruptly on it. Her face paled.

"I'm sorry." Suza rushed to a crouch at Ferth's mother's side. "I did not mean to trouble you."

Mira took Suza's hands and gave her a soft smile. "I miss them. Please tell me all you know of them. And you said, sons. How did you come to know them both?"

Suza pulled out another chair and sat, unsure of what she should say about her history with Ferth. She popped a berry in her mouth to give herself time to think. Mira slid the plate over, an invitation for Suza to eat. Suza gave her a grateful smile. She was starving after the journey. She'd eaten well when they'd arrived last night, but the rich food seemed to have only awakened her deep appetite. Callidon was easier to explain, so she started there. "I grew up in Skotar and worked—" she stumbled over the word, "for Queen Mavras's army. The queen stayed at Shi Castle, and the war chief, Laconius, led the troops."

Mira's face twitched when Suza said the name Laconius, so she hurried to move on. "But when I was stationed near the border, I found an opportunity to escape Skotar and join Titus's army. Your son, Cal, welcomed me. He gave me his tent the first night I showed up, scared and soaking wet from the Rugit River." Suza smiled at the memory.

Mira's lips curved up too.

"I didn't know him well, but enough to miss him."

Her face fell.

"He loaned me his clothes when my slav—shift dress got ruined. He brought me food and helped me settle in."

"He wan't usually such a gentleman…"

Suza flushed at Mira's insinuation. She'd thought Cal had liked her. He'd looked at her with desire. She'd felt the chemistry and wanted to see where the connection might have led them, but she'd never had the chance. He'd died, taking the dream with him and leaving his wild twin in his place. She sometimes wondered if Cal had lived, if they would have been good together, without the painful past she shared with Ferth. Cal felt like a fresh start, freedom from all her demons. But she knew deep in her bones that her heart had always belonged to the boy raised in Skotar, son of the war chief, protector of slaves, and conqueror of the Dragon. Her stubborn, tender, beautiful Ferth.

She missed him with a fierceness that stole her breath.

She was going to kill him for leaving her.

"And I see Ferth had the opportunity to loan you his clothes this morning." Mira's amused gaze dropped to Suza's outfit.

Suza's face went from warm to burning. She hugged her

ribs, feeling the cotton brush against her breasts. These were Ferth's clothes. She resisted the urge to smell the fabric in front of his mother. He must have stayed in this very room, slept in the same bed. If only he were still here. She swallowed the yearnings away, but the pain remained beneath her ribs.

Mira had a knowing look in those enchanting eyes. "That's a nice story."

Suza opened her mouth. Nothing came out.

"At least you shared all the *nice* parts."

Suza sighed. "I do not wish to add to your grief. You can be very proud of both of your sons."

"I am."

She took a bite of a roll, so she didn't have to look at Mira's searching gaze.

"And I understand if it's too painful to talk about Ferth."

The fork lowered as Suza tilted her chin, her gaze lifting. Mira knew.

"You were his slave." Her voice was barely a whisper. Tears filled her eyes. "The one that escaped. I'm so sorry for everything he might have done to you." Anguish underscored her tone.

Suza reached for the woman's hands again, clasping tight. "No. You misunderstand. He protected me." She thought of the scars on Ferth's back—his punishment for her escape. "He did not take advantage of me." That was true enough. "He is the best Draco Sang I have ever known."

Mira brightened at Suza's sincere tone. "Thank you."

"It's true. No other could be like Ferth, raised with a father like that." Suza flinched in recognition of what Laconius had done to the woman in her hands. "And overcome his beast after an almost complete transformation."

Mira looked as if she'd been suffocating, and Suza's words were healing air.

"I was there." Her voice caught. "When Cal went back to kill Laconius, I followed him into Skotar to try and help him, but I was too late." She hung her head. "Ferth turned on his soldiers to protect his brother. We got Cal out of camp, but the wound from Laconius's horn was too deep. Ferth carried him across the river, and they had a beautiful funeral service. They honored him like a king." Suza glanced up at the woman's silent tears. "I'm sorry."

Mira smiled, and her face seemed to glow. "I can see why Ferth fell in love with you."

It was like a punch to the gut. All the air felt like it was sucked out of Suza's lungs. She didn't speak. They sat there for long moments, sharing grief and companionship. Suza finally whispered the feelings that were bubbling over inside. "I love him. I love your son."

"I know."

"He left me."

"It is not enough for you to forgive him," Mira said. "He must forgive himself."

She had no response to that heavy truth. It pressed her further into the seatback.

"Your brother must be Uriah."

Suza nodded. "You know him?"

"Though we both now live at Titus's estate, I don't know him well yet."

"I would expect you to be there this morning, celebrating."

Mira picked at an embroidered blossom on the napkin, face downcast. "I don't usually work here anymore, but some mornings are heavier than others, and Darius lets me come work off the grief when it strikes."

Neither one of her sons had returned with the army last night.

Suza wrapped her hand around Mira's, grateful the

woman had shared honestly. Suza didn't want to party this morning. She wanted this connection of shared sorrow. They held tight to each other for a moment.

Mira cleared her throat, but her voice was still raspy. "Titus tells me Uriah is a great man. I look forward to getting to know him better."

Suza's lip rose. "As do I."

Mira chuckled. "The thing about time apart, it makes the sharing of stories all the sweeter upon reunion."

Suza put a cherry in her mouth and bit down, focusing on the pop of juice bathing her tongue and not the crush of sadness through her chest.

It was a pretty thought, but for now... for now, it didn't help at all.

TWENTY-TWO - TENDER

FERTH

Ferth woke and blinked at total darkness. He recoiled at the stink of herbs, acid, and sweat. The ground was hard below his thin blankets. His head ached, and his throat was dry. He felt the bandage on his shoulder and the soreness underneath. As he probed the tender spot, flashes of residual fire and agony flashed through.

"Hello," he whispered.

No answer.

Fear came over him, speeding his heart and breath. Had he been taken captive? Was he thrown in a dank cell below the earth? He reached out to his wolves through the mental connection and was relieved to feel it still pulsed between them like a golden highway. Rom and Lyko slept, and he did not wake them. At least they were alive, and he was not totally alone in this cold, dark world even if he had no idea where he, or they, were. He hoped this prison served breakfast. He closed his eyes and willed himself back to sleep.

"Ferth."

He cracked an eyelid.

A lamp lit up Keturah's face as she bent over him. "Good morning, son." She touched his brow and smiled. "No fever this morning."

It all came back in a flood, the shaking limbs, the bitter teas, and the worried faces of Keturah and Tobin. The delirium. "How long have I been here?"

"Three nights and two days."

"Whoa."

She helped him sit up while he braced against waves of lightheadedness. So weak. She held out a steaming cup. "Tobin wasn't sure you were going to make it. I knew better."

He read the lie in the sheer relief on her face as he took the drink with cool, steady hands. "Thank you, Keturah. I put you in danger, and you saved my life."

"I can't tell you how happy I am you came to me."

Ferth frowned. "I jeopardized your safety."

Dry fingers touched his knee, a tender gesture, but her voice came out hard. "Stop it."

"Thank you."

She nodded and settled into a more comfortable sitting position on the floor. "Tell me what's happened since you left here a commander in the Draco army."

He sighed. "I became captain when Jobu was assassinated by a fallen Draco and his wolf." Ferth took a sip for dramatic effect. "Turns out it was my twin brother."

Keturah inhaled.

"Yes. I have—had a twin that grew up in Elysium and *conquered* his beast as they call it there." A lump congealed in his throat. "He had a white wolf hewan. When he returned to kill Laconius, I stopped him, and Laconius hooked his belly with a horn. His name was Callidon—Cal. It wasn't until he became mortally wounded that I realized who he was and how much I wanted him. But it was too late. I had saved a cruel father and lost a brave brother." Heat built behind

Ferth's eyes. He let the tears fall, too tired and weak to stop them. Regret and sorrow ate through his body as he confessed his crimes. "I turned on the Draco Sang, my soldiers, and friends. I killed them to protect Cal and Suza—Shale."

She tilted her chin. "Shale, the slave from here?"

"Yes. She escaped and is in Elysium."

Keturah smiled.

"When I lost my beast—"

"*Conquered* your blood."

He exhaled slowly, letting the tears dry up. He needed to start believing and accepting that he was stronger for his humanity and his wolves. Better for it. Either way, it was time to make the most of it and move on.

"Tobin told me about Rom and Lyko. I can't wait to meet them."

"Where is Tobin?"

"He's been camping in the forest with your wolves, a woman named Allie, and his raven—"

"*His* raven?"

She shrugged. "That's what Tobin said."

Ferth chuckled. "Good for him. Them both, I guess." His shoulders relaxed at the thought that the others were safe.

"He was very uncomfortable in here. He wanted to stay with you, but I sent him away after the first night. He was fretting himself ill."

In his mind, Ferth felt Rom wake and reach out to him. He couldn't help smiling when he felt Rom's relief and joy at finding Ferth coherent.

"*I'll sneak out as soon as I can.*"

"*Wash first. I can smell you from here.*"

He wasn't good at sharing scents across the connection like the wolves were, but he tried to send the sharp musk that currently radiated from his armpit.

Rom coughed. *"You're getting better at that."*

"Thank you."

"No, thank you," Lyko said with a yawn. *"I'm almost sorry to have you back this morning. And the crazy things you said in your madness these last few days were highly entertaining."*

He wasn't going to take the bait. *"I missed you too."* Ferth chuckled aloud.

Keturah looked confused.

"Sorry. I'm connected to the wolves in my mind and was checking in with them."

"Handy."

"I'll say." It was a joy he couldn't begin to explain. A unique satisfaction that Keturah would never experience.

"And?"

"All is well with them, but they are anxious to put space between us and here."

Pain crept in at the corners of her eyes. "Of course. You must go. Hunt the great Dragon."

Ferth pursed his lips. His beard itched. It sounded so stupid when she said it like that. "Tobin told you?"

She huffed out a little giggle. "A noble cause." Clearly, she knew as well as he that Nogard was long dead and decomposed.

He forced levity into his voice. "I was going to invite you to come until you started mocking."

The humor fell off her face. "If I left, they would punish the others. I cannot do that to them."

Ferth hung his head, trying to hide his disappointment and frustration. He needed to get her out of here. She would love Elysium. Wouldn't she? A little cottage in a rural farm town. He could picture her there, sitting on a rocking chair, face toward the sunset. Would she be alone? She'd want him and her friends there for it to feel like home. The vision faltered a bit at the logistics. He pushed it away, problems for a another day. He hoped to live long enough to solve them. "I promised I would try and find Nogard's remains. But I will come back for you. I will free all the slaves." It would be his life's purpose. He felt it like a building tide in his soul.

Keturah touched his scruffy cheek, her eyes sad. She dropped her hand and stood. "Come. I'll set up a clean washing vat so you can bathe. You'll have to hurry if you don't want an audience. I need to join my group at breakfast, but I'll bring you something back."

Ferth finished the tea and stood on shaky legs. He left his weapons in her office and followed her into the laundry room. She started a fire, and he pumped water into an empty tub. After days of sickness and inactivity, his body protested the work. She left him with soap, a brush, and clean slave clothing.

He eased into the steaming water, his muscles melting in pleasure. The wound on his shoulder had shrunk to a puckered pink cut. He practiced rolling his arm, tender but with no shooting pain. He closed his eyes for a moment in gratitude.

He'd scrubbed clean, dressed, and strapped on his knife and sword when Keturah found him waiting in her office. His stomach tightened when she pulled a roll from her pocket and handed him a glass of goat's milk. He could eat an entire pig right now, but he took what she had to offer with thanks, knowing it came from her meager rations.

"I found Marko. He will meet you at the building doors."

"I owe you everything, Ma."

Her smile was proud, but underneath, sadness lurked. Ferth drew her against his chest. He was a head taller now.

She held tight, her fingers clinging to his back. "Do not come back here, my son."

He kissed her brow and held her a little closer. She felt too thin.

She pulled back. "Promise me."

"I cannot promise that."

She nodded, her face unreadable. "I will walk you to the doors."

They tracked the familiar halls in silence. Upstairs, Ferth cracked the outside door open. He stuck his face out and looked left then right around the courtyard. Four unfamiliar Dracos within view. Six slaves. The route to the gate looked as clear as he could have hoped. Marko sprinted under the copper dragon toward Ferth, sword sheath jangling against his thigh in his rush. He cleared the three steps to the doors in one stride. His face pinched in worry as he panted.

"We have a problem."

Ferth didn't have to ask what it was. His wolves began clamoring warnings in his head, and Mavras, the scorpion queen, strutted out of the citadel to his left. A moment later, across the yard, Laconius led the returning Draco army through the front gates.

TWENTY-THREE - QUEEN

JADE

*T*oday, Jade would murder someone, and she didn't have much longer to decide who it would be.

Sweat slicked her hands as she marched into Shi Castle at Laconius's side. She hadn't slept well the last three nights, her mind torn to pieces with indecision. Mavras was her aunt and queen, a family killer, and a traitor. Laconius was cold-hearted and power-hungry with no right to the crown. Jade had a greater claim to the throne than Mavras or Laconius. She thought again of her half-sister in Elysium, the true heir.

As she stalked across the familiar courtyard, Jade felt like she walked into another battle. With her two rhinoceros guards flanking her, Mavras approached the middle of the yard like an enemy army. The metal sheet on Jade's back, hidden under her clothes, weighed down on her like a giant hand.

Laconius stopped in front of Mavras and knelt on one knee. "My queen."

Jade felt a wave of hatred as Mavras's wide lips turned down in disapproval. Mavras hadn't come to battle. She'd hadn't fought and suffered. She had no right to judgment and disdain.

"I'm disappointed to see you back so soon." The queen looked over the tired army behind Laconius, her frown deepening.

"We will not make the same mistakes again," the war chief said. "Next spring, the humans will not have time to gather their numbers. We have killed their king."

"The king was a child, weak and inexperienced." Mavras's voice was a snapping hiss. "I have reports that the man who wears the crown now is not."

She made a good point. Jade didn't add that Captain Titus also lived.

Laconius's jaw tightened, and his fingers twitched at his side, but he stayed kneeling. He wore his torso bare to the chill, the fresh scars proving that though they had lost the war, he had battled hard.

Mavras's sharp gaze looked over the deep pucker above his heart where the assassin had struck. She flicked her focus away with cruel disinterest. "I heard about your son."

Steam plumed out of his snout nostrils as he huffed into the cool morning air. He rose to a stand. "The traitor has been killed." He moved to the queen's right side as planned before he turned and motioned Jade forward. Her heart flailed in her chest as she knelt at the queen's hooked feet.

Jade looked up. For the first time in her life, she stared directly into her aunt's eyes without fear, willing Mavras to *see* her. See the violet irises of the Regium bloodline. See the familiar, delicate features.

Mavras cocked her head. Her hairless brows drew together, studying.

"May I present to you Jade, Traitor's Bane. She has the true heart of a Draco Sang. She makes our father Nogard proud. She makes me proud." Laconius's deep voice rolled through Jade's ears, but the meaning of his words couldn't penetrate the steel shield on her back. She wanted to make her murdered father proud, her stalwart mother proud. Laconius could rot in the abyss with Nogard. "And from now on, she will be my daughter. I never had a son."

She hated him. He'd never deserved Ferth to start with. As she looked into his black eyes, she understood what he was saying. She would be his heir to the throne if she would give him the crown. She nodded with feigned devotion. Yes, she would give him a taste of power, but he would not keep it. She already had a father, and he had been a true king of the Draco Sang. He had loved her enough to protect her, save her even when he could not save himself. Laconious could never replace him—as king or father.

"A great honor for her," Mavras said, still searching Jade's face, her lips tight.

Jade bowed lower to hide the movement of her hands, pulling her blade from the strap over her chest. She inhaled, sprang to her feet, and lunged at the queen. Mavras's tail whipped up and wrapped their bodies. They were chest to chest, a lethal embrace. Behind Mavras, Laconius's sword severed one of the rhinoceros guard's spinal cords. Jade brought her knife to Mavras's throat as the queen stabbed the poisonous tip of her tail into Jade's back. The barb clanged against steel.

"This is for my father, Icor," Jade whispered as her knife cut into her aunt's thick, yellow skin. "And the sister you took from me."

Mavras's bug eyes nearly popped out of her head. She tried to speak, but bubbling blood drowned her words. Jade let go, and the Draco queen crumbled to the ground. Blood dripped off Jade's razor-sharp blade and splattered the dirt.

Laconius lowered the corpse of the second of Mavras's bodyguards. He turned to Jade and beamed. Disgust coiled in

Jade's belly. He picked up Mavras's sword, a family heirloom he had no right to touch. Jade flinched when he stepped up and put a forearm over her shoulders. She barely stood as tall as his exposed nipples. He lifted the engraved blade and turned to the stunned crowd. They had no love for Mavras, and they knew of Laconius's strength and ruthlessness. Murder was the most common way the Regium crown had changed heads. It was not right, but it meant Jade did not fear a riot.

"I am your king." He laughed in crazed delight. "And this is my heir."

She stared blankly. Another mark burned onto her soul. She'd thought it would get easier as the casualties rose. It didn't. With each life she took, she died a little.

She wanted to clean her blade. She wanted a bath hot enough to burn away the feel of wrongness on her skin and the rancor rising in her throat. But she wasn't close to being done. Not yet.

Laconius lifted his hands to the silent army. "Welcome home. Go take your rest, for tonight we celebrate."

The crowd began to murmur and break apart. Jade gratefully slipped out from Laconius's shadow. As was her habit, she turned toward the slave house in search of her mother. But it wasn't Keturah's loving face she saw. Ferth stood at the entrance, his body half-hidden by the partially open doors. His gaze bore into her. And there was nothing kind in his face.

TWENTY-FOUR - DESIRES

SUZA

Suza wanted to walk out the doors, join Xandra and find Ferth. Instead, she stood on a velvet box for her dress alternations, feeling alone and out of place. Her mind wandered to Xandra, who was soaring high above a sprawling farm to the northwest of Mitera.

"I can't stay here."

"We should go before the heavy snow hits up north," Xandra said.

"I don't know where we're going."

"Follow the call north. I will find Ferth along the way." Xandra's confidence seeped into Suza.

Xandra wanted to go, and Suza did too. But Uriah was happy. So were Imanna, Titus, and Mira. Everywhere she looked, Elysium was a country in celebration. Suza didn't belong. *"We'll leave in two days, the morning after the wedding."*

"Oh, that is lovely."

Her attention snapped back to the room she occupied at Darius's house. She forced a smile for Ferth's mother and Captain Titus, who'd just entered.

The woman adjusting the gown's hem looked up at Mira and nodded. "She'll steal the show tomorrow."

Mira chuckled. "Probably true, but since it's my show, I hope not."

The seamstress flushed and bent lower over her work.

Mira stepped forward. An amber ring glittered on her finger as she reached out. Suza took her hand. "Will you stand with my father during the service?" She turned the full force of those familiar glowing eyes on Suza. "I know we've only just met, but you feel like family. I'd like to be family."

Suza looked to Titus. He nodded. She wanted to be part of Ferth's family, but she didn't feel like she'd earned it yet. She surprised herself by saying, "It's your wedding. It should be exactly as you wish."

"Thank you." Mira smiled and stepped back. Titus put his arm around her shoulders. She gripped his waist as she beamed up at him, welcoming his quick kiss.

Suza's heart ached. Titus and Mira had waited eighteen years to be together. People were calling it an epic romance, but Suza called it a shame. And she refused to suffer the same fate. She had neither the patience nor the fortitude.

"I'll be leaving for Skotar in two days. If there are any messages you wish me to deliver to Ferth, I'd be glad to take them."

The bliss fell off their faces. They searched her countenance for a long time, obviously seeing the strength of her determination written there because when Mira finally spoke, she said, "I'll have a letter prepared, thank you."

Titus's frown was so deep his scars seemed to droop. "And I'll prepare a traveling pack, arrange a horse, and set up an escort to the border."

TWENTY-FIVE - BETRAYAL

FERTH

Ferth paced Keturah's small basement office. She'd left him there with his worries. She had work to do. Fortunately, Ferth's crew was camped to the northeast of Shi Castle and hadn't been found out by the returning army—yet. It was going to be much harder now for him to sneak out and join them, but he wasn't safe in here. He'd seen too many familiar faces in that returning horde. Jade had already seen him. He shuddered at the image of her face, splattered with the queen's blood.

She was Laconius's heir now.

His emotions churned. It wasn't that Ferth was jealous of the crown—he hoped he wasn't, he refused to be—but to see how quickly and completely his father replaced Ferth cut deep. He knew Laconius had ordered him dead, but this betrayal felt worse and far more personal.

Ferth had no place with the Draco Sang. He had no place with the humans.

The office door opened behind him. Ferth pulled his knife as he whirled. He didn't lower it as Jade stepped into the small space and closed the door. She'd washed. The fur on her head and neck glistened, and the scent of sage soap seeped over to him.

"What are you doing here?" he asked, still trying to assess the danger. The last time he'd seen her, she'd had an arrow pointed at his heart. Until she shot Thirro instead. And the time before that, he'd been her army captain, and the time before that, she'd been an underling, begging him for training tips. What were they to each other now?

She set a loaf of bread on the table and folded her arms, not reaching for one of the several weapons on her belt. "I thought I should visit my ma now that I'm home."

Ferth's blade lowered as his limbs went slack with surprise. "Keturah is your mother?"

And Jade hadn't shunned the human connection as most Dracos did. He thought of the time he'd caught Jade here with Keturah, and she'd pretended to be mad about the laundry. She'd really been visiting her mother. She'd been getting her own tin of Keturah's healing balm. He looked at Jade's features, the delicate nose and rosebud mouth, the violet eyes. She didn't look like Keturah or any human. She looked like a Draco, an unusually attractive one, but still a jackal.

"And what are you doing here?" Jade stepped forward, and Ferth flinched as the tip of his sagging blade touched her exposed collarbone. She wasn't wearing her leather vest, only a cream shirt unbuttoned at the sternum. "Here to take the rest of my heart?" Her lilac eyes dilated as she looked up at him.

How could he swallow a poisonous question like that? He stepped back and sheathed his knife, his insides churning. "I'm glad to see you healthy and well."

She snorted.

"You look good, Jade." He said it with sincerity. It unnerved him how glad he was to see her. He couldn't allow himself the luxury of needing companions. He couldn't keep Jade in his life any more than he could hold sunshine. "And I knew you would rise fast."

"Laconius believes I killed you."

His nerves flared to life. Should she decide to attack—as was her duty—he needed to be ready to parry. "I won't tell him otherwise. I'll be gone before morning."

Jade sighed. "No, you won't."

Ferth's fingers twitched toward his sword handle.

Her gaze tracked the movement, but she didn't unfold her arms. "You'll help me kill Laconius first."

Kill Laconius. His father. Avenge Cal and his mother. Ferth had thought of patricide many times, but it was still an act hard to contemplate, let alone carry out. And here was feisty Jade—she had more sense of justice in her little finger than most Dracos had in their whole soul, and yet she was the one proposing the murder. "So eager for the crown?"

She hissed, all kindness gone from her face as she flew at him. He did not pull a weapon. He thought of all their training sessions together as her claws went around his neck. Her scent rolled over his face. His hands came forward, and he gripped her narrow waist, not sure if he intended to draw her close or shove her away. She pushed him against the table. He didn't fight, not when he saw the pain in her eyes. His back came to rest flat on the table, her wiry form on top of him. Her face hovered above his. "You have no idea what you're talking about."

He opened his mouth, but nothing came out. Jade loosened her grip on his windpipe. He coughed out a chuckle. "Bad joke?"

Brows still crinkled tight, she looked him over, drinking in his face. Ferth went still beneath that predatory gaze. He had to tread carefully here. She was as tough as steel on the outside, but he knew she hid a tender heart.

"You left me." A broken whisper.

"I'm sorry." His hand slid up her back as if he could heal her invisible wounds with his touch. By the shift in her face, maybe he could. He loosened his hold, trying to put space between them as desire and hope flamed in her eyes.

Her voice came out low and gravelly. "Do you know why I didn't kill you in Mitera?"

Ferth didn't want to know the answer. Didn't want her to say it.

"I turned traitor for you."

He flinched against those violet eyes bearing down on him.

"Because I love you."

Her body melted on top of him as her mouth lowered to his. He tightened his grip on her waist to push her away. He loved Suza. But Jade's lips were so soft, and her eager tongue tasted of cream and salt. He thought for a moment that he could do this, give in. Suza was too good for him, but not Jade. He'd seen the satisfaction in her eyes when she'd slit the queen's throat. He wouldn't have to pretend away his faults. She had her own darkness too. Her fingers trailed down his neck, running over the lines of his chest. The flaring of heat in his body jolted him back to himself. He gripped her tight biceps and lifted her off. Her lips were deep crimson and flushed below starry eyes. She leaned toward him again.

"Jade, stop."

Hurt flashed across her eyes.

"I care about you. I would die for you."

Her jaw rippled.

"But I'm in love with someone else."

"Who?"

"She's not here."

"Where is she?" Her voice was hard.

"Jade." He reached for her, but she stepped back, folding her arms again.

"Where is she? Does she love you back?"

"Even if I don't see her again, this," he motioned to the space between them, "wouldn't be fair to you. I'm not going to use you like that."

"You're human now. I'm the one who's supposed to be using you." She threw up her hands in exasperation.

"I'm not human, though." The Draco Sang were very wrong in their belief about that. Ferth now knew he'd never lost the dragon blood. He'd overcome it, harnessed it. "And besides, you know what it is to love a human." He looked down at the bread she'd brought for Keturah. The end of it had gotten squished beneath his back. "So, you wouldn't force me anyway." He sent her a cocky grin. "Not that you could."

She eyed him. "No. You're still you. And I think I like you even better this way."

"You need to let me go." His voice came out pleading. "You deserve someone..." He wanted to say, who loves you like I love Suza, but instead, he said, "Who treats you like their queen."

She flinched at the word *queen.* He swallowed. He was doing this all wrong.

"My father was King Icor."

He was glad he was still leaning against the table.

"He knew he was in danger, so he helped Keturah hide my age and identity to protect me."

Ferth's mouth dropped open, thoughts spinning. He didn't waste time doubting her. He was too busy thinking of Imanna. The woman with the Regium brand. The woman who reminded him of Jade. There was a connection here. Jade was telling the truth, and there was more to the story.

"Laconius will kill me if he finds out or if he hears you're alive."

He tucked his questions away for later. Ice sliced down his spine and settled in his belly as he realized what he must do. He had to do finish what Cal started. Protect himself and Jade. He had to kill his father.

A plan took shape in his mind, risky and lethal.

TWENTY-SIX - ANTICIPATION

FERTH

"*N*o, absolutely not.*" Rom's voice was a clap of thunder in Ferth's head.

Lyko's fear sent a chill down Ferth's back.

Ferth stared at the cracked wall of Keturah's office, his new prison. His wolves seemed so far away. *"Jade thinks I should sneak into his bedchamber and slit his throat while he sleeps."*

"We are not cowards," Rom said.

Ferth could feel Lyko flinch before he let out a threatening growl.

"Cal was not a coward," Ferth said quickly. *"But this is not the same situation."*

"You can't die as he did," Lyko said. Deep pain gushed across the connection and caused Ferth to gasp.

He would not attack his father while he slept. Laconius would know exactly who took his life. He would know the truth—that his son, a *fallen* Draco, was more powerful than he.

"You bring him to us, or we'll come to him. You will not attack him alone." The intensity of Rom's words pressed into Ferth.

Ferth closed his eyes to better focus on his wolves pacing in a clearing a mile to the northeast. It was far too dangerous for the wolves to enter the citadel. There were too many here to defend the chief. He'd have to lead Laconious out, cut him away from the herd. It was time for justice for their brother, mother, and themselves. *"Tonight, we fight him as one."*

TWENTY-SEVEN - REGIUM BLOOD

JADE

Jade's gaze locked on the iron brand Laconius lifted from the desk. She held still, smothering her emotions as he turned it over in his thick palm. The royal brand—the skull and face of a dragon with a sword underneath. The brand Jade should have on her chest. Instead, she had a common Draco identification. *IJ06289.*

She'd earned her place as heir without the Regium mark.

"When shall we perform the branding?" Laconius asked. "Usher in the new royal bloodline."

Jade bite her tongue. He wasn't worthy of that symbol, but she wouldn't mind stabbing him in the heart with a red-hot iron. What else had he pillaged from her family, and how had he gotten his dirty hands on it?

"We could make a show of it." He leaned back in his chair. "Everyone loves a show."

She looked down at his bare chest, nodded to the mass of pink scars puckering the skin over his heart. "It won't take on top of those scars."

"We'll do it on my forehead. Like our first king, Attor, did to his son."

Jade held back a shudder as the image of her sister hit her like cold water. She sent him a vicious grin to cover the fear rising in her gut. She'd tried to talk Ferth into poisoning Laconius or attacking him while he slept, but Ferth refused. He had plans of his own, far more dangerous plans. But she couldn't fault him for his courage. "Tonight."

Laconius picked up the brand, turning it in the torchlight, so the iron flickered a foreboding red.

"After the feast, we will call for the forge heated," she said. "And we will affirm our new king." She looked at his chest wound. If only the assassin had struck true. "Everyone can see that no one call kill you. They will see your power expand." She swallowed back nausea.

Fat lips curled up to reveal his big, square teeth. "Jade, Jade, Jade." There was pride in his voice, and she hated how it got past her defenses and pleased her. He poured a clear amber liquid from the pitcher on his desk into two glasses. A chain with a lion's tooth lay on the table. Her eyes widened as Laconius filled the cups to the brim. He was a three-hundred-and-fifty-pound bull. She was not. He handed her one of the drinks.

"To being hard to kill," Laconius said.

"And to successful killings." Her stomach twisted in knots.

His grin was pure delight.

Jade brought the glass to her lips and took a sip. The velvet liquor burned down her throat and crackled up her nose. She lowered the cup. She needed to keep her head clear.

Laconius looked at her still-full drink with disapproval. He was going to make her drink it, and this much alcohol would send her straight to overcooked.

There was a knock at the door, sparing her for the moment.

"Enter," he yelled.

The slave, Kenji, looking haggard and sick, obeyed. He held a pitcher of mead in his hands. "The cooks have pulled the roast off the spit. Your feast awaits." He paused. "Your Majesty."

Laconius eyes glimmered with pleasure as he shooed Kenji away.

"Give me a moment," Jade said to Laconius. "There's something I need him to do." Before he could argue, Jade darted after the slumped shoulders that had gone back out the door.

"Kenji."

He turned, eyes red and sunken.

She stepped up close, blocking the glass at her chest from the view of the two guards stationed at Laconius's door, and spoke in a whisper. "Do you want to drink this?"

He blinked, focusing on the liquid in her hand.

"I'm going to toss it otherwise, and I just thought you could use it." She held it low between their bodies.

Kenji looked up and down the hall, empty but for the bored guards. He angled away from their view and, with calloused fingers, gripped the glass. He downed it in one swig, only a tiny grimace betraying his humanity. He sighed. "Thank you."

"Fill me up to the same line."

With steady, practiced hands, he poured her drink. The mead was cloudy and darker, but with the dim light and the opaque glass, hopefully, Laconius wouldn't notice.

"After the last of the food is served, come to me at the head table." She turned away from Kenji, smiled at the stony guards, and walked back into Laconius's room. She held up her glass in salute and then chugged it. She slammed the empty cup down on Laconius's desk and leaned forward, giving him a beaming smile as her nimble fingers slipped over the lion's tooth. "Well, I am ready for more. Come, *king*. Let's go indulge ourselves."

Laconius's grin turned greedy as he stood. He strapped his baldric over his chest.

They joined the gathered crowd in the great hall. Four massive murals spanned each wall, depicting in graphic detail the Draco's violent lusts. Jade joined Laconius at the head table. She was too nervous to eat much, but she made a show of it anyway. As the music darkened and the bodies around her loosened, she grew tenser.

When Laconius's celebration had turned sloppy and loud, she saw the slave lumbering toward her. She was glad to see Kenji's face had gained some color.

She held out her hand to him, and he took it, the amber fur on her wrist lighter than his skin. "Yes, you look good tonight." Her tone was suggestive and commanding.

Anger and betrayal flashed in Kenji's eyes, there and gone again. His face went as blank as the rest of the slaves.

Jade stood and turned to Laconius. "Excuse me, Father. I've something important to attend to."

He gave her a knowing smirk, his palm sliding up the spine of the slave sitting on his lap. "Call for the brand when you've finished with him. It is time."

She nodded, forcing her face to reveal nothing of her scorn. She put Kenji's hand on her waist as together they slipped out the side of the citadel.

She let him go as soon as they'd reached the privacy of the hall. "I need you to give this to Ferth. You will find him in Keturah's office in the laundry."

Kenji's eye widened.

A figure passed, and Jade pressed her body against the stones as she pulled Kenji to her. His mouth brushed her ear as his warm weight pinned her to the wall. It reminded her too much of Ferth and what she did not have. She closed her eyes, but that only made the memory worse. Ferth had kissed her back, melting her bones and filling her with hope before taking it away. She shoved Kenji off as soon as the footsteps retreated. Jade pressed the chain with the tooth into his rough palm.

"Tell him *the next bell.*"

Kenji nodded.

"If you mention this to anyone or fail to deliver, I will kill you. And I'll kill Pearl too."

"No need to make threats, Jade," he whispered. "I'll take care of it."

"Go."

He melted into the shadows while Jade went the other way, toward the suites. She pulled up short when a figure stepped into her path. Her pulse roared at the look on the fox Draco's face.

"Leaving so soon?"

"Hello, Dara."

Dara grinned, the torchlight catching on her pointed incisors. "Congratulations on becoming heir to the throne."

"What do you want?"

She picked at her teeth with a sharpened bone. "I'll let you know."

Jade's voice was as calm as the eye of a storm. "It's too late for that, Dara. It'll be your word against mine. And I'm heir. I've killed the queen. What are your claims compared to that?"

Dara's eyes darkened, and she hissed.

"Have a good night." Jade walked past, her muscles coiled, ready to pull a weapon if she had to. But the cowardly fox knew Jade had beaten her. Jade slipped through the royal wing. She only had a few minutes to steal the brand before she had to be at the gates.

TWENTY-EIGHT - REUNION

FERTH

Sweat slicked the iron in his hand—the royal brand. The tooth around his neck thumped against his chest as he ran. The lion's canine belonged to Eio, Laconius's enemy and Ferth's friend. Ferth sprinted with Marko straight down the exposed slope outside Shi Castle. He, Marko, and Jade had knocked the guards out in one surprise strike, but at any moment, they could wake, or another Draco could happen by. He tried to listen for the whistle of arrows but only heard the anxious silence of the wolves waiting in the trees. How long until Jade delivered the note, and his father came after him? He hadn't written his name on the threat, he couldn't put Jade in danger like that, but his father would find out soon enough.

Ferth exhaled as they slid out of the moonlight and into the shadow of the trees. He slowed to a walk, his disease-weakened body gasping for air.

"At least you smell better." Lyko prodded Ferth's waist with his snout.

Rom stayed ahead of Ferth, turning to lead the way and walking faster than Ferth wanted to move. They scampered up familiar trails and into the foothills. The northern pull in his chest felt stronger tonight, and Ferth's focus often drifted to the looming mountains ahead. The temperature dropped, reminding him of how little time he had before ice and snow impeded his hunt.

"Ferth," Tobin said, the same time Allie shrieked out Marko's name. She was a white blur in the night as she sprang from her seat on the fallen trunk and flung herself at the tiger.

Ferth turned away from them, remembering Jade. Guilt and anxiety twisted at the memory of her body on his, her tongue speaking to his lips. He pushed down the feelings. He could worry about that if he survived the night.

"Are you alright?" Tobin squinted to see Ferth's face better in the low light.

"It's time to get into position." He reached for his pack that Tobin had kept safe for him, but Marko swiped it up.

"You need your strength tonight."

Ferth didn't want to think about how true that was. "Thanks." He motioned the group to follow. He talked as he walked. "If he kills me, don't let him see you. Don't try to avenge me. Don't get yourselves killed. Marko will lead the group north. You will find where the thread leads, and you will finish the mission."

The only response was the soft pad of feet and paws on dirt.

They went up a steep incline, and the path leveled out into a valley. Azure Lake spread before him, its inky surface reflecting the moon and stars. A chill ran up Ferth's spine.

"Beautiful," Tobin whispered, his gaze transfixed on the still water.

"Dangerous." Ferth grit his teeth against memory. He'd been an underling, untransformed, and a shame to his father. Laconius had brought him here and thrown him into the deadly waters. Ferth still had scars on his calf where the lake Draco had bitten and clawed him. But he'd survived. And he would survive again. That determination was the only thing fueling him forward. He set his pack in a cluster of trees on the west side, away from where his father would presumably appear.

"Sharpen your sword," Rom said as the wolves circled back to the south to watch for Laconius.

Ferth was going to fight his father, the powerful, ruthless buffalo whom no one had beaten. Slowly voices trickled into his mind. Tobin had said something to him. Ferth snapped to attention as he finally registered his words, *I'll get you a drink.* Ferth whirled toward the lake. Tobin was crouching next to it, his cup outstretched.

Ipsum cawed and shot out of the trees toward Tobin.

Ferth yelled, "Tobin, get back!"

Tobin jolted in surprise, teetering forward over the water. Ferth darted at him, muscles protesting the sudden jump. Ipsum flapped his wings in Tobin's face, shooing him back. Ferth wrapped his palm around Tobin's shoulder. They stumbled back together.

"What? What it is?"

"Water Dracos," Ferth said between panting breaths. "The cruelest and most beastly Dracos, their humanity all but washed away when they are born of the water."

Tobin's focus snapped back to the depths. The water near the edge rippled ominously from below before the lake turned back to onyx glass. Tobin shuddered under Ferth's fingers. Ferth tightened his grip as they stepped backward and joined a wide-eyed Marko and Allie.

"I didn't see him go that way," Allie said, voice apologetic.

"I didn't think he would need the warning," Marko said.

"He knows nothing of Skotar," Ferth said. "Remember that if I...."

Tobin sat heavily next to the packs. Allie pulled out an onion bun from the pack Marko had brought. Tobin held it in his limp hands as he stared, pale-faced, at the lake.

Ferth forced himself to eat the bun Allie handed him. He ran a whetstone down his sword as he chewed. He focused on the count of his breath and the smooth slide of the stone. His pulse steadied. His mind cleared.

"He's here," Rom said.

Adrenaline seared through Ferth, but he forced his mind to stay calm. *"Alone?"*

"Yes."

Ferth allowed himself a smile. He'd known he could count on Laconius's pride as an ally tonight. The traitor stood and sheathed his sword at his side. He left his bow with his pack. Besides the small blade tucked into his boot and Cal's dagger at his hip, the sword was his only true weapon tonight. He put on his leather vest. "Stay hidden."

Fear wafted off Tobin in bitter tendrils as Ferth stepped away. Marko grabbed his forearm, and Ferth looked over his shoulder. Marko held out his baldric that held two throwing knives and a dagger. Ferth allowed the tiger to fit it over his chest.

"Thank you." Maybe collecting outcasts wasn't such a bad idea.

Heart pounding, he skirted the pool and walked out onto the rock ledge that overhung the black waters. The ledge his father had pushed him off. He stood like a conquering king on a pedestal, surveying his subjects below. At least, that was the impression he wanted to give.

"Be with me, brother," Ferth whispered to the wind as Laconius crested the path and stormed into view.

The bull looked up and stopped.

"Hello, Father."

TWENTY-NINE - FAMILY AFFAIR

FERTH

"You!" Laconius's angry bellow rolled across the lake.

"Yes." Ferth spread his arms and forced a smile. "I'm not so easy to kill. Aren't you proud of your son?"

Silvery moonlight washed over Laconious's fuming face. He swung his axe at his side as he marched forward. His wound was a mean slab of pink scars across his bare chest. Thighs as thick as tree trunks quivered with each step.

Ferth stepped off the rock and onto the grass, staking out better ground. Now that Laconius was here, his horns rising to shiny points, his eyes as wild as his curly hair, Ferth's nerves steadied, and his hesitations fled. This must be done. His back sang at the memory of his father's whip. His heart pounded out the beat of vengeance, but he couldn't forget the times his father had been proud of him. Those fleeting moments clung to him now like burrs.

"I'm glad you're still alive," Laconius said. "It will give me great pleasure to kill you."

The words cut like blades through Ferth's armor, and his last flicker of hope for reconciliation vanished. He knew it had been a foolish hope, a child's fantasy, but his lungs hollowed out at the loss, nonetheless. Laconius was five paces away now. Four. Three. He seemed to grow larger with each step closer. Heart beating frantically, Ferth pulled his sword free and lifted it.

Laconius's smile was full of condescension as he looked down on Ferth, as if his son were no more than a flea. Laconius attacked. Ferth deflected the crushing blow, the clang of metal ringing through his bones. His wolves crept closer as Laconius's axe curved down in a deadly arc. Ferth grunted as he blocked it and jumped free. Laconius struck hard and fast. At this rate, the fight Ferth had been anticipating his whole life wasn't going to last more than a minute or two.

Ferth's sword wasn't long enough to reach Laconius's body, and his exhausted muscles began to weaken beneath the onslaught.

"Pathetic." Laconius spat as he stepped aside to avoid an uneven patch of dirt. "Even as an abomination, I expected better from you. You've disappointed me again." He swung his axe against his son's sword in rapid blows.

"Now," Ferth whispered to the animals crouching in the grass behind Laconius.

Lyko dove for the back of the knees. Rom leapt, his claws tangling with Laconius's long hair, then digging into his thick neck and causing Laconius to roar and jerk back. Ferth snaked forward, getting into sword range. Laconius's bulging eyes tracked Ferth, his axe coming down even as the two wolves slashed at his back. Ferth blocked the axe with his sword, crouched to get closer, then pulled a knife from Marko's baldric and buried it in Laconius's side.

Laconius's left hand swung forward and hit just to the right of Ferth's sternum. Ferth was thrown off his feet and landed hard on his back. A rock pierced his healing shoulder. Laconius swung his axe over his head, but the wolves had already dropped back. Laconius ripped the blade from his abdomen, blood dripping into his pants. He charged Ferth without hesitation, murder flashing in his red-rimmed eyes. Then the wolves were in front of him, a shield of teeth, claws, and determination.

Laconius swung his axe, and the wolves moved to avoid decapitation. Ferth scrambled to his feet.

"Two wolves?" Laconius said.

Ferth didn't tell him about Cal, didn't want to taint his brother's memory. Laconius didn't deserve to know.

"I'll enjoy adding their teeth to my collection when I cut that chain off your neck." His greedy gaze dropped to the pendant Ferth wore.

"Spread out. Surround him," Ferth said. His breath came in sharp pants. Lyko darted left, Rom right. Laconius barreled straight at Ferth, forcing him onto the rock protruding over the lake.

"Ready for another swim?" Laconius's voice was taunting, but his breathing had turned heavy.

Ferth didn't speak, his entire focus on stopping the swinging axe. His wounded shoulder throbbed. The wolves again gathered behind Laconius, but he whirled on them, the bloody knife in his hand ready to fly. Ferth leapt and jabbed his sword into Laconius's back. Time slowed as the knife left his father's hand. Horror roared through Ferth as Rom leapt in front of Lyko, and the knife buried in Rom's belly. The gray wolf dropped. Agony seared across their mental connection, coming from both wolves. Lyko barked and whined, and a twisted sound tore from Ferth.

Ferth barely managed to keep hold of his sword hilt as Laconius whirled, the blade pulling free of his leathery back. Crimson rain splattered the ground around him, drops flinging into the lake, which had gone from smooth to stormy within seconds.

"Stay with me, Rom," Ferth said.

"I'll kill him," Lyko said.

"That would be great." Rom lay immobile, his words as weak as a candle flame, but Ferth felt a flood of relief at the flicker of life.

Laconius, mad with pain, slashed at Ferth. Ferth jumped back. His foot slipped on loose gravel, and he fell. He rolled to the edge of the rock as the axe shattered pieces of stone near his ear. Laconius lifted his axe high to strike again.

Maybe Ferth should have gone with Jade's plan and attacked Laconius in his sleep.

Lyko slammed into Laconius's back. They both went over the edge and into the lake.

"No!" Ferth twisted around, scrambling to his knees, and peering into the water.

Laconius roared as he churned in the water. He sluggishly swung his axe under the froth at foes Ferth couldn't see. Lyko clung to his shoulders. Laconius slipped under, only a mound of white fur remained visible above the red-tinted foam. Ferth turned and ran past Rom and down the slope to the lake's edge.

"This way, Lyko." Ferth dropped his sword on the grass and grabbed the branches of the overhanging tree that had saved his life not so long ago. The frantic wolf shoved off Laconius and paddled toward Ferth. Ferth sprinted to meet him, plunging into the icy darkness. He hissed against the cold but did not slow. Lyko was only two feet away when he was jerked under the water. Ferth's tree branch went taut, the end of the line. He let it go and dove, feeling for Lyko through their mental connection. The wolf was directly below him. He pulled a knife from Marko's baldric and kicked down until he felt fur. He gripped it tight in his fist and jerked Lyko up.

"It's got my leg!"

The wolf was running out of air, and they were both dangerously low on strength. Ferth felt along Lyko's body, aware they were both being dragged deeper despite his best efforts to swim upward. When he felt clammy skin, he slashed at it with his knife. With a piercing scream, the water Draco let go of Lyko. Ferth shoved Lyko towards the surface, his own body sinking with the effort. The Draco grabbed Ferth's thigh. Ferth slashed blindly, the water slowing his thrusts, until he felt its claws release. He shoved upward, his lungs burning, his heart frantic. With all his strength, he churned through the heavy water.

Finally, he burst into the moonlit night, gasping. Next to him, Lyko choked and sputtered, trying to tread water. Pain from Lyko's leg flickered across their connection. Ferth put his arm around Lyko, but his numb fingers were too stiff to grip the fur. He kicked, but his boots dragged him under. He thrust his face up, sucking in a breath, clawing at water but getting no traction.

He wanted to live.

Slimy fingers tickled the back of his neck, taunting and teasing. The water Draco didn't need to fight him, it knew it just needed to wait a few more moments before Ferth surrendered.

"Ferth!"

He jerked toward the sound of Tobin's voice. His friend stepped out from behind the lone tree at the edge of the lake, a rope coiled in his hand. Marko appeared behind Tobin as he hurled the lifeline across the water. Ferth caught the rope, and hope flooded through him. He ignored the creatures circling in the water as he forced the rope around Lyko's middle and his own. He didn't trust himself with a knot, so he wrapped the rope around his wrists and held Lyko against his chest.

"Now!" Ferth's shout was weak and water-garbled, but the rope went taut.

Ferth and Lyko sank in the water. He closed his eyes and pinched his lips, grateful his arms were numb as the rope dug into his forearms and back. He kicked weakly but didn't have the strength to reach the surface. Dracos clung to his legs and Lyko's fur as they were dragged back and forth. Ferth couldn't tell which way was up or who was winning this tug of war. His back scraped against gravel as he and Lyko rose half out of the water. He sucked in a grateful breath. When they came to a stop, frantic hands tugged at his arms, willing him to rise. Ferth lifted his head, blinking water out of his eyes. Marko stood knee-deep at their side. He slashed at the water with Ferth's sword, pushing the Dracos back and creating a perimeter, as Tobin's nimble fingers flew over the rope, untangling Ferth and Lyko.

"Come on, come on, come on," Tobin repeated.

Ferth made sure the limping wolf was clear of the water before he crawled out. He wanted to drop to the dirt and never rise, but Tobin wedged his narrow frame under Ferth's arm.

"Marko." Tobin's tone came out hard and commanding. "Get Rom."

Ferth reached out to his hewan, but the wolf was unconscious.

Lyko howled as if he could call down the stars. In the distance, wild wolves howled back.

Marko stabbed at the water one last time, then stepped back, following them out of the lake.

"Allie is building up a fire," Tobin said, his voice strained under the weight of Ferth's exhausted body.

"Laconius?"

"He went under and hasn't come back up…. Well, only a couple bits and pieces." Tobin pointed to a floating fragment of shirt and swirls of inky blood, so dark in the moonlight they looked like tar. The color of his father's soul.

The numbness in Ferth's muscles seeped into his heart. He'd killed his father.

Lyko limped at his side as Tobin dragged Ferth around the edge of the lake toward the beckoning glow of a golden fire. Just as the first wave of warmth hit him, two familiar figures stepped out of the trees and into the circle of light.

Keturah rushed to Ferth, but Jade stopped and pouted. "I'm too late." Her face pinched with regret as she looked over the ragged group. "He said he would wait for me to get my swords. I was trying to give you more time." Her voice softened. "I wasn't here to help you."

It meant a lot that she had come to his aid nonetheless. "Laconius is dead." Heartsick, he sank next to the fire and shooed Keturah away from his shoulder. "It's Rom. He took a knife in his side."

"Bring him to me." Keturah motioned to Marko who carried the limp wolf. She dropped to her knees by the fire and ripped open the basket she'd brought. "Boil water." Her face was set in hard lines, her voice steel. She pulled out a familiar tin along with a needle, thread, and clean linens.

A rush of love for the woman filled Ferth. He blinked back the heat that flared behind his eyes. "Please." He whispered it to his wolf, to the Dragon, to anyone and anything that might listen and send him aid. He couldn't lose Rom. His heart was as fragile as a hummingbird egg. He could not survive another loss.

THIRTY - WEDDING

SUZA

The smell of roasting sugar and the warble of violin music drew Suza through the grand entrance of the emerald palace and into the ballroom, Uriah and Imanna at her side. King Darius and his wife greeted them at the door and ushered them into the party. Fall foliage sat in vases on glittering tables, and candlelight reflected off the massive gold chandeliers. It was a gathering like nothing Suza had ever seen. The sound of conversation was like the murmur of honeybees, not the squabbling of coyotes. Rare gems and fine fabrics dusted arms and necks.

She was a world away from Skotar. From Ferth. It was no wonder he fled. She could not imagine him here, dressed in bright colors and mingling with this posh crowd.

Suza's silky green gown danced with her legs. It was a simple design, rounded neckline, long sleeves, and cinched waist. She felt beautiful in it, curvy and vibrant. She'd seen herself in the mirror earlier, but now she saw herself reflected in the lingering gaze of the other guests they passed.

Uriah and Imanna knew so many people. It shouldn't

have surprised Suza that her brother had multiple friends here tonight. She and Uriah were blood but separated by culture. This place, so foreign to her, was his home.

She would lay down her life for Elysium but would not spend her life here.

She watched Uriah and Imanna in their happy interactions with quiet curiosity—until her brother began introducing Suza to men. After the third man promised he'd find her when the dancing started, she glared at Uriah.

"Stop it."

"Why?" His brown eyes gleamed in challenge, but he didn't say Ferth's name. Ferth wasn't here. He had left her. Uriah wanted her to forget him and fall in love with one of the silk-wearing peacocks here in Elysium.

Imanna waved to a woman across the room. Uriah watched his wife walk away. Imanna wore a tight black band over the brand on her forehead and a cap of delicate lace draped over the top of her head that fell over her wavy brown hair and half of her face. The scalloped trim ended at the tip of her nose, leaving only her red rosebud mouth entirely visible. The effect was intriguing and alluring, the focus of many stares.

"Let's get a drink before the ceremony begins." Uriah motioned Suza toward the tables in the back of the room. They didn't make it three paces before a man stepped into their path.

"Yosef," Uriah said, greeting him with the humans' handshake.

Uriah looked handsome with his clean-shaven face and brown suit, but Yosef... Suza blinked as the young man chatted with her brother. He wore blue pants and a white shirt that was open in front, revealing a wide span of his toned chest and abdomen. No brand or scars marred his caramel skin. A blue sash wrapped over his shoulders, biceps, and waist, tying the tunic in place, and making him look ridiculous.

Suza was still staring at his exposed sternum and heavy pectorals when Uriah turned Yosef in her direction and his eyes, blue as his sash, settled on her. Her breath hitched. He had the most beautiful face she'd ever seen, with a full mouth and glossy black hair swooping over his forehead.

"Meet my younger sister, Suzaena."

Yosef held out long fingers to her, but Suza wasn't comfortable surrendering her fighting hand to a stranger. After a stern look from Uriah, she lifted her right hand and placed it in Yosef's. He brought his left hand up so his uncalloused palm cocooned her fingers.

"Uriah, I can't believe you've been hiding your enchanting sister from me all this time."

Uriah's nervous gaze flashed to her.

She smiled, and Yosef's focus dropped to her lips. "He's very protective of me."

Yosef turned her hand palm up, and she resisted the urge to snatch it away. His fingertips tickled across the scabs and scars still healing from battle. "It looks like you can protect yourself."

Her body betrayed her, soaking in the compliment like water in a dry sponge. Heat seeped up her arm as he bowed, brought her hand to his mouth, and pressed a kiss to the center of her palm. Her fingers curled up under his chin, brushing soft skin.

He looked up through thick lashes. "But I find myself without defenses."

"Nice line," Uriah said with a teasing chuckle.

Yosef grinned, showing bright teeth as he straightened, and Suza suffered another jolt of attraction as his gaze caressed her face. "Do you think it worked?"

"It was a good start," she admitted, gently tugging her hand out of his.

Yosef laughed, a deep sound she wouldn't have expected from a man tied up with ribbons and half unwrapped. "You're something entirely new."

She liked that thought. Maybe she could *become* new. Bury the past and start over. She tried for the coy smile she'd seen other women wielding, but it felt odd on her face.

A tinkling bell drew their attention across the room, and the talking ceased. King Darius spoke in the sudden silence. "Thank you all for coming tonight. It is an honor for me to welcome you to this long awaited, much anticipated, event."

Behind the king, Titus stood stiffly in his leg brace, but he wore a wide smile. Next to him, Mira kept her face smooth, but her eyes shined like polished gold. An image of Ferth flashed through Suza's mind and heart. She took a step away from Yosef.

"We, as people of Elysium, owe a great debt to Captain Titus," Darius said. "He is one among many who risked everything for our freedom." Darius took a breath and smiled. "And he is Draco Sang."

A murmur ran through the crowd. Uriah went still at Suza's side.

"It is time we opened our eyes and let go of our prejudices. As king, I will not allow mistreatment of the Draco Sang who are law-abiding citizens. We need their unique talents and strengths. We would have lost this country if we did not have the loyalty and sacrifice of the Draco Sang." Darius's voice rang out like a clear morning bell. "Starting today, all hewans have my protection. They have the right to walk free, and their human is responsible for their actions and will be held accountable in the law. We will treat them with the gratitude and respect that they deserve." Darius let the weight of his words settle over the room.

Titus discreetly wiped at his eyes, but to the left, Raja Forysth was scowling, her pudgy face sour. Clearly not everyone liked the new policy.

"With that said." Darius's voice lost its steel edge. "There is someone I'd like to welcome." He glanced at Titus.

The captain's mischievous grin had Suza bracing as the crowd looked to the back door. It opened, and Eio padded in.

A gasp of surprise sounded amongst the people, but it was quickly stifled. Many in this room had fought at the border and seen Eio. He was a war hero.

"We welcome Captain Titus's hewan, Eio," the king said.

The golden lion moved slowly, like a relaxed river in late summer, giving people a chance to exhale. Eio stalked past Suza, and she lifted her fingers in greeting. He stopped and turned his face up to her. He grinned, mouth full of sharp teeth, and Suza could feel the tension rising around her. She gave a genuine smile and bowed to the regal lion.

"Hello, Eio." She said loudly, her voice carrying through the room.

He purred and licked her face.

Suza laughed quietly and wiped her cheek with her sleeve. She rubbed Eio's ear with her other hand. "Nice to see you too."

He turned, and her fingers slipped off yellow velvet. His paws whispered against marble, the only sound in the room as he approached Titus and Mira. Eio took up position on Mira's side, and she buried her hand in his mane, her countenance shining with delight.

"Please, take your places," Darius said. "The couple will make their promises."

"Stand with me?" Yosef whispered to Suza.

"I'm sorry, but I'm assigned to stand with Closford." Before he could argue, she turned and whisked away to find Ferth's family.

Closford leaned on a cane and one of his grandsons as family members surrounded him. Suza hesitated, feeling like an intruder. She moved to leave when Mira caught sight of her and motioned her forward.

"You look beautiful." Mira kissed her cheek. "Thank you for being here. I feel like a part of Callidon and Ferth are here with you."

Suza's heart gave a squeeze as she swallowed.

Mira blinked the sorrow from her eyes and turned to her sister. "Elssa, this is Suza. Can she stand by you?"

"Of course." Elssa held out a friendly arm, and Suza took Ferth's place.

The room went silent as Titus guided Mira to the center of the circle of people that formed around them. The couple faced each other, holding hands. Titus spoke first.

"I, Titus Mackson, give myself to you, Mira Closdaut. I give you all that I am, my future, my whole life."

"I, Mira Closdaut, give myself to you, Titus Mackson. Thank you for waiting for me. I'll try to make it worth it."

A woman a few feet behind Suza muttered, "That was short."

Suza's heart melted. It was perfect, no need for long-winded promises or wordy caveats. Their vows were simple and powerful. And true. She couldn't look away from Titus's face. She had never seen joy like this before.

His eyes glittered like the blue of a summer sky, and his countenance shone like sunlight. Titus slipped one hand around Mira's waist while the other cupped her jaw and tilted her chin up to meet his mouth. The kiss ached with tenderness, and Mira's body went soft against him. Titus traced his thumb across her cheekbone as he pulled back just enough to whisper, his lips brushing hers with the words.

Unable to look away from their enchanting embrace, grief and desire pooled in Suza's belly like fire and water.

When Titus pulled back, he drew Mira against his side, and turned a beaming face to the crowd. The churning in Suza's heart did not abate. She wanted a love like that, born of sacrifice and persistence. The call north inside her soul tugged and jerked. His name bloomed in her chest and swirled over her tongue like a gathering storm. She covered her mouth with her hand and let the pain out in a silent, choked plea.

Ferth.

"Come, friends," Titus said. "We gained victory at the border. We are free to live and to love. Let's prove it tonight!"

A cheer rose.

Suza didn't want to feast or dance. She wanted to vomit. Xandra was miles outside the city, unsympathetic and eager for Suza to leave.

Yosef caught sight of Suza and angled toward her. She pretended not to see him as she wove into the dense crowd. She wanted away from his silky smile, his pretty face, and scarless skin. He had nothing on Ferth's vibrant eyes and gritty strength. Ferth was fire. She felt like a frozen woman, crawling toward his warmth, hoping she wouldn't get burned.

She found Uriah and Imanna visiting with one of the older rajas. Uriah took one look at Suza and excused himself from the conversation. He pulled her to the side of the room, to the shadow of a pillar. Imanna appeared at his side, concern pinching her eyes.

"I'm leaving," Suza said.

"Now?" Uriah asked.

"Leaving the party now. Leaving the city in the morning." A beat of silence hit. Suza reached out and took their hands. "Please come with me." Still no response. Suza lowered her voice as she turned wide-eyes on Imanna. "You are the rightful ruler of Skotar, and your country needs you. The people there are brought up in greed and violence. They need help. Mavras will gather another army this winter. The Dracos will come down again and again."

Imanna's lips thinned, and her violet eyes turned haunted as her free hand went to her belly.

Uriah's hand tightened on Suza's in warning, but she plowed forward. "Now is the time to strike."

"I'm having a baby in six months." Imanna's voice was incredulous.

"Then you don't have much time."

Imanna's jaw hardened.

Uriah didn't speak, and it was then, seeing the glimmer in his brown eyes, the forward lean of his strong shoulders, that Suza realized he was willing to come with her. He wanted to follow his little sister, protect her. But the higher duty fell with Imanna and his child, and Suza respected him more for it. She would not ask him to leave his wife.

"Goodbye." She reached forward and hugged Imanna's ridged shoulders. "I understand your decision." She turned to Uriah.

He drew her into his arms, wrapping her in warmth, then he kissed her face, pressing hard as if he could smash his blessing of protection into her cheek and make it stick. "I love you."

She sent him a grateful smile. He was free and happy. He was honorable and kind, and he was more than she could have ever dreamed of. She'd had time with him, a gift she'd cherish. "I love you together or apart. Forever and ever."

Sudden tears glittered in Uriah's eyes at her words, the words their mother used to say.

How true they had become.

THIRTY-ONE - BECOMING QUEEN

JADE

Jade woke in the middle of the night to a silent camp. She stared at the wide sky. The tasks before her seemed as impossible and vast as the stars, and even more overwhelming.

"You'll make a great queen."

She turned toward the quiet voice. Ferth's eyes twinkled like the stars as he leaned against a tree trunk, his hand rested on Rom. He looked as handsome and unreachable as a dream. And the answer to all her problems. She rose from the grass and crawled to his side. He did not recoil, but he did not reach for her.

She listened to the steady breathing of the others as they slept around the cold fire, gathering her words. "And you will make a great king."

When he didn't immediately refuse, hope sprouted. She leaned closer, keeping her voice low, intimate. "Think what we can do together. Laconius was preparing you to rule."

He scoffed quietly.

"Skotar needs you."

He said nothing.

"And you are powerful."

Ferth ran his hand down Rom's back. Jade wanted to touch the gray fur, feel how soft and warm it was.

She clasped her hands between her knees. "Together we can free the slaves. Bring stability and strength to the country. We can rule together." She wanted his help and companionship. She was weary of isolation, and Ferth made her feel seen and understood. He was intelligent and ruthless. The only person she could trust besides her mother.

A long moment passed before his voice rolled deep and quiet, like far off thunder. "Growing up, my dream was to become king of Skotar."

Hope soared through her heart.

His hand moved in slow circles over his limp wolf. "I wanted the power. I looked forward to controlling the Draco Sang. My word would be law, and disobedience would bring swift retribution. I tasted a portion of that dominance as captain in the army. I was effective, but at times, cruel."

Jade leaned away at the bite in his tone as he spit out the last word.

"I played with mercy and justice, depending on my mood. I toyed with lives." His far-off gaze refocused on her, and her heart sank at the rejection she saw in his eyes. "I am tempted, but I cannot become your king. I will not allow myself to be corrupted by power again."

"That's exactly why you're the best man for the job."

"No. I do not wish to fight for the rest of my life." He shook his head sadly. "My place isn't by your side... or in your bed."

It hit like a slap, causing her to feel ugly and small. Cast aside.

"I'm sorry. My heart is elsewhere. I cannot give it to you, not even for a kingdom." He sighed. "I will serve Skotar in my own way."

"You're making a mistake." The words hissed out of her. The urge to fight him rose like a violent wave. She would force him to her will.

He looked her in the eyes, unafraid. "Maybe."

She held back her fury, but her breath came out sharply. She growled, deep and menacing.

Marko woke with a start. "What? What is it?"

She swirled away from Ferth. "Nothing. Go back to sleep."

The Draco studied them with cunning eyes before rolling over.

Jade looked back at Ferth, wondering if she might change his mind, but his jaw was set in a stubborn line. "Fool."

He chuckled. "Maybe."

She shook her head and padded over to sleep next to her mother.

The next day, Jade went hunting.

She needed to get back to the castle and deal with the chaos another dead ruler would cause. She'd already been gone a night and a day. Beto would be managing the training yard, and most of the Dracos probably hadn't noticed or cared that their new king hadn't emerged from his chambers today. No one knew she was queen. She wasn't ready to make the claim. She liked being here with this strange band of travelers. She liked the feeling of acceptance and peace and safety—qualities she'd never attained before.

Her breath clouded in the early winter morning as she stepped into the circle of their small camp beside the lake. She dropped the dead magu she'd killed and stretched her back.

Tobin jumped to his feet. His blue eyes locked on her, scanned her for injuries, and she felt a wave of warmth at his care. "Thank you." He motioned to the meat.

She gave him a half smile.

He beamed at her, his gaze adoring and open. He'd been looking at her like that since they'd met last night. It was a shock to see anything but resentment in a human's eyes, but he looked at her like she was his lover. Jade had never seen anyone so unguarded with their thoughts and emotions. It was a sweet change after the constant scheming of the Draco Sang. She felt her body respond to his attention, and she bit her lip as she turned away.

Allie added logs to the fire, causing it to spark.

Marko wordlessly lifted his knife and approached the animal. With swift, deft movements, he began skinning it.

Keturah slept curled up next to Lyko for warmth, her body sprawled in a manner only accessible to the deeply exhausted. She'd been up all night and most of the early morning tending to Ferth and his wolves.

Jade found Ferth awake and watching her. He lay on his back, shoulder freshly bandaged, head against a trunk, hand still on Rom's chest. His fingers rose and fell with the wolf's shallow breaths. He had not left Rom's side since the fight last night. Ferth's bond between his wolves was a palpable thing. Not for the first time since this spring, Jade wondered what her hewan might have been like. What if she had conquered her blood instead of surrendering to it? She would have a jackal at her side, a trusted friend. She pushed the regret away, burying it deep in her mind with the rest.

She raised her brows at Ferth in a silent question.

He shook his head. Rom had not woken.

She sighed, picked up the kettle, and walked over to the lake. A short sword out and ready in her hand, almost wanting a water Draco to attack so she could hash out her feelings with violence, she filled up the pot with water. She lugged it over to the fire to boil.

She intended to sit by Ferth—try to salvage friendship— but Tobin's attention stopped her. When she met his guileless gaze, he patted the seat next to himself on the split log. Feeling that intoxicating flutter in her belly again, she sat next to him, close enough that their knees touched.

"Will you come north with us?" Tobin asked. "Into the mountains."

She tilted her chin to look at his face. A few straggly strands of beard peppered his jaw. His nose was pointy, his face narrow. He looked so small and weak compared to Ferth, until she looked into his blue eyes and saw an entire universe worth exploring. "What do you expect to find on this hunt?"

"Nogard." He said it with so much confidence that Jade swallowed the mockery on her tongue.

"I can't. I'm the queen of the Draco Sang now." She gazed out at the lake half expecting Laconius to storm out of the crystalline depths and call her a liar.

"Queen," Tobin breathed.

"Sorry to disappoint you."

"It's okay." But his forlorn expression remained.

She laughed. A true laugh that bubbled up from a long-lost place. She caught Ferth watching her, and a flush crept up her collar. She sobered, peeled off the bench, and walked over to help Marko skin the magu. This work was beneath her station now. If she didn't act like a queen when she returned to Shi Castle, she wouldn't be queen very long. The brand laying on the ground next to Ferth's pack seemed to soak up the sunlight, leaving only shadows around it.

Keturah and Lyko roused with the smell of cooked meat, and Jade handed her bleary mother a cup of steaming herb tea. Keturah sipped it as she checked on the sleeping gray wolf.

"His pulse is strong. No fever." He didn't wake with her gentle prodding. "How's your shoulder?" she asked Ferth.

"Fine."

Jade handed him a cup.

"Thank you."

Silently and begrudgingly, she forgave him for rejecting her and not loving her as she wished. She crouched next to him and her ma. "I need to return to secure the throne."

Keturah's face snapped up from her cup to look at her daughter. "If you go back alone, you'll be killed."

"Possibly, but I don't think I will. There will be a some unhappy Dracos, but since the war, not as many as before. Most just want a steady ruler who will leave them alone. And I am the Regium heir."

Jade thought of her half-sister. "The only one here at least."

Ferth raised thick brows, his eyes cunning. She wondered if he'd met Imanna at the Lion's camp. She couldn't hold his gaze. She didn't want to talk about her sister, the sister she'd never see again. She picked up the heavy iron. Her chest tingled with anticipation.

"It's time." Her voice came out weaker than she'd hoped.

"You don't have to do this," Keturah said.

"Yes, I do." She glanced at Ferth.

His jaw rippled, but he didn't deny it.

She turned the rod over in her hand. "I am a Regium. They will look for the royal seal on me. The Dragon's blessing. I will appear weak if I don't submit to this marking. Pain has power. Symbols have power. And I need all of it I can get."

Keturah sighed in defeat. "I'll get the dye."

While the iron heated, everyone else ate strips of steak, but Jade was too nervous. She paced the tree line, thinking about what might happen when she waltzed into Shi Castle, delivered the news, and took the crown. She considered asking Ferth for Laconius's tooth necklace, another symbol with power, but she dismissed the idea. It was the only thing Ferth had left of his father. Ironic that it belonged to a human's hewan. She thought through her list of potential threats. Captain Mina was probably the biggest.

The glow of red iron drew her attention. Ferth had lifted the brand, checking to see if it was hot enough.

"Is it ready?" Jade asked.

He nodded solemnly and set the brand back into the crackling fire.

She swallowed and clamped her teeth. She sat cross-legged on the cold dirt and pulled her shirt over her head, leaving a band covering her small breasts. A breeze ruffled the short fur on her back. Like her face, she didn't have fur on her breasts or belly, and her Draco scar was visible above her heart. She went to lay down on the hard ground, but before she could, Tobin sat behind her. He put gentle hands on her shoulders and guided her head down to his lap. His warmth seeped into her and settled her nerves.

Lyko took Ferth's place next to Rom and pressed his body close to his brother's. Ferth came to kneel on Jade's left, Keturah on her right. Marko, Allie, and the raven watched from over their shoulders.

Keturah wiped Jade's chest clean with a hot linen. The bitter stench of vinegar stung her nostrils.

"Your hands," Ferth said.

She stuck them under her legs, but he shook his head. Tobin reached out and gripped her wrists, but Ferth shook his head again. He was right. She could tear free of Tobin's grip in half a second.

"Kneel on them," she told Tobin, staring up at him from his lap.

He didn't look happy as he shifted her forearms under his shins. "This is not what I had in mind for this trip."

Jade grinned at him, and he slid his hands under her head,

cradling her. The unexpected pleasure over her scalp was a stark contract to the dread in her belly.

"Ready?" Ferth asked, his face a grimace.

"Do it," Jade said. Her gaze locked on Tobin's steady blue eyes. *Never let me go.*

THIRTY-TWO - BURNING FRIENDS

FERTH

Every muscle in Jade's body went rigid. She stared at Tobin with such intensity, Ferth felt relieved that her violet, fiery gaze was focused elsewhere. Keturah forced a leather strap between Jade's sharp teeth then looked to Ferth and nodded grimly.

He really didn't want to be doing this.

He picked up the glowing brand. Heat radiated off it in sinister waves. He checked the orientation so that the dragon head was on top, and the sword was cutting through her old brand. He exhaled sharply, put a steadying hand on Jade's left shoulder, and brought the searing iron down on her skin.

As she screamed against the strap in her mouth, she bucked, her skin sizzling. Ferth rammed his knee into her lower abdomen, holding her down as he lifted the iron away from her skin. The smell of burning flesh clogged his nose, and Lyko buried his snout in Rom's neck.

He set the iron back in the fire as Keturah leaned over Jade and poured inky green liquid on the fresh burn. Tears poured down the sides of Jade's eyes as she hissed into the leather.

"It's okay," Tobin whispered. "You're okay." He brushed his hands over her brow and velvety scalp. "I've got you."

Ferth picked up the brand. "Again, Jade."

She whimpered.

He went slower to make sure the second burn was exactly on top of the first. She arched as the heat touched the already angry flesh. Tobin grunted as he worked to keep Jade's arms pinned under his shins.

"Three," Keturah said. "Two. One."

Ferth lifted the iron, and Keturah exhaled her relief when she saw the dye had turned a deep purple within the burn. Jade's eyes fluttered closed. Ferth set the red brand on a rock to cool. Tobin lifted his knees, and Jade's arms rolled free, limp as worms. He pulled her higher into his lap, his arms going around her bare shoulders and waist.

"It's over," he whispered. "You were so brave." He kissed her brow. "It's over."

Keturah worked the leather out of Jade's mouth. She'd bitten clean through it.

Tobin's lips trailed over Jade's cheek. "You're okay."

She opened her eyes and looked up at his face hovering inches above her own. "Thank you." She lifted her chin and pressed her mouth to his, a closed-mouth kiss that lingered… and lingered.

This was a good thing, Ferth thought, but he couldn't quite kill the flicker of unpleasantness at the sight it. She'd been kissing Ferth just yesterday. He'd never let it happen again, but *still*. They broke apart, and Keturah knelt close. Jade flinched when Keturah smeared cream on the cooling burn. It was goopy and yellow, not her usual healing balm.

"This will stop the skin from healing, so the scar keeps," Keturah said. "Let it dry before you put your shirt back on."

Ferth pulled Jade's black-handled knife from his pack and held it out to her. He couldn't thank her for killing Thirro, even though he was grateful for the choice she'd made. He couldn't return to Shi Castle with her, but he wished her only success.

She nodded to him, as if she finally understood the complexity of his emotions. She slid the weapon into its place on her right hip.

Allie brought Jade warm tea, and Marko handed her bits of steak.

"Will you come with me?" Jade asked them as she laid against Tobin's chest. "Marko, I could use you at my side, and Allie, you will no longer be a slave. Things will change."

THIRTY-THREE - GOODBYE

SUZA

Suza put on her laundered clothes—tight pants and a leather vest over her tunic. She strapped on her sword belt, the familiar weight a comfort. After breakfast, she left Darius's fine house and walked toward the stables. A small group stood out front by three saddled horses. Three? Titus had mentioned an escort, but two? And where were they? Only Uriah, Imanna and her hewan, and Mira and Titus stood there.

Suza had never ridden a horse before, but she'd seen humans ride them these last few months. They made it look easy, but now, facing the long legs, heavy muscles, and dark eyes, trepidation skittered down her spine.

"Thank you for the horses and supplies," Suza said to Titus. "Thank you for everything you've done for me."

He leaned forward and pressed his lips to her brow, and a wave of longing struck her. She'd finally found a father. Could she really leave so soon?

She turned to her brother, and her courage failed. Then she noticed he wore sturdy boots, riding pants, and an arsenal of weapons. Her heart soared with hope, her face alighting.

"Yup," Uriah said. "We are your escorts. And not just to the border."

She meant to speak, but a gushy squeak came out. She flung herself at him, his sword hilt knocking her in the stomach. "Thank you."

He chuckled and stepped out of her hold. He motioned to Imanna, whose face was drawn. "She wants to see her country before the baby is born."

"I'll make no promises on how far we will go with you," Imanna said. "I will return home the moment I feel I need to."

Home. The true queen of Skotar belonged here, in the human capital.

Suza nodded. "Of course."

Imanna turned to Titus and embraced him. "Goodbye, father."

"I love you," he said. "And I trust you to follow the path that calls. Don't come back here on my account." His mouth pinched as if he were unhappy to have said those words. Titus couldn't hide the emotions simmering in his eyes. He wanted her to stay. He'd had enough of the women he loved leaving him. He pinched his lips into a thin line and held Mira a little tighter to his side.

Imanna nodded in understanding. "You would be reason enough." She didn't promise to return though.

Titus looked to Suza. "There are letters for Ferth in this saddle bag." He patted a pocket on one of the packs the gray mare carried. A heavy winter coat was strapped at the back of the saddle.

"I'll do my best to deliver them."

"Leave the horses with Captain Mills at the border camp."

"And a letter from you so we know all is well," Mira added.

"Come on, Sis," Uriah said. "We want to get to Salvick before dark. They have a nice inn." He stepped to the side of the gray horse and motioned her forward.

"I've never ridden a horse before."

"I assumed. I'll hold the lead rope, and this mellow girl will follow without complaint."

Tears of relief welled in Suza's eyes. She didn't have to be quite so brave.

"Put your foot in the stirrup."

She obeyed, and Uriah hoisted her onto the tall beast. She swayed uneasily, cursing Ferth inwardly. This felt like his fault. She added it to the mental list of things she was mad at him about. She couldn't wait to let him have it.

Imanna used a mounting block to climb onto her glossy black horse. She waved to Titus and Mira as she clicked at her horse and started toward the street. Her hewan, Kira, walked at the horse's side. Suza clung to the saddle when her horse suddenly moved to follow. She chided herself for being skittish but remained tense until they'd exited the city gates and crossed the bridge into the countryside.

Xandra shot out of the sky and dove at Suza. The hawk startled her horse, who jumped, and nearly caused Suza to fall from the saddle.

"How nice of you to drop in." Her voice dripped with sarcasm across their mental connection.

Xandra perched on the leather band Suza had tied to her left forearm. *"How nice of you to leave your emerald tower."*

Suza rolled her eyes.

Xandra's voice went soft as she swiveled her head north. *"And so, we go."*

"I won't be a slave again, and I can't let anything happen to Uriah or Immana." She willed it, so please let it be. Any trouble they found would be her fault. The reality of the danger they

were heading for settled like heavy chains around her shoulders.

"We'll be careful and avoid being seen. We'll find Ferth. Everything will be fine." But Xandra couldn't hide her worry from Suza.

Suza didn't look back as Mitera shrank behind them.

THIRTY-FOUR - HOT ENOUGH TO STRIKE

JADE

Jade stopped at the secret caves west of Azure Lake to return the royal brand to its rightful place among the Regium horde. It had gone missing when Mavras murdered the Regiums. How Laconius got the brand, Jade would never know. She picked through piles of treasure and found the ring Keturah had shown her two years ago—when Keturah had told her the whole truth, and Jade had realized how much her father had cared for her… and her mother. He'd trusted the slave with his secrets, his fears, his gold, and his daughter. Icor had known Mavras was out to get him, and no one could know who the baby growing in Keturah's womb belonged to—not until the iron was hot enough to strike.

Jade's thoughts lingered on her unknown father as she wove her way back to Ferth's camp, where she picked up Keturah, Marko, and Allie. Together they trekked down to Shi Castle.

Pockets heavy with silver, Jade strode straight into the citadel, where dinner was in full swing. Captain Mina sat in the royal chair at the head table, Dara and Beto flanking her.

Jade inhaled courage, feeling that the invasion of Elysium was a mere precursor to the real war she'd started when she'd murdered her aunt, Mavras. Even before that, when she'd learned the name of every slave.

The fighting was nowhere near over.

"You're in my seat." Jade's voice cut through the chattering noise. Heads of various sizes, textures, and colors turned in her direction, but she kept her focus on Mina. She didn't slow her step as she approached the high table.

"Move."

Mina didn't move. "Where's Laconius?"

"Dead."

Soft murmurs rippled through the room.

Mina's face twitched before she shifted it back to feline arrogance. She raised delicate brows and said, "Are you about to tell me you killed him?" She laughed and others joined in.

"I'm telling you," Jade's voice was low and sharp, "that if you don't move out of your queen's seat, I'll kill you." She wasn't bluffing. She'd strike like the asp, bold and fast and deadly.

"My queen?"

Jade might have to kill Mina just because of her insulting tone. Jade walked around the table, drawing closer to the usurper. Marko followed her, a silent weapon in her wake. She liked him.

"Hello, Kenji," Jade said to the man pouring Dara a drink. She stopped within striking distance of Mina, and tugged her shirt open at the neck, revealing the inflamed purple burn to the room. "Yes. I was Laconius's heir, but it wasn't him who gave me Regium blood. It was my father, King Icor." Jade held up her left hand, where Icor's ruby ring sat on her finger. The ring that had been passed down from ruler to ruler for centuries. Icor had given it to Keturah to keep it hidden from Mavras's searching eyes all these years.

Beto jumped to his feet at the sight of it. His ram-like gaze moved from the ring to her face. He must have agreed with what he saw because he set his shoulders and said, "My queen."

Jade nodded to him, her heart lurching in gratitude. Beto was a big win. Huge.

This was going much better than she'd anticipated.

"Liar." Mina spat the accusation out, but her eyes were fearful. She stood and pushed the bone throne back as she pulled a long, jagged knife from her belt.

"It's true," Keturah said.

Mina glared at Keturah across the table. "You impertinent slave, I'll have you—"

"Careful what you say. That woman is my mother, and she is no one's slave now." Jade pulled one of her short swords free and felt Marko move to her side. "You may take your rightful place down there." She motioned to the lower tables, packed with stunned Draco Sang. "Or Beto will escort your corpse elsewhere."

Mina's nostrils flared as she lifted her blade.

Jade cursed inwardly, but her face betrayed nothing of the fear sprouting through her veins. The only way she knew how to get where she wanted to go was straight through the heart of the opposition. Ferth might have had more finesse, but he hadn't taught her diplomacy. He'd taught her dueling. How to survive. How to win.

Short sword in one hand, knife in the other, she glanced at Marko with a look that meant stay out of this. He stepped back, understanding that Jade had to earn her own respect.

Mina charged with a sudden jab at Jade's belly. Jade jumped to the side, knocking into a chair. Mina didn't unsheathe her short swords—an insult. Arrogant mistakes had already cost the Dracos too much.

Jade pushed away from the table, narrowly missing

Mina's follow up strike. Mina's dagger cut into the wood of the chair. The half second it took her to pull it free cost her. Jade darted under Mina's arm and without hesitation, never hesitation, she thrust her knife into the cheetah's armpit. Mina gurgled an anguished growl, eyes wide.

Jade hated killing. The heaviness of life bleeding onto her hands. The sounds of regret and failure leaking from her victims along with their vibrancy.

Mina whirled, the nasty blade lashing toward Jade's face. Jade blocked it, then sliced down with her sword and cut along the bottom of Mina's forearm, shaving off fur and flesh.

Jade hated this.

Mina's eyes flared red with anger and fear. Her scream echoed through the citadel. Jade sliced her neck, ending the gut-wrenching cry. Ending the life.

Jade turned away from the mess on the floor and the ache in her breast. Blood was smeared over her left hand. She wiped it on her cheek and through her furry scalp, painting a deadly image for her new subjects to see. She was glad Tobin had not come. She didn't want him to see the truth about her and what she was capable of.

With gore decorating her face and her gaze cold as Dracosteel, Jade scanned the room. There were a few faces tight with the threat of violence. The thrill. Dracos deciding whether they could gain anything by challenging the new queen. Most of the Dracos seemed to have changed their tone in her favor. Mina's death had not been for naught.

Dara hadn't moved from her seat next to the throne made of bones.

"You will move from my table," Jade said.

"Why?" After a pause, Dara added. "I am here to serve you, my queen."

"I don't want you here, and you're in Marko's seat."

Marko grinned, showing his canines.

Dara growled, but she stalked away from the table. She was a follower, and not much of a threat.

Beto turned to leave.

"No, Beto, you may stay." Jade looked toward the women still waiting on the other side of the wide table. Brave women willing to risk everything to stand by her. To stand for freedom and change. Her heart tightened.

She would not fail them.

"Allie, Keturah, please join us as well."

Unhappy outbursts greeted the remark.

"Quiet!" Jade leaned forward, her knuckles braced on the table.

"I am queen, by blood and by battle, and what I say is law. Every human in this country belongs to me. They are *mine*." She hissed the last word with all the acid she could muster.

"You are no longer allowed to touch the humans or control them. If you don't like it, you may come to me and see how you fare. Or you may leave." She sure hoped they'd pick the latter. It might be a very short reign otherwise. Mustering another breath, she said, "As of this moment, every slave in the country of Skotar is free."

Draco Sang leapt to their feet in outrage.

Jade lifted her chin. The battle line had been drawn. Her heart, her truth, laid bare. Now came the gathering of forces and defenses. She studied the varied reactions among her people, noting the Dracos who sat calmly, accepting the new changes.

A slave tried to free himself from a wombat Draco, but the Draco punched the human so hard, the boy crumpled to the ground in an unconscious heap. The other slaves looked paralyzed with fear.

Jade yelled, "Listen!"

Thank the stars, they did.

"I am hoping that many of the humans will wish to stay here, and work for pay as equal citizens among the Dracos." The treasury of Skotar didn't have as much as she'd hoped. The war was expensive, but Jade wanted to open trade with Elysium and start filling the coffers. In the meantime, she knew where the secret Regium horde was hidden. She silently thanked her father.

More dissenting voices barked at her from around the room. The slaves were weak humans. They were meant to serve the Dracos, et cetera, et cetera....

Jade's voice was frosty. "If anyone touches a human without consent, their hands will be cut off. If other body parts are involved, those parts will be removed as well."

Slaves shoved away from the lower tables. Many of the Dracos stopped them. A pig Draco at a nearby table grabbed a male slave. Jade's belly tightened. The Draco would make a perfect example.

"Marko, cut off her hand." Jade's blade needed a break, and she hoped to prove that she wasn't fighting alone.

Marko's face was grim, but he didn't hesitate. Yes, she liked him very much. Surrounded by tense silence, he marched toward the table. When Marko got near, the Draco dropped the slave. Marko grabbed the pig's left wrist. She squealed and tugged, pushing against Marko. She pulled a knife, and Marko whirled, yanking her wrist back so the pig hissed in pain.

"Would you rather I cut your throat?" Marko asked, revealing his delightfully rough voice for the first time.

The Draco's eyes went wide, and she dropped her knife. It clattered on the stone floor.

Marko surveyed the room, his shrewd gaze landing on Kenji. Marko grinned at him. "Kenji, was it?"

Kenji nodded, face uncertain.

"Would you like to hop over here and help hold this Draco still?"

From embers that had simmered for years, fire roared to life in Kenji's dark eyes. He set the pitcher on the table with finality before stalking to Marko. Kenji grabbed the pig's beautifully carved Dracosteel knife from the floor.

"A gift for your assistance," Marko said.

Kenji grinned, showing the gap in his front teeth.

"Turn her to stone, please," Marko said.

Kenji held the knife so tightly against the Draco's throat that he drew blood.

Marko slammed her left arm down on the table, drew back his rapier and with one clean sweep, cut off the Draco's leathery hand. The pig howled. Jade held her breath, tensing against possible mutiny.

But the Dracos let the remaining humans go. Jade and her friends had won this first battle. The Draco Sang accepted her as queen. For now.

But it was clear the fight for the humans and the country wasn't over.

"You might want to see a healer," Marko said as the pig Draco's blood splattered plates of food and dripped off the table onto the floor. He wiped his blade clean on her shirt. "Then come back and clean up the mess you made."

The pig wrapped her arm in her red-stained shirt and stumbled out of the room.

"Thank you, Marko," Jade said. "You too, Kenji." She owed them both for casting their lots and their strength in with her.

Marko strode back to Jade's side. Pearl joined Kenji, and they turned to leave.

"Kenji."

He looked over his shoulder at Jade.

"Would you please ask the kitchen staff to come see me? Tell them I'd like to offer them jobs."

Kenji nodded, his face flushed with happiness.

"I won't blame you if you walk straight out those gates after that, but I'm hoping you," Jade looked at Pearl, "both will stay and see me in the morning about jobs as well."

They made no promises, but hope bloomed in Jade's chest as she watched Kenji and Pearl, hand in hand, walk freely out of the room. Tentatively at first, and then with growing confidence, a string of humans followed them out the doors.

She didn't feel like eating, but she forced down Mina's plate of food for appearances. Every person in the room was watching her, calculating.

The kitchen staff of twelve red-faced, weary humans plodded into the room and stopped in front of the head table.

"Thank you for coming," Jade said.

"We're free?" Herc asked. He wore a filthy apron, and his gray hair was tied back in a ponytail.

"Good evening, Herc."

His mouth dropped open in surprise. Yes, she really did know them all. She'd been the one who'd left him eucalyptus oil when he'd developed that cough last winter.

"I'd like to compliment you on an excellent meal." She picked up a roasted bird leg. "Have you eaten?"

He snorted. "No, your highness. Not yet."

Jade motioned to the full platters on the high table. "Come eat with me while we talk." There was a rarely used bench on the other side of the high table. Marko and Beto pulled it out for the humans, who sat nervously and touched nothing.

"I suppose I can't order you to eat," Jade said. "Since you're free now." She looked to Beto. "Will you pour them mead?" A test.

His expression remained hard and unreadable, but he stood and lifted the pitcher Kenji had left. Wordlessly, he filled each cup to the brim.

A good sign.

With slack jaws, the humans watched the head war trainer serve them.

Beto finished, set down the pitcher, and returned to his meal.

Beto was powerful and respected at Shi Castle, an important ally. But at the lower tables, there were too many Dracos watching her like predators scouting prey for Jade to breathe easy.

Herc nodded at the other humans, and they reached for slabs of meat. It became a rush of face stuffing after that. Long moments later, their eating slowed.

"I'd like you to stay on as cooks in the kitchen. You will be paid and treated with equal standing as the Dracos." As much as she could help it. "If you leave, you fend for yourselves. I can guarantee no protection to you on your journey to Elysium." It was nearly overwhelming to think how much work she had ahead of her. If she survived that long.

"This is our home," Katy said.

Herc glare at her.

She ignored him. "I'd like to stay and cook for you."

"Thank you," Jade said.

"Where will you get the coin?" Herc asked.

"We're dragons," she said with a half-grin. "I have my hoard of treasure."

Herc didn't smile. Jade dug into her pocket and pulled out twelve silvers.

"For tonight's meal." She tossed one to each of them.

As they cradled their first bit of wealth, and therefore true freedom, Jade knew she had won another critical victory.

THIRTY-FIVE - DARKNESS AHEAD

FERTH

Ferth woke in the darkness that comes before the dawn. It was quiet. Too quiet. Tobin, Lyko, and Rom slept close, all four of them huddled for warmth under their single wool blanket. Ferth didn't want to risk further injury to the still-unconscious Rom or he would have moved their camp farther away from the lake that had swallowed his father whole. A torn boot had washed up on shore, the only trace left. Ferth wondered what horde of treasures and weapons the water Draco must have collected through the years.

He ran a gentle hand over the bandage wrapping Rom's torso. The wolf didn't stir with the touch, but Ferth couldn't feel any fever or additional swelling. He scanned the spindly trees before his gaze locked on the lake mere yards away. The black surface distorted the stars. Laconius had once told him that a person could see their future in the reflection of Azure Lake. As the warped darkness seemed to reach for him, engulf him, Ferth could only hope that wasn't true. A chasm seemed to open deep inside his soul. Maybe it was the loss of Rom's steady presence, the loss of an unknown brother, the loss of a kind mother, or the loss of the woman he loved. Even the loss of a cruel father. Endless cold felt like a fitting future for Ferth, a man who destroyed every connection. Twisting despair clawed through his mind. His pulse rose against the pain, but his body was utterly still.

"Ferth?"

He jolted at the hoarse voice.

"What's wrong?" Rom asked.

Ferth rolled on his side, his hand finding Rom's face and tilting it up just enough to see his hewan's brilliant eyes fixed on him. He let out a grateful sob. *"Rom."* All at once the tears came, and he buried his face in Rom's neck.

"I'm okay."

"I almost lost you and Lyko. All because of my arrogance and pride."

"What happened?" Rom asked, ignoring Ferth's self-pitying declaration.

Ferth explained, sharing the memories with words and imagines. A shutter ran through Rom when he heard about how close Lyko and Ferth had come to drowning. Ferth went quiet for a while before he said the words that were eating a hole in his heart. *"We killed our father."*

Rom grimaced as he rolled over, leveling his gaze with Ferth's. *"It had to be done."* He licked the brine off Ferth's cheeks with a warm, rough tongue. *"Our father was poison for us and for Skotar. We'll feel the grief of it for a time, but we will not allow space for the bitterness of regret. We carry too much of that already."*

"That's fat that weighs so heavy on you," Lyko said.

Ferth choked on a short laugh, wondering how long Lyko had been awake and listening.

"Welcome back, brother," Lyko said. *"If you hadn't slept so long, you would have gotten to see Ferth brand the jackal."* He shared the memory, including the smell of burning skin. And

the kiss. *"Tobin's in love with Jade, and she's the new queen of Skotar."*

"So, I missed everything," Rom said.

"Pretty much," Lyko said.

"Don't pout," Ferth said. "You're just in time to hunt for dusty old dragon bones."

"And it's going to snow," Lyko added.

THIRTY-SIX - RETURNING

SUZA

Suza stared across the icy Rugit River delta at the country beyond.

Skotar.

Her home and her sorrow. It had been nine days since she'd left Mitera, nine days to prepare to make this crossing. It had not been enough. Trepidation and anticipation swirled through her body as the cold north wind slapped her face. Ice frosted the river edges and snowflakes danced through the air. Across the low delta, the land was dense with forest below a silvery sky. The scene was beautiful and dangerous. Just like Skotar.

"Ready?" Uriah looked between his two anxious traveling companions.

Below her furry hood, Imanna's face hardened with resolve. Uriah took her hand and together they walked into the river. Kira followed with a whine. Suza checked her bow was strung and easily accessible from where she'd secured it on top of her pack. On the southern banks, the human sentries watched, faces unreadable. They must have thought her insane to willingly go north.

Thanks to the winter, the river bottom was hard and stable. Suza's sealed leather boots kept out the wet, but not the cold. She wiggled her numb toes as she walked, grateful the water never rose above the top of her knee-high boots.

She tensed at the sound of Uriah's sword whispering free of his scabbard. He kept Imanna behind him as he took his first step onto enemy soil.

Their homeland.

Heart pounding, she scanned the trees for her hewan. *"See anything?"*

Xandra patrolled ahead of them. *"No. The campsite is empty."*

They followed the path the Draco army had pounded smooth. They walked, nervous and searching, until they reached the abandoned clearing where the Draco Sang army had camped—where Suza had lived mere months ago. The smell of beast and sewage lingered, but now, nothing living seemed to venture within miles of this cursed place. She closed her eyes and pictured the rows of tents, the hundreds of ferocious warriors, the quiet slaves, and the Draco with half a wolf face and a whole human heart.

Uriah let out a long sigh and sheathed his sword. Imanna chuckled nervously. It was windier in the clearing, so Suza lead the group to the safety of the trees. The clouds overhead thickened, and snow fell in earnest. A mile later, Suza didn't argue when Uriah suggested they make camp in a circle of tall pines. He pulled the tent from his pack and set it up for the three of them to share. Waves of gratitude hit Suza. She would have been a terrified ball of nerves if Uriah and Imanna hadn't come with her.

Xandra flew down and gave Suza a fresh-caught sea bass. She didn't like Xandra fishing in any waters north of the Rugit, let alone the High Sea, but she only said, *"Thank you."*

Uriah stretched a tarp over their heads to keep the snow

off while Suza and Imanna rummaged for dry wood and built a small fire. He fileted the fish and set the meat to roast. They ate in silence. Xandra pecked at the leftover fish bones, and Kira ate the head. As soon as the fire fizzled out, the three humans and two hewans crawled into the tent. For the first time in weeks, Xandra deigned to join her. Uriah lay in the middle, his front warming Imanna and his back radiating heat to his little sister. Within minutes his breathing steadied into slumber, but Suza stared at the brown canvas for a long time, listening to the silent fall of snow.

Where was Ferth? How could she possibly find him? What had seemed so easy while sitting in Darius's castle, now seemed foolish and impossible. She'd thought her heart would know. She'd thought love had connected them, but she felt only one constant tug in her heart, the urge that every Draco felt but must ignore, lest they follow its perilous call into the deadly northern mountains.

There was only one place she could think to go now.

Shi Castle.

The place of her enslavement.

THIRTY-SEVEN - WOLF PACK

FERTH

Ferth sat with Tobin on a frozen boulder, watching. He'd taken his pack off, and his hand twitched toward his sword hilt, but he knew better than to interfere as Lyko fought.

The wild pack was small, three wolves. Two females and a male. One of the females was young, a year and a half old. Ferth got his information from Rom, who was standing a foot in front of Ferth, also watching. Rom was tense, but so far he hadn't engaged—thank the stars.

Rom had only started walking without a limp a week ago, but Ferth couldn't fault him for being ready to back up Lyko if he needed him. So far, the white wolf was holding his own against the wild male. The older female, four of five years old, Rom guessed, watched from the other side of the fight, her eyes bright and unreadable.

Lyko barked as he circled the mottled brown wolf. Lyko was bigger, but the wild alpha looked grizzlier, a feral sheen in his eyes. Ferth had hoped to avoid this confrontation, but the small pack had been following them for the past four days, interrupting their sleep and drawing closer each night. They'd had no choice but to engage.

Maw open, the brown wolf lunged. Lyko swatted its head away, his claws drawing blood. The male fell back, and Lyko jumped on him, biting his shoulder and tearing at flesh before pulling back and circling again. The older female barked.

"*Is she happy Lyko's winning?*" Ferth asked.

"*I don't speak wolf well,*" Rom said.

Ferth laughed hard.

"*This is a fight,*" Lyko said. "*Not a comedy show.*"

Ferth continued to let the laughter roll through him, loosening his chest.

"*But I'm reading underneath her icy stare.*" Rom sent his own glare to the female across the clearing. "*I think she likes Lyko better than her alpha—which isn't saying much.*"

"*Of course she wants me,*" Lyko said. "*Why do you think she been following me for days?*"

Rom snorted.

The male flung himself at Lyko, but it was a desperate, wild strike. Lyko knocked him back with a kick to the belly. Lyko howled in triumph. The brown wolf was slow to get up, and when he did it was with his head down and his tail between his legs. The clearing was silent except for the sound of Tobin cracking nuts open for Ipsum to eat out of his hand.

The defeated male let out an unhappy growl before slinking south into the sparse trees.

"*Well,*" Lyko said. "*That was fun. Time to meet my new ladies.*"

"*Are you serious?*" Ferth asked.

Lyko sauntered over and started sniffing the adult female. She was a beautiful honey color, lean legs and long ears. She eagerly greeted him back.

"*You don't have to watch,*" Lyko said.

The female licked his white face and purred.

Rom growled. *"This is so unfair."*

Lyko shrugged with pure arrogance. *"I can't help that she likes me because I'm beautiful and strong and heroic."*

"Lucky for you she can't hear your idiotic chattering."

Ferth imagined there were plenty of wolf pheromones wafting across the clearing as the creatures rubbed their heads together. The wolf pup lay in the snow as Lyko and his female walked side by side out of view. Ferth blocked his mental connection to Lyko immediately.

Rom sulked and huffed as he paced around the boulder.

"Go introduce yourself to the other female."

"She's too young."

"I didn't say mate her."

Rom glared at Ferth, the expression oddly human on his long face. Finally, the gray wolf slunk over to the young wolf. The female pup lifted her head but didn't rise. Rom lay down in the snow and pressed his nose to hers. Then they both turned their faces away. Mere inches apart but staring in opposite directions.

"There," Rom said. *"Happy?"*

Ferth chuckled, drawing Tobin's attention. "Rom's jealous."

Rom snarled.

"So am I." Tobin popped a nut into his mouth and crunched.

They went quiet, each male left alone with his thoughts. So, Lyko got the girl. Ferth couldn't help but wonder if Cal would have too. He'd seen the way Suza had looked at Cal when he died in her arms. She'd gone back to Skotar, risked her life and freedom, for Cal. She wouldn't do that for Ferth. And Ferth could never forget the kiss Suza had given Cal. Her quivering lips trying to breathe life into his brother had seared like a brand on his heart. She'd known Cal for only a few days, but it had been enough for his death to cloud her in grief and regret. Loving Cal would have been so much easier than loving Ferth.

For the first time, Ferth was glad Cal wasn't alive to take the girl he loved. It was a terrible thought, and he quelled it the moment it sprouted. He didn't really mean it either. He'd give anything to have his brother back, and Suza wasn't his anyway. He'd been stupid enough to let her go. Feeling wretched and small, he stood, stomping feeling back into his legs.

"Let's head out. Lyko can catch up."

Rom stood. *"Or not."*

Lyko marched into the clearing, chest out and chin up, the female at his side. *"That was—"*

"Don't want to know," Rom said.

Lyko strutted past Rom and stood in front of Ferth. The younger female came up beside her mother.

Ferth stared down at four wolves. Skies. Four wolves.

"Meet my mate." Lyko's voice oozed with pride. *"I've named her Amber."*

"How creative." Rom's voice dripped with sarcasm.

"Nice to meet you," Ferth said aloud.

"Yeah, she only speaks wolf." Lyko laughed.

"And you speak wolf?" Ferth raised a brow.

"I spoke it well enough a minute ago." Arrogance rippled over Lyko's shoulders.

"Gag," Rom said.

"We're leaving." Ferth turned on a heel and led out, following the increasingly insistent pull in his breast. The females followed, and Ferth was glad to have them, anything to make these mountains feel a little less creepy and haunted. The shadows grew barbs and the fog chilled right through to his bones.

THIRTY-EIGHT - CHANGES

JADE

Jade couldn't leave the citadel. The rebel Dracos had the castle under siege. They'd set up the slave house as their headquarters, a strategic move as well as a symbolic one. They held twenty-three humans hostage. Emil, who had been a commander in Mavras's army, had declared himself king.

A knock sounded on the front doors of the citadel. Tense, Jade moved to join the group gathering at the entry.

"It's a trap," Dara said.

Jade was pleasantly surprised the fox Draco had sided with her in the great dividing of Shi Castle.

Pearl looked through a slit in the old wood. "It's my mother." Her voice shook.

Kenji pulled her away from the door, away from potential danger. He'd shaved his long hair off at the scalp. If it weren't for his broad-shoulders and twenty-one years, he would've looked like an underling. Jade wondered if that was his intention. He looked bigger than two weeks ago. Sleep and plenty of food had done that to many of the humans.

Pearl wrested her arm out of his grip. "We need to let her in."

Jade looked through the hole in the door, but her field of vision was narrow and choppy. Catrie stood huddled on the step. Jade couldn't see any Dracos except the flyer on the roof across the courtyard with an arrow pointed at the human. Jade stepped back and pulled her short sword free. She nodded to Marko, and he pulled the heavy door open a foot. Beto stood behind him, weapons ready.

"Hurry." Marko motioned.

Catrie darted inside, and he slammed the great door closed.

Pearl rushed into her mother's arms and clung tight.

Jade's brow furrowed as she glanced around. Where was the trap?

Pearl pulled back. "How did you get free?"

Catrie's voice was grainy and dry. "They sent me to deliver a message."

Jade's blood ran cold. After two weeks of fruitless stand-off, whatever scheme Emil had cooked up wouldn't be pleasant.

Pearl kept her arm around her frail mother as a support.

Catrie cleared her throat. "The Draco garbage in charge over there would like you to know that every morning at sunrise, he'll hang a human from the roof of the slave house."

Pearl brought a thin hand to her throat as her pale eyes popped.

Jade's fingers tightened on her hilt.

"It will end when you give up the throne to Emil and pledge loyalty to him." Catrie ran a hand down Pearl's long hair, but she looked at Jade. "He wants you to know that he'll show you mercy and let you live."

Beto snorted at what they all knew was a lie.

"He says you will have a place in his kingdom, and he will forget this unfortunate incident."

Jade said nothing. She needed time to think. Emil had more Draco Sang under his banner than she. She had the food stores, but Emil could hunt the forest. He had access to the water wells and baths. Jade had stone walls. She claimed most of the underlings, but he had full-fledged, war-hardened Dracos. But it didn't matter how the weights hung in the balance. Jade would never surrender. She couldn't.

She sheathed her short sword and motioned them all to move into the great center room where breakfast sat on the tables. "Eat, Catrie. Rest." Pearl and Kenji stayed with the worn-out woman.

Beto, Dara, and Marko followed Jade to the room Mavras had used as her command office. Jade perched on the desk. Beto folded his arms around a chest as big as a barrel. No one spoke. No one looked happy.

She couldn't give in or negotiate. She would win or she would die. All the humans' fates were tied with hers, and there were far more humans in Skotar than twenty-three—twenty-two now that Catrie was free. Nearly a hundred humans took shelter within the walls of the citadel and called her their queen. She could let Emil do his hangings, and then he will have lost his leverage. He would be cutting off his foot if he killed the slaves. But could Jade stomach it? She had already swallowed terrible things in her short life. She'd killed more humans than she could count. What was two dozen more? Was this a necessary sacrifice to save the rest? Lose this battle to win the war? Peace was bought with blood, was it not? She knew no other way.

"What if we agree to his terms?" Dara asked.

"No." The word dropped from Jade's mouth with finality.

Dara held up a forestalling hand. "What if we set a trap for him? We lure him into a fight with a promise of peace."

"He has more fighters," Beto said.

It was a three to one ratio of Draco Sang warriors. Impossible odds.

"The humans will fight with us," Marko said.

That just meant more dead humans. Discouragement settled over Jade like a cold mist. For weeks she'd climbed over and through every idea they could think of. She'd schemed and planned and dreamed. It wasn't enough. She didn't have the power to free the humans, control the Dracos, and keep the throne.

She needed help. Not for the first time, she wished Ferth were here instead of off on a fool's errand.

Her errand seemed just as foolish.

The ring on her middle finger glittered darkly. Icor had saved it for *her*.

She knew she was the queen Skotar needed. She would give her life for this country, but she was not ready to give it her death.

THIRTY-NINE - FIRST MARK

SUZA

Suza plodded through the snow, head down, legs heavy, heart heavier still. She was cold, tired, and discouraged. Three days from Shi Castle, and it felt like three days to their doom. This hunt for Ferth was a terrible idea, and she'd dragged her brother and his pregnant wife—the true heir of Skotar—into it. A fact that would get Imanna killed by Queen Mavras faster than a hog at festival.

Xandra's voice broke through Suza's brooding. *"Three Dracos eighty yards to the northwest."*

Suza's fatigue fled as she relayed the message to Uriah and Imanna, stopping them in their tracks.

"One's a hound Draco with his nose pointed right at you," Xandra said.

"What are the other two?"

"A snake and a deer. They don't look like nice folks. They don't seem to subscribe to the practice of washing either. I can smell them from here."

"Then you're too close."

Xandra ignored Suza, swooping closer to the incoming Dracos.

"I think they're lawless ones," Suza said aloud.

There were many Dracos in Skotar who lived in the wilderness, eating off the land and fending for themselves. They avoided subjection by staying in small numbers, not worth the ruler's time. But they still lived by the universal Draco Sang law, unwritten but ubiquitous.

By strength and wit—whomever had the most of both had power.

"They're coming for us," Suza said.

Uriah muttered something about Poe under his breath. He rarely spoke of his grizzly bear hewan who'd died saving Zemira and her baby. Suza wished the bear were here right now too. Uriah grimaced as he looked at Imanna. "Hide behind those trees, Suza and I will ambush them."

"I can fight." Imanna's tone was curt with insult.

"Yes, my love. I know. But I can't risk…"

"Stop it, Uriah." Imanna turned to survey their surroundings. "Now, what's the plan?"

They could hear the Dracos closing in, cracking branches and crunching snow.

"Kill or be killed." Suza pulled her twin blades free.

Imanna lifted one sword in her left hand and kept her trusty knife in her right.

Kira's body coiled next to Imanna, and the sleek black dog bared her teeth to the northwest.

The Draco Sang came into view all at once. One blink there was nothing but blue sky and spindly trees, the next, three feral beings filled up the view, weapons high and toothy mouths open in battle cries. A month ago, Suza might have frozen in fear, but today, without hesitation, she bent her knees and lifted her swords.

The dog Draco stopped when he saw them and lifted a hand to halt his companions. "They're humans." The dog sniffed the air. "But they don't smell right." He raised his voice. "Who are you?"

"That's none of your business," Imanna snapped.

"Runaway slaves," the snake Draco said, his voice a slithering hiss that whistled around protruding fangs. Suza recoiled at the thought of anyone kissing that mouth.

"Shall we keep them for ourselves or turn them in for a reward?" the deer Draco asked.

"I kinda like them," the dog said. "They smell good."

"They look good," the snake said.

"One for each of us," the deer added.

The dog Draco looked at the dog hewan and laughed. "And look at the little pet. She's mine."

Kira growled.

"Oph." The Draco bit on his knuckles as he chuckled. "She did not like me saying that."

Anger roiled through Suza. Vinegary memories of objectification and Draco mockery spread like acid over her bones. The Draco Sang saw nothing but weakness and personal pleasure in humans. She looked forward to teaching these three an important lesson.

"We won't be going anywhere with you," Uriah said.

The Dracos stopped their chortling. The dog Draco noticed their drawn weapons as if seeing them for the first time. "So, we shall have some fun first." He paused. "And then we shall have some more fun later." He laughed. He threw his head back and howled. It ended abruptly—on the edge of Imanna's knife, which quivered in his exposed neck.

"He was getting very annoying." Her voice was calm, but her cheeks flushed, and her fingers trembled at her side.

Her first kill? Suza wondered.

The Draco crumpled to the red-splattered snow.

Two seconds later, the other Dracos snapped out of their shock and attacked. Uriah and Suza stepped in front of

Imanna and lifted their blades. And suddenly, Suza was back on the battlefield, fighting in tandem, working together as brother and sister. Uriah blocked, and Suza stabbed. Uriah swung from the left; Suza surprised from the right. The fight didn't last long. The Dracos weren't trained or disciplined. They'd grossly underestimated their opponents—a fatal mistake.

The skirmish ended quickly. Uriah retrieved Imanna's trusty knife, cleaned it, then returned it hilt first. "That was a thing of beauty, my sweet. A story for the children." She flushed as he kissed her.

Suza pulled nuts and soft apples from her bag while Uriah searched the bodies, collecting coins and a high-quality axe. "May the Dragon keep you," he muttered half-heartedly over the corpses.

After he washed his hands in the snow, Suza gave him a palmful of walnuts. Fighting made her hungry, and Imanna was always hungry these days, it seemed. They sat and ate in silence for a while, each dealing with the deaths in their own way. Imanna's eyes looked glazed over, and she seemed to sink farther and farther into her furry hood.

"It's time," Suza said. "I understand, and I thank you for coming as far as you did. It was more than I expected."

Uriah's lips turned down, but he looked to Imanna to speak.

Imanna's eyebrows drew together. "Time for what?"

"You want to return to Elysium." Her heart sank. With Uriah and Imanna, she was something formidable, capable of taking down Dracos. Without them, she would be alone.

"No," Imanna said. "Not yet." She stood, shoulders straight. "I'm looking forward to seeing my castle now more than ever."

FORTY - ALPHA

FERTH

They camped at the base of a jagged mountain range. It was still early in the afternoon, but the steep cliffs barred their way, and no one had the strength of courage to venture into their only path forward—a narrow canyon that was as welcoming as a monster's maw.

There was no fuel for a fire, so they sat in miserable heaps in the cavity of a jumble of rocks that looked like the dark canyon had coughed up. The female wolves were still with them, part of their pack now. Lyko was alpha—at least among the wolves. Ferth couldn't tell who had more power in the pack after that. Rom in actuality, but Lyko's mate acted like she was the second in command. Rom and Amber didn't get along at all. That was clear.

The youngest wolf, Aisha—Rom had named her—was a sweet little thing that liked to cuddle, a wonderful trait in this frozen abyss. As if she'd read Ferth's thoughts, Aisha crawled into his lap and curled up.

"We're going to go hunt," Lyko said, indicating Amber with his nose.

"Is that what you're calling it these days?" Rom asked. The

wind shifted and Rom lifted his head from the snow, ears twitching.

"What is it?" Ferth asked.

Before Rom could answer, Ferth felt it. Instead of the clear southern breeze that had pushed them along, the creepy canyon seemed to come alive and exhale an icy rot. It smelled of death and nightmares.

Lyko snarled. *"You'll be grateful when I come home with your dinner."*

Rom rolled to a stand, his muscles rippling. *"I don't need you to feed me."* His lips pulled back.

"Oh, now you want to fight? Finally, the urge strikes the high and mighty Rommy baby?" Lyko's tone was mocking, but he hadn't moved from his stance by the southern path they'd come from, the only direction any living creature might be found.

"Go ahead, run away, coward."

Ferth looked between his wolves in dismay, his own heart pumping out a battle cry. With effort, he forced away the rising tide of blood lust.

Lyko made a deep foreboding cry and lunged at Rom. The wolves crashed together, and the mass of roiling fur slammed into the hard snow with the sound of shattering ice. Lyko's mouth closed around Rom's already half-severed ear. Along their mental connection, confusion, frustration, and pain pulsed like funeral drums. Amber circled the brothers, her incessant barking escalating their emotions. Rom kicked at Lyko's weak leg.

Ferth jumped to his feet, Aisha grunting as she flopped onto the ground. "STOP!" Ferth yelled it out loud and slammed the command down the connection. His body shook with the force of it, and with the effort not to pull his own sword free and start swinging.

Madness. This place was thick with it.

Rom's and Lyko's panting breaths drowned out the eerie whistle of the mountain pass. Still intertwined, they looked at each other. Lyko licked a fresh drip of blood off Rom's ear.

Rom buried his head in Lyko's neck. *"I'm sorry, brother."*

"I don't know what came over me," Lyko said.

Tobin's eyes were so wide the blue irises looked lost in a sea of white. He turned to the mountains and with a gravelly voice said, "The Dragon is near."

FORTY-ONE - ENFORCED WITH STEEL

JADE

Jade leaned back on her cushions and let out a pent-up breath, her muscles relaxing. It had been a long day, and tomorrow would be worse. The first hanging. She'd intended to spend the day working on how to save the humans and bring Emil and his horde to heel, but instead she'd dealt with endless problems that had cropped up inside the citadel.

She'd had to replace the treasurer after she'd caught her stealing. Jade needed to get coins from the hidden horde, but she might never get the chance to leave the castle. She'd had big dreams for this country. She wanted to open trade with Elysium, turn her timber, stone, and Dracosteel into silks and spice.

The door opened and a young man sprinted in, tripping on the rug in his haste. "Your Majesty." He panted as he jerked out a quick bow.

Jade's pulse rose, and she nodded for him to speak. Whatever it was wouldn't be good.

"It's my sister, Leah. A Draco took her to his room." The boy twitched with agitation.

To let this pass was to invite the rest of the Dracos to join Emil's rebellion. She rose from her cushions. Next to her, Marko lowered his mug of mead and stood.

"Lead the way." She strode toward the open door. The sooner they got there, hopefully the fewer crimes she had to punish. The less pain the girl endured.

In the hall, the young man bumped into two people kissing as he whisked past. The silhouettes shifted into familiar figures as they separated.

"Frankie?" Kenji said. "What's wrong?"

Frankie picked up his pace as he tore down the west wing. The nicest suites in the stronghold. The leaders lived here.

Jade groaned inwardly.

Kenji and Pearl joined the group as they ran down the hall. Muffled screams came from three doors down.

Frankie let out a pained cry.

Marko tried the handle. Locked. He pounded the wood. "Open now for the queen."

A pause in the shuffling behind the closed door. "The *queen* can wait her turn." Maniacal laughter followed the crude words.

Jade's blood boiled.

FORTY-TWO - FORWARD

FERTH

Ferth and his band stared into the unnaturally dark canyon. Motes of ice floated in the air, and the whistling wind spoke of horror and decay. The gap in the mountain was wide enough for two or three men to walk abreast. They couldn't see an end to the gloom. The tug in his chest called him in, but every other fiber of his being screamed at him to run.

He must venture into the canyon. Go forward into the trap.

"Just a stroll through the mountains." Ferth's voice sounded like it came from far away.

Tobin didn't respond. He was whispering to Ipsum and stroking the raven's crown. Compared to the void between the cliffs, Ipsum's black feathers practically looked like summer.

"You don't have to come," Tobin said to the raven.

Ipsum shook his head.

"Fly south."

Ipsum shook his head again and pecked at Tobin's coat. Tobin opened it with a shudder and let the bird nestle against his chest. When they'd arranged themselves, he looked to Ferth.

"We are ready."

"I will never be." Ferth thought they should turn back, but the idea wasn't stronger than the all-consuming pull north. He clenched his jaw and faced his doom.

"I've been through tighter," Lyko said. *"We came out in a secret paradise. So, I'm going to hope for the best."* He trotted into the canyon without a backwards glance. In a blink his white fur was swallowed up in inky blackness.

Heart thrashing, Ferth pulled his hood low over his head as if it were a shield and followed the wolf. They made a straggly line heading into the twisting shadows. Aisha let out a sad whimper before the dark swallowed her too. And so, like fishes into the pot, Ferth and his band of beasts and men trudged deeper into the steepening mountains, into the malicious fog.

Into hell.

Ferth squinted, trying to keep the world in focus. His companions were shifting silhouettes. The ground seemed to blur and refocus as he shuffled to keep his feet connected to the earth. No one spoke. The chill penetrated deeper than sinew and bone. It pervaded Ferth's soul, sucking away his energy and joy. And still the hook in his chest raked him forward over the jagged rocks and cold dirt.

His boot hit something in the path, and the zing of metal echoed through the canyon. Ferth crouched, straining his vision. Bones, weapons, and leathers lay scattered over the dead earth. A lump formed in his throat as he remembered the warnings. All who went this way perished. And here they all were.

Perished.

"Keep walking," Rom said.

Ferth exhaled and stood on wobbly legs. With aching

slowness, they trudged past corpse after corpse. What had killed them? The swords and axes lay next to the bodies, unsheathed.

The darkness coalesced into a vision of his father. Laconius stood blocking Ferth's path, his hair wet and matted, his face twisted in a scream. How had he gotten out of the lake? Ferth fumbled for his sword, his heart racing triple time.

"What is it?" Tobin asked, his voice coming as if from another world. He walked in front of Ferth and through Laconius's misting form. Ferth's father laughed as he dissolved.

Ferth shook his head, blinking ferociously. "I saw my father."

"That Draco is good and dead." Tobin's voice sounded suddenly clear and shockingly chipper. He gripped Ferth's elbow and urged him forward. "Put that sword away before you hurt one of us."

Humbled, Ferth obeyed.

"It's creepy in here. Let's get a move on. No more stalling."

"Stalling?" Ferth was sane enough to sound offended.

"You could seriously not be slower."

Ipsum squawked in agreement before the pair turned away and strode out in front of Ferth.

Simply a lovely walk in nature, Ferth told himself, forcing his rooted feet forward. No big deal.

And then the visions came again.

His childhood flashed before his eyes. Not a single joy could be found. He saw slaves whipped and raped. He saw children shunned and scolded. He saw hewans killed and people destroyed. He didn't just see it; he relived it. He was a child again, crushed from the loss of his mother and disappointment of his father.

He stopped walking. His whole body trembled with convulsions. Tears froze as they tore out of his eyes. Rom whined, and Lyko barked. Rom came to Ferth's side, and he fisted a gloved hand in Rom's fur.

"*Stop it,*" Lyko demanded.

"*I'm not doing anything,*" Ferth said.

"*Well, stop it anyway.*"

The sharpness of Lyko's voice made Ferth think of Cal. Regret and sorrow filled him with despair. He'd killed him, his brother. Ferth had ruined everything.

He should be dead. Not Cal.

"*Once, when Cal was seven,*" Lyko said. "*He ate the leaves off an osill vine near the giretorbie pits. It made his poop turn purple.*"

"*Why are all your stories about poop?*" Rom asked.

"*Excuse me for trying to lighten the mood. Big baby over there is about to poop his pants.*"

"*I am not,*" Ferth said, insulted.

"*Just checking.*"

Surrounded by darkness and death, they stumbled on. Rom at Ferth's side, Lyko behind, flanked by the two females, and Tobin ahead, a phantom in the mist. When the wicked cold began to claw through his mind again, churning up misery, Ferth begged his wolves to keep talking.

"*About excrement?*" Lyko asked.

"*My expectations are low,*" Rom said.

"*I want to smell mint and rosemary,*" Ferth said.

"*Picky,*" Lyko said. "*And not something I can remember well enough.*"

"*But you decided to store various poop smells.*" The poignant smell of rosemary and the freshness of mint drifted from Rom's mind.

"*Now who's the showoff?*" Lyko said.

"*Sweet paradise,*" Ferth whispered as he reveled in the scent of spring.

Rom and Lyko sent more, each trying to outdo the other.

They plunged Ferth in a bath of blossoms, herbs, and fresh rain.

Tobin's voice cut through the fantasy of smells. "How are you doing back there?"

"You know, just fighting my demons with flowers."

"How lovely. Keep it up. Because I can see the end."

FORTY-THREE - CONSEQUENCES

JADE

Why were people so anxious to rule, Jade wondered as she pulled her knife free of the dead Draco's throat. She hadn't wanted to kill him. Of course, she hadn't asked for his treachery and disrespect either.

The Draco's naked body sagged against the bed.

"You can't create a law without enforcing it," Marko said at her elbow, his rough voice apologetic. "He knew what the consequences would be."

She wouldn't have had to kill him if he hadn't pulled a weapon on his queen when they'd broken up his little *meeting.*

The girl was now wrapped in a coat and walking out under the protection of her brother's arm.

Jade's shoulders slumped. She'd told them she would protect them, and she'd failed. Again.

But she would not give up.

"Hang his body from the top floor window," Jade said to Marko. "We'll beat Emil to the punch."

Marko nodded grimly.

"Thank you."

FORTY-FOUR - STILL ALIVE

FERTH

Ferth and the wolves broke out of the canyon, gasping for air.

"We're still alive." Lyko's tongue lolled out the side of his mouth and his breath came out in frozen clouds.

"Low expectations," Rom said.

"Let's hope there's another way out," Ferth said.

"Excluding death," Lyko replied.

"Obviously."

Tobin stood a few paces away, watching them with an unimpressed expression.

"No big deal for you, eh?" Ferth staggered farther away from the canyon, but the oppressiveness in his chest didn't lift. Sadness seemed to permeate his whole body.

"I'm fine." Tobin rubbed at his arms. "Hungry and cold. Typical outdoor-in-winter conditions."

"You don't feel that the world is ending? You don't want to melt into the ground instead of face the pain?"

"Didn't peg for you the dramatics." Tobin squinted. "Are you sure we got all the infection out?" He reached out a hand to feel Ferth's forehead, but Ferth batted him away with a scowl.

Tobin grinned. Irritation flared through Ferth. This kid was nothing but a weak human, and he dared mock Ferth? He had the audacity to show no fear in this place of terror? He shoved Tobin's shoulders so hard the boy fell hard on his butt.

There, now he was afraid.

Tobin held up his hands in surrender, but from the opening of his coat, Ipsum let out a battle cry that had Ferth reaching for his sword again. Tobin had brought them here, and he would pay for that mistake. Ferth leveled his Dracosteel at Ipsum's face. He'd shove it through them both, two birds with one stab.

"Oh, come on now. Don't hurt the boy," Lyko said. *"It won't make you feel better."*

Ferth whirled on Lyko. *"How the blazes would you know anything?"*

The wolf rolled his golden eyes. *"Oh, very witty there, chief."*

Rom padded up and checked his shoulder hard into Ferth. *"Get control of yourself."*

Ferth's nostrils flared as he stumbled. *"Don't you feel the fire in your veins?"*

"Sounds like you need to see a healer," Lyko said.

The filter of bloodlust cleared enough that Ferth could hear Lyko's teasing tone and sense that both his hewans were wound up tighter then bow strings and teetering on the edge of joining him in fit of violent rage.

"Tobin is human." Rom's voice quivered. *"He has no dragon blood to torment him."*

Gathering back a small bit of self-control, Ferth pondered that theory. It could be possible. Rom was proving himself often correct.

"Get up," Ferth said to Tobin, his tone unpleasant.

Tobin scrambled to his feet, face wary. "I'm sorry. This place is unnatural. I feel it too. The air is stale, like a tomb."

Ferth battled with the shivers and lost. "Thank you for that peppy thought."

"Sorry."

"Stop being sorry."

Tobin held his hands up and took a meek step back.

Ferth fought the urge to knock him down again. Instead, he hissed and turned away, searching for something less pathetic to destroy. This mission was a mistake.

They stood in a massive bowl-shaped mountain. The world was gray—the snow a lighter shade than the rocks, and the sky a medium slate. Ferth could not remember a life before this endless, colorless freeze. When he looked to his traveling companions, they were bleached of animation or vibrancy.

Ferth could see no way forward. "After all that, we ended up in an empty valley." He hurled a rock. It clanged against the cliff face and dropped to the ground with an unsatisfactory *thud*.

"I don't think it's empty." The gray wolf's nose lifted in the air, his face pointed north.

Worse. It was covered in dead bodies.

They stepped slowly, setting their boots and paws with caution. Even Tobin's baby face had dropped into grim lines. Ispum, now on Tobin's shoulder, didn't so much as ruffle a feather. They passed more Draco Sang corpses, some preserved with gory freshness in the snow. Weapons lay strewn about like spilled rice.

The group stopped when Ferth gasped. Part of the mountainside wasn't mountain at all. On the north side of the valley, blocking a wide path between cliffs, lay a massive dragon.

His scales and wings were bleached to a chalky white. His claws and horns looked like decaying bone.

Nogard.

"He's dead," Tobin said, his voice both awed and disappointed. The boy made to step closer, but Ferth's hand snaked out and grabbed his wrist.

One crusty, pale eyelid popped open, and the Dragon's giant red iris fixed directly on his prey.

FORTY-FIVE - ANOTHER FATHER TO KILL

FERTH

Ferth's sword came free of its sheath with a whine, and he gripped it with numb hands. The Dragon's body looked more like stone than flesh. Impenetrable. If he went through the eye, would the weapon be long enough to reach past the skull?

"Do it." Nogard's voice blasted through Ferth's mind like a hot furnace.

The hair on Rom's and Lyko's backs rose, and they both tensed. Tobin didn't flinch. Clearly, he hadn't heard the voice of hell intruding on his mind.

"Go through the missing scale on my back near the top of my wing. If you aim true, you'll find my heart."

"You've poisoned this place." Ferth refused to speak mind to mind.

"I've poisoned a lot more than that, son."

Son.

The word tore through Ferth like a cannon ball.

"Stopping my breath will bring me peace. It will stanch the flow of fresh corruption in the air, but it won't cure the world. The blood

has drained out of me. I cannot draw it back. Every child must root the beast out of their own breast."

Ferth's sword lowered a fraction. He wanted to lie down and die. Utter hopelessness wrapped him.

"I've waited a long time for you," Nogard said.

Rom brushed against Ferth's side. A touch of warmth. A spark of life. Instead of curling up in a ball, Ferth looked around at the spray of corpses. "You've had a recent change of heart?"

"Is he responding to you?" Tobin asked.

"In my head."

"What is he saying?"

"Not recent." Nogard's voice was an icepick hacking at Ferth's insides. His eye, the only vibrant thing about him, rolled as he gazed over the graveyard.

"They could not conquer their blood. How could they have conquered me? They did not even get close enough for a fight but died by the suffocating power of their own fears, their bodies turning too bitter to eat. You come here not seeking glory, power, or treasure. I sense the love and courage in your heart. It blinds me. Release me from my prison. I am tired of being unhappy and alone."

"Ferth?" Tobin slid closer but kept his gaze on the dragon.

"He wants me to kill him."

"That's lucky."

Nogard laughed, a grating whine that sent a painful shiver down his nerves.

"You better do it soon before I change my mind and your luck changes. All of you standing in front of my nose like dinner reminds me how hungry I am. And how sweet the smell of honor is." The Dragon inhaled. The air in his nostrils rattled like the wind. *"It's been a long time since I've had wolf."*

"I'll kill him myself," Lyko said.

"Adorable." Nogard closed his eye on Lyko's snarl. *"Aim true. I'll give you one strike."*

Sweat slicked Ferth's palms despite the cold. He side-stepped, moving down its narrow head to its body. Its scales were no longer a glossy black like in the stories. They were stony and matte, flaking and cracked. Ferth scanned the Dragon. Lying down, it rose taller than Ferth. Long wings lay folded in sheets. Where the top of the right-wing joined near the spine was an indent, a change in texture the size of a palm.

"Does it seem too convenient there's a weak spot right above his heart?" Rom asked.

"Everyone has a chink in their armor somewhere," Nogard said.

"Butt out," Lyko snarled.

The Dragon exhaled, and the world turned colder. Bitterness that tasted like regret coated Ferth's tongue. Sadness welled with shocking force through his breast, and he felt the unwelcome desire to worship this beast, give the Dragon his strength and life. Tears filled Ferth's eyes as his ribs squeezed his heart.

The female wolf pup whined.

"Do it, now." Rom's voice quivered.

Ferth's sword seemed to turn to lead as he tried to lift it. His energy bled out through his pores, and his shoulders sagged. His vision blurred to shapeless whites.

Lyko came up behind him and rammed his head against Ferth's back, knocking him out of his stupor.

"You've done harder things." Rom pressed Ferth's hand with his wet nose.

"No, I haven't."

"You conquered him already," Lyko said.

Ferth looked down at his wolves standing at his side, their expectant faces, their hope. He took a deep breath, gathering his strength and determination. Ferth coiled and leapt, kicked off the Dragon's forearm, and landed on Nogard's back. The wings shifted, and the dragon shuddered to life. The four wolves barked as Nogard surged off the ground with a sound of crashing rocks. Ferth swayed and stumbled, gripping a horn on the dragon's spine.

"You took too long," Nogard said. *"And I've always been a coward."* The Dragon roared, but not just in Ferth's head. The penetrating boom blasted the valley. Smoke poured from his snout.

"Do something!" Tobin yelled, clutching his ears and stumbling backwards.

"I'm trying," Ferth muttered. The target on Nogard's back undulated beneath his feet as the beast stretched and stomped.

"We'll distract him," Lyko said.

Ferth's heart throbbed in frantic alarm. *"Get away. Run!"*

Lyko and Rom didn't listen. They rounded on Nogard, one on each side. The spiny face swiveled, tracking its prey. Lyko darted in first, clawing at a crusty nostril.

Nogard laughed until he coughed out embers and smoke. He inhaled. And inhaled. His body rolled back. His wings lifted behind Ferth's calves, preparing to strike.

Ferth was out of time.

He knelt, wedging his knee against a sharp spike to gain a semblance of balance. Gripping his sword in both hands he lifted it high. Not allowing for fear or hesitation, he brought it down, his focus glued to the tiny target. Dracosteel pierced leathery flesh. Nogard shuddered, throwing Ferth. His serpentine neck snapped forward, aiming for the darting wolves. Flames licked the frozen ground. Holding tight to the stuck sword, Ferth's body swung. His side slammed into the beast's back with a painful smack. He didn't let go.

"Ferth!" Tobin's shout was full of fear.

Nogard's forepaws smashed the ground, flinging Ferth against his sword. Ferth grunted as the blade sliced into his coat. He scrambled to his feet, nearly losing his balance, and tumbling to his death. With a wild lunge, Ferth pitched his weight on top of the partially impaled sword. With his body folded over the hilt, the weapon shifted deeper.

Nogard roared with pain, fire shooting out of his snapping maw.

Pulse sky-high, Ferth reared back and pounced again. The handle rammed into his gut as the sword slid into the Dragon all the way to the hilt. No blood came out of the wound. Nogard pitched forward. His long neck slammed into the ground with a plume of ice and dust and sparks.

The Dragon went still.

Ferth knelt on his heels, panting. He hissed at the pain in his belly, his shoulder, his hands. His fingers trembled and his heart thrashed against the cage of his ribs. He pinched his eyes shut, opened them. Nogard remained still. Rom and Lyko appeared next to the beast's side. Dragonfire had singed the fur on Lyko's right, but they were alive. Ferth raked a shaky hand through his hair and exhaled.

"Tobin!" Ferth's voice cracked as he yelled the name. He desperately scanned the valley. Dismay curled through his chest. No, not Tobin. Not another brother lost.

But the young man and his raven stepped out from behind a boulder.

Ferth gasped in relief and jerked forward, leaning on his knuckles.

"I'm here. We're fine." He didn't look fine. He was whiter than Nogard's corpse.

Ferth's shoulders lowered. That was too close. Ferth needed to get Tobin to safety, out of his dangerous company.

Ipsum flapped up, circling the old prince's body, making his inspections.

"*Nice shot,*" Rom said.

"*Good luck getting that back out.*" Lyko eyed Ferth's buried weapon.

Ferth tugged on the hilt, but it didn't budge. Not even a sliver. "I love this sword."

It was intricately carved on the base of the blade and the ivory handle. The Dracosteel gleamed in a hundred rippling layers. A sword worthy of a Draco captain. Or the Dragon Slayer.

"*Nogard's last victory,*" Rom said.

"He's not keeping my sword." Ferth yanked as hard as he could on the hilt, succeeding only in straining his muscles more. He brushed errant hairs out of his face as exhaustion slammed into his shoulders. "But it'll keep until morning."

"Morning?" Tobin's eyes went wide with panic.

"I'm not ready to face that canyon again." Especially not at night. The sky had already shifted to a charcoal gray. "And I'm tired." Ferth slid off the cold body.

"Sleeping next to a dragon, even a supposedly dead one, seems like a bad idea."

"We've had worse ones." Ferth sighed. "But you need not stay." He knew Tobin was anxious to return to hot water and baked goods. "Your hunt is over. I'll help you cut out the eye you promised to take home to your mother. Even she won't be able to deny what you found. You did well. We would never have succeeded without your determination and faith." He sent Tobin a wry smile. "And healing skills. Thank you for tending to me. I wish you a safe journey home." He tried to keep his face placid, hide how much he would miss Tobin. He couldn't ask the human to stay in this dangerous, wild place. Tobin deserved a far better world than Ferth had to offer.

Ferth held out his hand in the human way. "It was a pleasure fighting beside you. And I'm sorry I threatened you. I should not have let the Dragon get to me like that."

Tobin opened his mouth, closed it, opened it, and hurled out the words, "You take that back, Ferth. You can't send me away because I refuse to leave." He folded his arms. "I might not have fancy blood, but I have every right to be here."

Ferth held up his hands as he reeled back. He blinked, brows tight.

"I'm not as strong and skilled as you, but I've earned my place here." The boy's nostrils quivered like butterfly wings.

"Tobin." Ferth's voice was soft. His chest swelled with hope.

The human whirled away, but not fast enough to hide the red creeping into his eyes.

Ferth reached out and put a hand on his shoulder. Tobin turned. Curling his chin down, he buried his face in Ferth's chest. Ferth wrapped his arms around the sobbing body.

Tobin's hands clung to his back. "You almost died."

"It wasn't *that* close." A smile tugged at Ferth's lips.

"Yes, it was. And it was worse at the lake. And don't forget Gristlecove and the infection."

"It's been a treacherous couple of weeks. But I'm still here, and some things are better forgotten."

"I can't forget." Tobin pulled back, his eyes swollen. "You're my family now." Rom came up next to him, and Tobin set his hand on his head. "I hate my mother's cold halls." He looked at Ferth. "Please don't make me go."

"I didn't want you to feel you had to stay. You deserve better than the dangers I manage to find at every turn. You just listed all the reasons you should go back Mitera, to safety. But do I *want* you to leave?" Ferth grinned, huge and full of joy. "No. You're the only brother I have left."

FORTY-SIX - UNCHAINED

JADE

Jade woke with a start. Something was different this morning. Maybe it was her dread over seeing another innocent human hang from the roof. Today would mark number three.

Confused, she rubbed at her chest. The call of the north was gone. Vanished. Her heart felt light and free. Unchained. She sat up in bed. The warm eastern sun caressed her face.

What had Ferth done? Was Tobin all right? Every time she looked through the window and saw the gates, she found herself searching for them, wanting them to return. She padded to the window, but she didn't see her friends at the gates. Emil and his horde of rebels gathered there.

Jade jerked on her clothes and weapons and rush from her room. Down the hall, a Draco underling held the door open for a human.

The slave stopped and thanked the underling.

"You're welcome." She smiled, then her grin blurred. The underling bent over, clutching her knees as brown mist rose from her skin and then coalesced into a bird with long tail feathers and an orange belly. The bird chirped, soared through the door, and disappeared into the rafters of the main hall.

Her hewan, as Ferth called them.

Jade wondered what had caused this girl to conquer her blood. That act of kindness and respect had been so simple and small. Jade had freed all the slaves, continued to fight for them, and yet she remained morphed and ugly. She pushed away her jealousy, horrified to realize she now wished she'd chosen differently before it was too late and she'd become this monster.

The boy stared at the girl, his eyes big. "Congratulations." He beamed. "Beautiful bird. Was that a flycatcher?"

The underling looked to the queen, her face drawn with fear and ashen with shock.

Jade wasn't going to hunt the hewan or punish this girl. She took the whole thing as a good omen. She opened her mouth to start proclaiming promises of a bright future, but Kenji rounded the corner.

"The rebels are gathering at the gates for a hunt." He jogged toward her.

"You're sure it's to hunt and not attack?"

"They're out of food."

Jade knew. They'd been watching the rebels as closely as possible these last weeks. She started toward the great hall, then turned and grabbed the underling's wrist. The girl jolted. Jade let go and tried a smile. Her gaze dropped to Jade's sharp canines. Jade closed her lips and swallowed her frustrations. She'd missed the lessons on charm and gentleness.

"You did well conquering your dragon."

The underling's eyes bugged.

"We'll honor you and your hewan properly when we have the chance. Well done."

"Thank you, my queen." The girl lowered herself in the deepest bow Jade had yet received.

Beto appeared down the hall, and Jade motioned him to join her.

"My queen." He dipped his horns to her.

"The rebels?"

The tiny skull he wore on a chain jostled against his exposed sternum. "The time to strike will be as soon as they've left for the hunt. We can take over the entire keep."

She nodded, thoughts churning. She and Beto stepped into the main citadel and faced the gathering group of Dracos, underlings, and humans. Her people.

"Do you feel it?" She pointed above her heart. "Can you sense the northern call anymore?"

Brows furrowed and paws rubbed chests. Dracos began to shake their heads.

She smiled because she felt like smiling, probably the best omen yet. She silently thanked Ferth. "The chain is broken. The tether gone. We are free."

Confused faces all around.

Her grin grew. "Now is the time to strike."

Hands went to hilts.

"But not to fight. This morning, we make a bid for peace. Unity is worth great risk to attain." Those words weren't met with a surge of enthusiasm so, she tried again. "Today we end the rebellion."

A cheer rose.

There we go. "Follow me." She hoped they would obey that command forever. After instructions, she moved through the entry, opened the heavy front doors, and strode out into the courtyard.

The Dracos marching under the copper dragon turned and faced their queen. She left her weapons sheathed. At her sides, Marko and Beto scanned for archers. She spared a glance for the rotting humans she hadn't been able to save. But no more. She would turn their sacrifice into success.

"Sisters and brothers." Jade's voice rang out over the cold morning. "I have an invitation for you all. Come. Join us and feast." The faint smell of hot bread wafted from the open doors, underscoring her offer. Prey would be scarce this time of year and this close to the stronghold. The hunt would be hard. "Let's put aside this quarrel and join together as the great family we are."

"No." Emil elbowed his way to the front of his pack. "We will not bow to a queen who licks the boots of humans."

She did her best to look down her nose at him from her station across the yard. It helped that on the steps, she stood higher than he. "I do not lick any boots. Why would I when I have roasted venison and creamy greens to enjoy this morning and strong mead to wash it down with?"

Murmurs started up among Emil's followers. He frowned as he looked over his shoulder.

Jade plastered on a massive smile. If they attacked, she would be forced to retreat behind stone walls. She would not win against the strength of his warriors. "Come, join me."

An unfamiliar Draco spoke, "What will your punishment be?"

Jade was glad the female Draco had asked.

"You must accept my authority and rule as queen. You will no longer fight against me, but for me." She spread her arms. "For all of us. We are a family. Including these humans, who were born and raised here, same as we were."

The Draco sheathed the dagger she held. "I accept." She marched toward Jade.

Emil stepped in front of her. "You will not."

She looked over at him in distain. "I'd rather fight you than her. You've treated us worse than Mavras." She spat at the ox's face and continued toward Jade.

The Draco knelt on the stairs and bowed her scaly head, baring her neck to the queen. "You have my loyalty, Your Majesty."

With a lump in her throat, Jade nodded. "I will strive to deserve it." She moved aside and motioned the Draco inside. "You know where the feast is served."

A reptilian grin spread over the woman's face as she sauntered inside.

A slew of rebels followed. Enough that Jade began to breathe easier. She would win now in a head-to-head fight. Assuming the new recruits would stay true. She felt they would. She felt it in the place in her heart that was no longer shackled to the Dragon. The rising sun blazed with the promise of not merely a new day, but a new era.

Emil watched with rising anger as Jade sweet-talked his army away from him. The doors of the slave house opened, and the Dracos who had been left behind as guards strode out, along with the humans. They too, joined the cause of food and freedom.

Unable to surrender his pride, Emil cursed Jade soundly before taking his few remaining followers and stormed out of the Shi Castle stronghold and into the unforgiving winter.

She sent him a friendly wave goodbye, hoping to never see him again but knowing she wouldn't be that lucky. She could not relax yet. She posted guards at the gates and ordered the murdered slaves taken down and treated to a proper burning. She took down the Draco corpse too. Time to clean this place up.

The future was bright, and optimism clutched her with an unfamiliar hope. She still had mountains to climb, but for the first time, her dream of a healthy, happy Skotar felt attainable.

FORTY-SEVEN - SHI CASTLE

SUZA

At dusk, they camped three miles southwest of Shi Castle, outside the range of the stronghold's dormant farmland. Avoiding more run-ins with Dracos had caused them to travel slower and take a more round about approach. They were a day later than she'd planned, but they were finally here. It seemed too soon.

"*It's time to find Ferth,*" Suza said to Xandra.

"*I don't want to leave you alone.*" The previous Draco attack had shaken Xandra.

"*That's a first,*" Suza said.

"*Har har.*"

"*And I'm not alone. Go find him.*"

The hawk brushed a soft wing across Suza's cheek. The gesture felt awfully final, and the pit of foreboding in Suza's belly deepened as Xandra flew to the east and disappeared. If Xandra didn't find Ferth, would Suza be forced to turn around after coming so far? Three humans approaching Shi Castle on their own, like tributes, was asking for slavery. And the whip. But how could she return to Elysium so completely unsatisfied?

An arm's length away, Imanna sat down on a fallen log and rubbed at Kira's ears.

Uriah set up a canvas tent, then settled next to Imanna, pulling her close under his arm. "It's colder than I remember."

"Fewer inns than I'd hoped," Imanna said with a teasing tone. They'd had to avoid all settlements and Draco waystations. Imanna sighed and looked up at the tall thin trees. "But more beautiful than I expected. There's something about the wildness, the complexity of nature here that strikes somewhere deep inside." Her purple eyes glowed in the dusky hues of sunset. "I feel so alive here."

"That's the element of danger talking," Suza said, her voice light, though Imanna's words resonated. She felt the same way about this untamed place.

"It helps we've avoided—mostly avoided—all Dracos," Uriah said. "And stayed away from the strongholds."

"Would it be so bad?" Imanna asked. "We could present ourselves as emissaries from Elysium."

Suza couldn't help the snort that honked out of her nose.

Imanna's delicate face crumpled. "I know I'm ignorant and my hopes make me sound like a fool."

Uriah glared at Suza.

"It's a nice dream, Imanna." She forced her voice into seriousness. "And I would never fault you for your idealism, but a Skotar where human and Draco Sang live together in any sort of equality is never going to happen."

"Not with that attitude," Imanna muttered under her breath as she turned away.

Suza bristled. Imanna was a spoiled princess from Mitera. She had no idea what Draco brutality was. She had no idea the powerful legacy of violence her Regium blood carried.

Imanna dug around a bramble of vines with gloved fingers, clearing away leaves and snow. Suza couldn't see what she'd found until Imanna held up a single plumloch flower. Golden veins ran through the lengths of the dark, purple petals. They were wilted at the edges from frost, but the flower hadn't succumbed to the winter yet. The velvety blossom transported her back to Ferth's war tent. She'd found one near the outskirts of camp. The striking beauty amid such ugliness had lifted her spirits. More inexplicable, it had reminded her of Ferth, her Draco Sang master. If only she could find him here too, a treasure hidden among the rocks and ice.

"Nothing as majestic as this has ever graced the green castle," Imanna said. "What is it?"

Uriah face squinted up in thought. Finally, he shrugged. "I can't remember."

"A plumloch," Suza said. "The last to bloom in late fall and the most glorious."

Imanna put her nose near the glittering pollen. Her nostrils flared as she leaned back at the sour smell.

"And not loved for its fragrance," Suza added, biting her lip.

Imanna coughed and handed the flower to Uriah. "Like you in the morning. Late to rise, handsome as heartache, but don't get too close before a bath."

Suza laughed, the tension in her chest easing a bit.

"I'm here," Xandra said. *"Going over the wall."*

And just like that, Suza's shoulders cinched back into a knot. *"Stay away from the archery range... and the guards with bows... and everything else."*

Xandra didn't respond. She'd stayed hidden for three years while Suza was a slave at Shi Castle.

Suza leaned back against the bare tree trunk and closed her eyes. After much practice and intense concentration, Suza could see through Xandra's eyes. She wasn't good enough at it to pay attention to the world around her at the same time, but she trusted Uriah and Imanna to protect her, and she needed to see Shi Castle. She *needed* to see Ferth.

Xandra perched on top of the great copper dragon that stood as sentinel above the gates. At first, Suza couldn't place what was different. The courtyard was mostly empty. It was dinner time. A tall Draco with the neck of a giraffe and gangly arms was going around lighting the courtyard torches as the day bled into night. A Draco Sang doing the tedious job of a slave? Dread pooled in Suza's belly.

"Where are the slaves?" she asked, willing Xandra to see more. Had they all been killed after rebelling at the Rugit River?

Xandra tipped off the green-tinged statue. Cold wind tickled her wings as she soared down. Light shone from the windows of the slaves' barracks, but slaves weren't given torches at night. Single candles didn't glow like that.

So, the Dracos had move in and taken over the humans' home. This was worse than she'd thought. All those people— her friends. Murdered.

She tried to tell herself it was better in the long run. No slaves in Skotar anymore. The Dracos could shovel their own filth. She ignored the nagging thought that the Dracos would find more slaves soon enough. Steal them from across the now permeable border.

"I don't smell Ferth," Xandra said. *"And his wolves make plenty of stink."*

Despair welled up like a threatening wave, and Suza made to pull away from Xandra to spare her hewan from sharing her grief, but before she could retreat to her cave of misery, Xandra's sharp gaze focused on two familiar figures coming down the path from the citadel.

Suza stopped breathing. Kenji and Pearl were holding hands. Holding hands. In public. *"Is that a sword on his hip?"* She couldn't believe it. She reached for them. And fell forward, blinking. Uriah and Imanna came into focus, faced worried.

Uriah lifted Suza from the snow. "What is it? What's happened?"

Suza shooed him away as she found her seat again. "Shh. Give me a minute." She pinched her eyes shut, focusing on the connection. Kenji and Pearl were still there. Not just alive, but full of energy and color.

Kenji leaned down and kissed Pearl. A Draco walked by and scowled but did nothing. Nothing.

"What's happening?" Suza's voice quivered with confusion and the yearnings of hope.

Xandra's voice was as soft as her feathers. *"The slaves are free."*

FORTY-EIGHT - RISK

SUZA

*S*hi Castle came into view at the top of the hill. Nerves skittering and heart roaring, Suza walked so close to Uriah she kept bumping his elbow. At least he didn't mention it. She followed his lead, matching her pace with his confident strides, lifting her chin. On the outside, she was the picture of poise, but inside, fear was a living monster, prowling and snarling. She was marching them to their deaths.

"I think you need to stay here. I'll check it out and come back," she said.

Uriah put a steady hand on her shoulder. "Xandra is already scouting. And we've already had this conversation. And we already decided not to have you go alone."

She swallowed but didn't argue. She plodded forward, straining to hear the whistle of arrows. The copper dragon loomed in menacing warning. It was bigger than she remembered. The gate was open, no surprise at midday. A skunk Draco stood guard. He glared but made no move to stop them. Why would a cat block a mouse from entering its den?

Heart racing, Suza stepped across the threshold and

under the dragon's wing. She almost turned back at the sight of the towering white citadel. Uriah's hand had moved to his sword hilt. A moth Draco crossing the courtyard saw them but kept walking.

"The humans really are free," Uriah whispered, relaxing his stance.

"But how?" Suza asked. Mavras would die before she'd let that happen. Maybe she had. Where was Laconius? *If it looks like a trap and smells like a trap....*

"Hello." Suza flinched as Imanna's sweet voice carried across the cold air. The rightful ruler of this place waved to a middle-aged human who'd just walked out of the nearest building. "Can you help us?" She smiled at him.

He scowled but nodded and came over. His coat was of a finer make than Suza had ever seen on a slave before.

"We are emissaries from Elysium here to meet with the queen," Imanna said.

The man's brows rose. "Well, she does work fast, doesn't she? I think you'll find her at the training yard."

"Something is seriously up," Suza whispered to Uriah as Imanna thanked the man.

"Let's go find out what," Uriah said.

Suza couldn't see how this might end well, and yet she refused to turn back, not without answers. "I really hope I don't regret this."

Uriah let out a dark chuckle. "You and me both."

"It looks like the training fields are this way," Imanna said, indicating the direction Kira's nose was pointing.

Suza knew this place like the back of her hand. She could find the nooks and hiding places with her eyes closed, but she nodded mutely and let Imanna lead the way.

"Already making yourself at home." Uriah gave his wife an adoring smile.

"I think I like it here." Imanna turned on a narrow heel and strode forward like she owned the place.

"Is she serious?" Suza whispered. "Or is this how she deals with fear?"

"Let's hope it's the nerves talking," Uriah said, his brows knit. "If she starts taking a shine to having a queendom, we've got real problems."

"I think we already have problems." Suza pointed a sword at where Imanna had come face-to-face with a towering crocodile Draco.

Uriah cursed and darted to his wife, Suza close on his heels.

"Nice scales," Imanna said, only the slightest quiver to her voice. She pointed a finger at the Draco's muscled arms. "So shiny."

"And they're very smooth." He licked his lips. "I'll show you the rest if you want."

"No, thank you," Imanna said politely at the same time Uriah roared, "She doesn't!"

The Draco held up his hands in surrender. "Alright, no need to call in the tiger." He turned and walked away muttering, "Everyone is so touchy these days."

"Really, dear," Imanna said. "That was an overreaction."

Uriah glared at her. "Nice scales? So shiny?"

She turned her eyes into pools of innocence. "Is it my fault you haven't taught me proper Draco manners?"

"There is no such thing."

"So, I should have punched him in the brand like I've seen them do?"

Uriah exhaled in exasperation. "No touching Dracos."

"This way," Suza said, walking past them and cutting between two low buildings. The clash of metal rattled her nerves as the training yard came into view. She stopped in her tracks. Humans. There were humans training alongside the Draco Sang. "Kenji!" His name flew from her mouth like a song.

He turned from his opponent, earning a smack on his shoulder. He flinched, but his gaze didn't leave Suza's face. Recognition hit and with it a smile bloomed. She ran, heedless of all but the fierce joy propelling her forward. Kenji dropped his practice weapon and jogged to meet her. He held out his arms, and she flung herself into them. He lifted her up, her face smashed against his sweaty cheek, his ruined ear so close it was blurry. He set her down, but she kept her palms wrapped around his meaty forearms.

"You're alive." Bliss distorted her words.

He laughed and then flexed. "More than that."

"I'll say. But how?" She looked over the mix of underlings, Dracos, and humans. "What has happened here?"

Kenji turned Suza to face the familiar figure who'd approached. "She happened."

"Jade."

The petite jackal grinned like a self-satisfied fiend. "I prefer Your Majesty."

Before Suza could form words out of the tangle of stunned thoughts, Imanna's gasp cut across the space. Suza shifted to welcome Uriah and Imanna and introduce them, but Imanna had already stepped up. She only had eyes for Jade. Imanna was staring, her brows tight and her jaw loose.

Jade's smile seemed nearly too big for her delicate face. "Hello, sister. Welcome home."

FORTY-NINE - SISTERS

JADE

Her sister had come. Here. To Shi Castle. Jade was smiling on the outside, but inside, she was a whirlwind. Why was Imanna here? To claim her throne? A Draco abomination too weak for her beast could never rule the Draco Sang. Jade cringed at herself. She needed to stop thinking like that. The Dracos who had conquered their blood were not weak.

With sudden clarity, Jade realized she did not want to give up the crown she had suffered and killed for. She'd given her soul for this power. She had plans for this country. What did Imanna want with it?

Jade recognized the man from the healers' tent in Elysium. Uriah looked much more formidable on his feet. He took a protective step in front of Imanna as she whispered, "Sister."

"You are Sacora Imanna Regium, are you not?" Jade asked.

Imanna looked around, fear swelling on her face.

"You are safe here," Jade said. "Or as safe as I can keep you."

Imanna swallowed, but when she spoke again, her voice had gained strength. "Who are you?"

"I am the daughter of King Icor and the human, Keturah. I was born a year before the murders, but our father had the foresight to keep me hidden. I grew up in the caves just north, tended by a trusted slave. I joined the underlings under the pretense that I was a tribute from the lawless ones. I killed Mavras when we returned from the war. Laconius named himself king, but his reign was *short*."

Imanna stared. "I have a sister." Some of the worry in Jade's breast leaked away at the tenderness in Imanna's voice.

"As do I."

Imanna reached for Jade, but Uriah blocked her arm. "What did I say about touching Dracos?"

"You're a Draco. You like it plenty when I touch you."

Jade chuckled, liking her new sister very much.

He scowled.

Jade turned to Ferth's runaway slave. "I didn't expect to see you back here, Shale."

"It's Suza. And I didn't expect to be seen, but with humans walking free..." She looked around, her eyes still registering disbelief. "I thought I'd risk a meeting."

"What can I do for you?" She glanced at Imanna. "Here for the crown?"

"I'm looking for Ferth," Shale—Suza blurted. "Have you seen him?"

Jade studied the woman, seeing her as if through Ferth's eyes. Luscious brown hair curled around a stunning face. Vibrant eyes were like the forest in summer. She stood with her spine straight and her head held high. Brave enough to walk into Shi Castle without claws. Jade pushed away the burn of jealousy. This was the woman Ferth loved. Jade had the sudden urge to kill her. She inhaled deeply. She'd solved so many of her problems that way. Old habits were hard to kill, harder than people. "He's not here." Her tone came out colder than she intended.

Suza's eyes dimmed.

"Well, thanks anyway," Uriah said. "We'll be going."

"How you talk, Uriah." Imanna brushed his hand off her arm. "Surely the queen can spare a nice meal for her travel-weary older sister?"

The way Imanna said "older" had the hairs on Jade's arms rising. "Of course. Tonight, we will celebrate your safe return."

FIFTY - STAY CLOSE

SUZA

*S*uza was tense from her scalp to her toes. Any minute she would wake from this dream to feel the crack of the whip on her back. This couldn't be real. No human slaves? Jade was queen and yet she hadn't killed Imanna. Pearl and Kenji were alive and *happy*. She and Uriah were guests at a feast at Shi Castle, not servers or entertainment.

"Stay close to me," Suza whispered to Uriah and Imanna as they climbed the white stone steps to the citadel. "This is weird."

"A good weird," Imanna said, smiling at everything she saw.

"An unbelievable weird." Suza maintained her threatening scowl. Imanna didn't have a clue.

Uriah held open the massive double doors, and Suza and Imanna stepped into an enormous room full of Draco Sang. Imanna stopped. She grabbed Suza's arm and slid flush against her side as she gawked. Her gaze snapped from the violent murals on the walls to the rowdy creatures on the benches. Drums pounded, dishes clattered, and Dracos howled. The smell of sweaty fur and roasted fat tainted the air.

"We are not in Elysium anymore," Imanna whispered.

Despite the tang of fear and the oppressive memories, this felt more like home to Suza than Mitera ever could.

"Suza!"

Her neck snapped in the direction of the deep, gravelly voice, still familiar after four years. She coughed out a surprised laugh as Marko, her best friend from Gristlecove, came barreling towards her from the head table. Only now he wasn't an underling with bad skin and the propensity to talk about his feelings in the middle of the night. Now he was a tiger Draco Sang. And he was coming at her fast. He flung his arms out in welcome. She only hesitated a moment as she took in the size of his muscles and the fierce cut of his eyes before she closed the gap, leaping into his arms and surrendering to his embrace.

"Suza, my beauty." The contrast of his raspy voice and the tender words sent a laugh bubbling through her. "I'm so happy to see you alive and..." He squeezed her waist. "Strong."

He set her down, his striped face turning grave. "You never sent word. I feared the worst."

"I'm sorry. I..." She'd been afraid and ashamed of her slave status. She hadn't wanted to trouble him.

He leaned forward and kissed her cheek with thick lips. The fur on his chin tickled. "I'm sorry I didn't come after you."

A lump clogged Suza's throat at Marko's friendship and affection after all these years.

"Introduce us to your friend," Imanna said. She dragged Uriah at her side like a shield as she stepped up to the frightening Draco.

"Marko, this is my brother—"

"Uriah!" Marko beamed. "Well, if Gristlecove weren't already dead, this sight would surely kill him on the spot."

Suza and Uriah turned to stone.

Marko looked from one face to the other. "Oh, you hadn't heard? A fallen abomination, er, I mean, a Draco Sang separated from his beast, like ah, you. What am I supposed to call you? Anyway. His name is Ferth."

"Ferth." Suza's voice came out squeakier than a rusty nail on tin.

"Yeah." Marko cocked his furry head. "You know him? Well, he killed your father and freed all the slaves. Helped most of them go to Elysium, but my Allie and I couldn't really go south." He pointed to a woman sitting at the high table. He waved, and she smiled at him.

Suza couldn't move a muscle or breathe.

"What with me being a Draco, of course. So, we followed Ferth here. He needed fixing up on account of Gristlecove cutting him with his nasty blade—you know how he liked to keep that thing dirty."

"He beat me to it," Uriah said, his voice awed. "Just like he said he would."

Suza's insides had turned soft, and her knees wobbled. Ferth loved her. She smiled as she held the pleasure of that knowledge to her heart.

He loves me.

"Then Jade killed Mavras. Then Ferth killed Laconius."

Suza's chin dropped to her neck. "He what?"

Marko didn't seem to hear her. "So, Jade made herself queen, and set all the slaves in Skotar free." He exhaled as if the story had exhausted him. "Allie and I decided to stay." He flexed furry biceps. "The queen needs my muscles." He looked expectantly at the stunned faces as he continued the show of shifting bulk. His gaze drooped when he didn't seem to get the excited reactions he was hoping for.

Suza couldn't speak over the frenzy of thoughts. Her Ferth had been through battle after battle. And she hadn't been there. He'd gone to Gristlecove for her. He'd been wounded again. For her. It should have been her. Was he okay? Where was he now?

"You're impressively built," Imanna finally said.

Marko turned to her, his face brightening.

"And it seems a lot has happened," she added.

"Not the least of which is you're the lost princess."

"Shh," Imanna said. "Let's keep that quiet for now."

"Yup—everyone already knows. However, I am quite good at keeping secrets." Marko winked at Suza. "Aren't I?"

Suza felt that he wanted an answer, so she nodded dumbly, her mind still spiraling around the news of her beloved. Her heart called for him, but she got no answer.

"What secrets do you have on my sister?" Uriah asked, a friendly grin breaking through his shock.

The tiger smirked, and Suza knew she was in trouble.

"No time for that now." She waved a dismissive hand.

"Later," Uriah said.

Suza could only hope for a later where she would have all her people together to share stories and to make new ones.

Marko looked up at the high ceiling. "Is she here?"

Suza squinted in confusion. Understanding came late. "Oh, no. Xandra is currently hiding on the copper dragon. She's doesn't like confined spaces, and she doesn't feel safe here, despite what you may say."

He leaned forward and lowered his voice. "Smart girl. And a beauty. When can I see her again?"

"Again?" Uriah's brows rose.

"Marko saved us," Suza said. "He found me in my room the night that Xandra was born. She was flopping around squawking and clawing at the walls. I was scared and irrational. Wounded from the whipping and grieving for our mother. Marko calmed Xandra and comforted me. He brought us broth and tended my wounds. He snuck Xandra out of the barracks and kept my secret."

"Thank you for being there for her when I could not." Uriah's voice was hoarse. "I owe you a great debt."

"Nah." Marko waved a meaty paw and grinned, canines flashing. Imanna leaned back at the wide display of teeth. "I thought it was an adventure. And Suza is still the bravest woman I've ever met." He turned as a petite figure stalked into the room. "Although that one there is giving you a run for your money. She's got big ideas for this place and the guts to fight for the humans too." Marko landed a heavy hand on Uriah's shoulder, and Suza noticed her brother couldn't help his flinch. "Come, let's eat."

Suza was forever grateful to Uriah for the arm he offered her. Even leaning on him, she stumbled over her emotions as she walked to the queen's table.

After weeks of travel, Suza gorged on the familiar wild meats and allium stews. She chugged foaming mead, clearing her throat and her mind. Pearl and Kenji came over, and it was a sweet reunion. Their optimism and health calmed her anxieties, and a deep comfort settled low in her belly. The only thing missing from this perfect picture was Ferth.

Where was he? He seemed to be traveling the path before her, preparing the way for her, but staying just out of reach. Next to her, Uriah picked up his mug. He scraped at unidentifiable crust near the handle.

"Not quite home?" Suza whispered to him.

He set down the dirty drink without partaking. "I miss Mitera, the smell of flowers along the streets, the shining glass, the silk sheets." He chuckled as he looked sideways at her. "You must think me soft."

Suza pinched his iron bicep. "Like pudding."

He pursed his lips then turned serious, dropping his voice

and leaning closer. "I'm afraid that Imanna will wish to stay." He sighed. "And where she is, I am."

The siblings turned and watched as Imanna threw her head back and laughed riotously, clutching hands with the queen and pounding her other fist on the table like a true Draco Sang.

FIFTY-ONE - WASHED CLEAN

JADE

"*A* long journey calls for a deep soak in the mineral pools," Jade said, standing from the dinner table with a pat on her flat belly. "Follow me."

Marko stood, ushering Uriah, Imanna, and Suza to go before him. The three guests and Imanna's dog, Kira, walked along the starlit path with a hint of reluctance in their step.

The pools came into view like inky mirrors, and Jade sighed in anticipation of her favorite nightly ritual. Draco Sang crowded the largest pools—they'd set aside the two worst springs for the humans now that they'd been forced to share. The queen had her own, the smallest and hottest pool, conveniently off to the side for privacy.

Marko took up his usual position as sentry, not looking very fierce at all sitting on a rock bench with his head tilted back on a boulder and his dreamy gaze on the stars. Jade stripped, leaving her weapons within easy reach, and slipped into the burning bliss. She sighed and waded forward, careful not to let the steaming water touch her tender brand mark. The smell of sulfur mixed with the sage that grew around the edges. When she finally opened her eyes, her three guests were standing on the edge, fully dressed and looking uncomfortable.

"I thought humans were big on cleanliness," Jade said.

"Not so much on nudity," Imanna said.

"Even with it being near black out here?"

"Of course." Imanna shrugged off her coat. "We're being silly."

"Don't soak for too long," Jade said. "You don't want to overheat the baby."

Uriah jerked, stepping it front of Imanna as if warding off a blow. Kira's ears shot up.

"How did you know?" Imanna asked.

Jade shrugged. "You cradle your belly sometimes. It was a guess."

"Turn around, Uriah." Suza was down to her bottom layer at this point.

Dim moonlight glinted off the woman's stripes, scars, and Draco brand. Jade's jaw loosened as she stared.

"Oh yes." Suza sank into the heat. "I've always wanted to come in these. They are as divine as I imagined."

"You're Draco Sang?" Jade asked, still dumbfounded. "Or did they misbrand you as a child?"

Suza hesitated, which was answer enough. Of course she was a Draco. Ferth wouldn't settle for anything less than dragon blood, and the strength to conquer it. The beautiful woman seemed to angle her shoulders so her brother wouldn't see her scarred back. She paddled further in the steaming water.

Uriah waded in. The water came as high as his toned belly. He looked bigger and fiercer without his shapeless coat. Faint silverly light danced on the handsome features of his face and muscles as well as his brand.

"If you're both Draco Sang, what's happened to your abomina—hewan things?" Jade asked.

"Poe died," Uriah said. "Fighting this war."

"I'm sorry." Jade surprised herself by truly meaning it. "So many senseless deaths." She'd stolen more than her share of lives.

Suza didn't answer about her hewan.

Jade could understand Suza not trusting her, but it hurt more than she cared to admit. She wanted to be part of this family. "How is it that each of you didn't end up like me?" She ran a leathered palm over her furry scalp.

The Draco humans looked at each other. Suza spoke first. "Uriah and I are children of Lord Gristlecove. I conquered the dragon when I took my mother's lashing. I came here as a slave after that."

"I escaped to Elysium when I was nine," he said. "Captain Titus found me and taught me that we can control our beast instead of being controlled. So I did."

"Do you regret it?" Jade asked. "Especially now that Poe is gone, and you must live with the loss."

"Never." Uriah's jaw twitched, just a ripple in the wan light. He sank lower in the water. "I am my own master. No selfish dragon deserves to control me."

Jade swallowed the bitter taste of regret that bubbled up her throat. She'd never felt so ugly or ashamed.

Imanna drew circles in the water with delicate fingers. She'd left the headband over her brow. The royal brand over her heart was immaculate. Irrefutable. "My mother managed to smuggle me out before Mavras killed her and our father."

It warmed her to hear Imanna say *our father,* to claim Jade as her sister.

"Mother's faithful guard, Urdig, a goose Draco, flew me over the border into Elysium. The plan was for me to grow up in secret in the wilderness, and then when'd I'd transformed, I'd return to Skotar to reclaim the throne. Titus found us living in the marshes outside of Kiptos. Urdig was no nursemaid, and he couldn't be seen by humans. Titus let Urdig live and return to Skotar, but he kept me. He raised me as his own daughter. He gave me the choice. If I wanted to submit to the Dragon, he would help me return to Skotar, or I could follow his path to inner peace and total freedom."

"You don't make it sound like an abomination at all," Jade said.

The rustle of reeds and the ripple of water were the only reply.

The Draco humans were quiet as they dried and dressed, as if leaving Jade space to sort through her confused emotions. Marko led them to the citadel and showed them to the finest rooms.

Jade bid them a good night.

"One more thing." Imanna's tone was soft, soft as the kiss of a viper.

Adrenaline shot through Jade's veins at the cunning look in her older sister's eyes. She'd known the weather would change. In her experience, days like today didn't keep. Something sour would surface. This was Skotar.

Dread crept down her collar.

Imanna's lavender eyes locked on hers. "In the morning, we will duel for the crown."

FIFTY-TWO - FINISHED

FERTH

Without the nightmares that had plagued him these last weeks, Ferth slept like the dead. He woke to a sky that was more blue than gray. He stretched, bumping Lyko and Amber out of the way as he stood. He left Tobin tucked in the one blanket they had to share. The Dragon's corpse was still there. He sighed, disappointed that it hadn't dissolved during the night. He tromped over and climbed on top, several scales ripping free beneath his boots. He tugged at his sword still stuck in its back, but to no avail. He stomped back down, kicking off more scales.

Tobin had gotten to his feet and stood wrapped in the blanket, eyes bleary and sunken. It was time to get him back to a real bed.

"I really hate to lose that sword," Ferth said.

"Better than your life," Tobin said.

"Yes, but not what I want to hear right now."

"Sorry."

Ferth squinted at the bloodless corpse that had fathered them all. He pulled out his knife. "I know you promised your mother an eye, but can I talk you into a tooth instead?"

"You can."

"I better not lose a good knife too," Ferth muttered as he crouched. But just in case, he left Cal's blade safely at his hip and grabbed a throwing knife. He pulled at the dragon's head to shift it but it didn't move. The lips seemed welded together as he cut at them, marveling at the stony texture, and the lack of blood. He sliced away a chunk of mouth and cheek to reveal a section of grizzly teeth.

"This is gross," Tobin said. "I don't think I want it anymore."

"Get me a rock," Ferth said. "I'm going to need to do this hammer and chisel style."

Tobin made a gagging sound, but within seconds a rock appeared in Ferth's hand. He set the tip of his blade at the base of an impressively white, triangular tooth. Slamming the rock into the hilt, he chipped the tooth free. When it came loose, he carefully worked it out of the jaw. He wiped unruly hair and bone dust off his forehead as he stood and turned to Tobin. He set the palm-sized tooth in Tobin's hand.

"There you go."

"Thank you."

They stood in silence for a moment. "Well, that's about it. Shall we go?"

"I thought you'd never ask."

It felt wrong to walk away without so much as a tribute. Nearly petrified dragons probably didn't burn, but Ferth could at least show the Ancient One the respect of trying. He rummaged through his pack for flint and a stick, then approached the massive face once more.

He had no idea what to say. "We honor you for your strength and endurance. For surviving all these years. That was very impressive." Tobin, Ipsum, and the four wolves gathered around him. "Thank you for providing the opposition that makes us powerful."

"That feels like a stretch," Lyko said.

"You can thank him for getting to have me as a hewan," Rom said.

"I just did," Ferth said.

Rom huffed.

"Wrap it up," Lyko said.

"May you find mercy with the Mother," Ferth said.

"Very nice." Tobin gave a nod.

Ferth set the twig on fire and held it to the dragon's cracked lips.

"You can't seriously think that's going to work," Lyko said.

"Do you see any kindling? Or trees at all?"

Lyko didn't have a chance to answer before the dragon's head alighted in a whoosh of flame.

"Whoa," Tobin said, jumping back, his jaw hanging.

Blue flames spread along the neck, engulfing the body in seconds.

Tobin spread out his arms. "Ahh. I'm finally warm again."

It was when the heat from the massive fire melted the ice off a nearby Draco corpse that Ferth had the idea to clean up the place. The wolves helped him find them all, and one by one he threw his fallen predecessors into the pyre. Embers floated and twirled in a wild dance. The sun came out from behind the clouds as if called forth by the golden tribute.

The Dragon and Dracos burned down to nothing but a trail of rapidly cooling ash and assorted weaponry. Ferth's blackened sword lay in the center of a wide path. Ferth stood where Nogard's head had been and gawked at the new world that opened before his feet.

Awed speechless, he and his companions padded forward, sliding over smooth marble cobblestones, their vision fixed on a white castle built on a raised plateau in the center of a wide valley. Pines and aspens covered the ground, and a waterfall crashed from the high northern cliffs into a lake before unravelling down the valley like a ribbon of cobalt silk. The castle was crafted from the same white marble as the road they walked on. It glittered in the sunlight like a multi-faceted diamond.

"What is this place?" Tobin asked.

"It's Nogard's home," Ferth guessed. "He built his kingdom for one." A pity. What a sad way to spend a life. With a sudden strike of insight, he realized he wanted to stop running, stop hiding. He didn't want to follow Nogard along this path of loneliness and pride.

"It's beautiful," Tobin said.

It was so magnificent it nearly stopped Ferth's heart. It tempted him like the pull of a seductive dream, but instead of running forward, exploring the fantasy like a nursery child, he turned his back. He would find Suza first, and if she were willing, he would bring her here. They would walk through those magnificent doors together. Or not at all.

FIFTY-THREE - UNCHAINED

JADE

"Good morning, Majesty." Marko said as he stepped into Jade's bed chamber. "Breakfast first or sister slaying?"

Jade scowled.

"Not funny?"

She swung to a sitting. "The crown is rightfully hers."

"But she is not the right one to wear it." Marko's rough voice gave his words power.

"Thank you for the vote of confidence." He believed in her. Many here did. The number of freed slaves who stayed was a testament to that.

Allie walked in, her hair unbrushed, but her eyes bright. "Let's get you into your fighting leathers, shall we?"

"You both are being annoyingly chipper," Jade said.

"It seems better than the alternative," Allie said.

"Which is?"

"Anxious and despondent."

Jade pursed her lips as she turned her back and slid off her night shift. "I don't want to fight her." She put on her tunic and faced her friends. "But I want to rule Skotar." She couldn't walk away now.

"Well, I don't know what to tell you. I'm not good with decisions. Ask Marko."

He nodded dutifully. "Can't even pick her favorite breakfast."

"It's the job of the queen to make hard decisions," Allie said.

"And to choose well," Marko added.

"Alright, I've had enough advice from the both of you this morning." Jade's voice was curt.

When she was fully dressed for battle, she strode out, nearly chewing a hole through the lip she worked between her teeth.

The three Draco humans were already at the training fields when Jade arrived. An impressive crowd had gathered. The rumor that Icor and Sacor's oldest daughter had returned from the grave had permeated the stronghold faster than the north wind. Jade had debated keeping this duel quiet, but if Imanna was to take the crown with any hope for success, it would have to be in a very public display of power. And it wouldn't hurt for the people of Shi Castle to see just how far Jade was willing to go to keep her queendom. Her steps faltered at what she must do.

Jade and Marko strode into the square marked off for the duel.

Imanna handed her coat to Uriah.

"Please don't do this," he begged. "Please."

"I love you." Imanna took his stricken face in her hands and kissed him hard on the mouth. She pulled away and turned her back on his ashen features.

Suza took Uriah's elbow, but he didn't seem to notice her. Kira stood at Suza's elbow, ears pulled back.

Beto, the training master, cleared his throat. "This is

Sacora Imanna Regium, daughter of King Icor and Queen Sacor."

A riot of gasps, squawks, and howls rippled around the spectators. "She's an abomination!" a Draco yelled. "She's not worthy of her blood," another said. "Imposter!"

Imanna pulled her tunic down, revealing her royal brand. Then she ripped off her headscarf, and the crowd went quiet. She pointed to the symbol on her head. "My mother gave me this mark before she saved my life. She sent me away because the true heir was not safe in her own kingdom. She marked me like Attor did his son. She wanted there to be no doubt as to my identity and my rights."

Stunned faces stared, and begrudging respect built among the crowd.

Beto's voice rang across the clearing. "Sacora Imanna challenges Queen Jade, daughter of King Icor and Keturah, to the crown."

Keturah pushed her way to the front near the rope on the ground. Kenji put his arm around her. She worked her chapped hands in front of her stomach as she watched. Jade did not want her here.

"As is tradition, each will choose one weapon. The duel ends with surrender."

The crowd booed.

"Or death."

A cheer.

Beto turned to Jade. "Your Majesty?"

Jade's heart slammed against her chest. She suddenly felt so tired. When would the killing stop? When could she rest and enjoy her victories?

"I'll use a dagger." This was personal. Jade handed Marko her short swords and the handful of knives she kept on her person.

"I'll choose the same as my little sister." Imanna attempted a cocky grin, but it fell flat.

Beto nodded and motioned everyone away from the ropes. He was the last to step out, but not before he said, "May the strongest blood triumph."

The sisters circled. Imanna moved with agile grace, her weapon comfortable in her hand. Many had made the fatal mistake of underestimating Jade. She would not fall into the same trap and misjudge the petite human before her.

"Come on," an impatient Draco yelled from the crowd.

Imanna darted forward. Dracosteel blades clashed. Imanna got a fist in Jade's belly, but Jade ripped hard on Imanna's braid, sending her sprawling on her back. Normally Jade would have jumped to end it with a quick, fatal strike, but for the first time in her life, she hesitated.

Imanna sprang to her feet. She didn't snarl or threaten. She crouched, arms up and eyes focused. This was a woman worth knowing. Jade wanted years together. She wanted to meet the baby growing in Imanna's belly. Jade was not a child killer.

Jade rushed in, feigning right and striking left. Imanna blocked, slipping in a jab that had Jade leaping back. The dance continued, engage, disengage, engage, disengage. The rush of their heavy breath became the music of the dance. Jade slashed at Imanna's side, but Imanna twisted out of the way, snaking her dagger at Jade as she moved. Pain seared across Jade's forearm. She jumped back as she glanced down at the stripe. Red dripped down her fingers. She wiped them on her pants as best she could while blocking Imanna's next round of rapid strikes.

"Tell me, sister," Jade said. "How many men have you killed? How many Draco Sang?"

Imanna's silence was answer enough.

A part of Jade resented her sister her innocence. "And yet

you expect to kill me now? The first one is the hardest." Jade bared her sharp teeth. "I know."

Imanna lifted her chin, her lovely face calm. She slashed again, their clanging blades playing a familiar song. The next attack brought them in close. Jade angled her dagger down towards Imanna's breast. Imanna blocked the blow, but Jade had better leverage and held her ground, stepping closer. Imanna's dog barked but didn't break the line of the rope. Imanna brought her second hand up to their locked blades, trying to hold strong.

Jade pushed down, and her blade sank closer to Imanna's throat. Pale eyes locked on Jade's, searching and steady. Jade's blood flamed, her jackal nature rising in a triumphant wave. Her left hand rose, wrapping around Imanna's throat. Her surroundings turned to haze. The entire world narrowed to this embrace. This shared breath. Jade's blood howled for her to finish the job. Kill. Jade's gaze dropped to Imanna's neck and the image of her blood-stained touch on her sister's white skin.

Finish it. The familiar roar of violence and victory forced her forward another inch. *Take what you've earned.* Her blade touched Imanna's collarbone, splitting skin.

No.

Jade jerked back, throwing Imanna to the ground as she disengaged.

"No!" The word came out as a howl. Jade dropped her knife.

"I surrender. The crown is yours. Hail the new queen of Skotar!" Jade's voice broke as her body trembled.

Her nerves itched. Amber and gray swirled before her face, blinding her. She held her breath as she watched the fur on her hands fade and her claws retreat into human finger-nails. Her strength gave out, and she dropped to her knees. She closed her eyes as the tumult of uncertainty and confusion crashed through her aching head. Her gaze snapped up at the feel of a rough tongue on her face.

A jackal. *Her* jackal.

A glossy panel of black fur ran down the beast's back, and rich amber covered her face and flanks. Violet eyes pierced Jade to the core.

"I liked being queen."

Jade heard the jackal's words in her mind. She stared, her emotions overwhelming.

"She's beautiful, Jade," Imanna said.

"I'll finish this." The jackal lunged.

"No!" Jade sprang to her feet. Kira darted between Imanna and the jackal. Jade landed on the jackal's back, her hands wrapping its bony forearms. They went down together and rolled. The animal thrashed and yipped. Jade clamped her thighs hard on the long torso. *"Stop it! You will not attack Imanna. I surrendered for the both of us."*

"I don't approve."

Jade's voice turned hard. *"Her dog listens to her. Ferth's wolves listen to him. You will listen to me. I will not be made a fool by you."* The jackal stopped fighting, but Jade was afraid to let go. Fake submission and then strike. She might have played the very same trick. Jade's gaze rose to the stunned crowd. She had to save this situation before they turned on her and killed her jackal. The animal went still, as if having the same thoughts as Jade. *"We've got to play this right."*

"What are we going to do?"

Jade let go of muscle and fur. She stood and smoothed out her vest. She scanned the sea of faces. She couldn't look at her mother's beaming face, glittering with tears. She couldn't go to the embrace she wanted most. Not yet. She made her voice commanding. "We have been wrong about our blood. Why are we yielding to the dragon when we should be conquering it?"

"You lost your heritage because you surrendered the crown."

Jade looked at the beetle Draco who had spoken. Iridescent scales covered his bare shoulders and back. Antennas wiggled in the air above his bulging eyes.

"We've been blinded by our lusts. Look at you."

The Draco shrank back, as if suddenly embarrassed, but then he stepped forward with a snarl. "You're a coward and an abomination!"

Jade picked up her dagger from the dirt. "*You* I will not hesitate to kill. Come here."

He didn't move.

"You will see I have not lost my prowess and skills, but I have gained much." Her gaze flickered to the sleek jackal.

When the beetle was smart enough not to come into the fighting square, Jade lowered the blade. She motioned Imanna to come out from under Uriah's arm.

Imanna did, but before Jade could present her as queen, Imanna spoke in a loud voice. "I do not accept the crown. Jade will remain the queen of Skotar."

Jade's head twisted toward her sister.

"Bow to your queen." Imanna led by example.

After a moment's hesitation, the crowd began to bend like spring wheat. Pearl clapped, and Kenji let out a bellowing hoot that filled Jade with warmth.

"Why are you doing this?" Jade whispered.

"I don't want to rule." A smile spread. "Well, maybe a little. But I wanted to prove to you, and too all of Skotar, that you are worthy. Worthy of your hewan and worthy of the crown. I can return to my home satisfied that I have done my duty to my people. I am at peace."

"That's a risky game."

Imanna's smile grew. "I still have the reckless Regium streak."

"Much to my chagrin." Uriah's face was still blanched unnaturally pale as he stepped up to his wife's side. His fingers shook at his sides. Jade wondered at the courage and strength of the man who had held himself back from crossing the line. The mountain of respect and faith he gave to his wife. A man worthy of her sister. Jade looked in his intense brown eyes, and a moment of understanding passed between them. If he had stepped into the ring, Jade would have made the kill. She knew it. He knew it. She nodded at his bravery.

He dipped his chin. "Congratulations." He held out his hand in the human way.

Jade took it, warmth spreading up her arm at the touch that no longer revolted her. "I thought it was too late for me."

Imanna raised her voice so all could hear as she said the words that changed everything. "It's never too late."

A murmur rolled over the Dracos.

"It is within your power to control your blood and conquer your heart. To live up to the great potential within you."

Emotions rose in the crowd, many curious and open to Imanna's words, but more were angry.

"You are all dismissed," Jade said. When no one moved, she looked to Marko and Beto.

They both stepped up, issuing commands that would not be easily disobeyed. Finally, the Dracos scattered. Jade sighed. This morning she had only added to her many tasks.

"What are you going to name her?" Uriah asked.

Jade studied the animal that stood calmly, but inside was a cunning storm. "Jack."

"Jack the jackal," her hewan said. *"Are you serious?"*

Jade grinned. *"I like it."*

Uriah chuckled. "Nice to meet you, Jack."

Jack ignored him.

Keturah stepped into the fighting square, and Jade held out her arms. Her mother pulled her close.

"My girl. My brave, brave girl." Keturah's face pressed into her daughter's hair, now brown curls like Imanna's. "I am so proud of you."

Jade melted against her mother, her whole body filling with exquisite lightness. Tears leaked from her eyes. "This is what you were trying to teach me all my life."

"If I had known all it would have taken was a duel, I would have attacked you long ago."

Jade laughed as she pulled back and took her mother by the hand. Her smile was so big it hurt her cheeks. She'd never hoped to experience this kind of joy in her life. She'd never been worthy of it before. "Come on. All these *feelings* are making me hungry."

FIFTY-FOUR - LOVE

SUZA

Uriah and Imanna didn't leave Shi Castle immediately. Suza was sure they were giving her time to make her decision. And attempting to get her to change her mind. But she wouldn't be returning to Elysium with them. Skotar was Suza's home, and with the slaves free and the queen a Draco human—the queen of Skotar was a Draco human—Suza kept saying it, kept pinching herself, but the dream never dissolved. She knew it was real because Ferth wasn't here.

After four days of the Regium sisters scheming to bring not only peace between their countries, but friendship, Uriah and Imanna packed their bags. It would still be dangerous traveling. The lawless Dracos prowling the forests had increased since Jade had outlawed many of the Dracos' favorite things.

The queen assigned three guards to escort Imanna and Uriah to the border—Kenji, an underling, and a Draco warrior. They all stood together under the copper dragon. It didn't seem so menacing today. Maybe it was the fresh poop Xandra dropped on its head as she perched between its horns, unnoticed by the group below. But as Suza searched the intricate statue, she thought maybe it was something more. A tentative hope had hatched in her breast. The future seemed brighter than ever before, her heart lighter.

"You are always welcome here," Jade said as she embraced her sister. At their feet, Jack and Kira rolled in the frozen snow like litter mates.

"Come to Mitera," Imanna said. "I want this child to know you."

Jade's eyes glistened. "I hope to." She looked over the courtyard, the jumble of low buildings, and the massive citadel. "It might be a while before I can leave here." She sighed. "A long while."

Uriah stepped in front of Suza, blocking her view of the sisters. She looked over his face, trying to memorize the lines, the warm brown eyes—same as their mother's.

"I don't want to leave you here."

"I don't want you to go."

He drew her against his chest, and she let herself be held for a long time. When he finally let her go, she discreetly wiped at her cheeks before facing him again.

"I expect a letter with every exchange," she said.

Jade and Imanna had organized a postal system to exchange letters at the border every month.

He scowled. "Your expectations were always too high for me."

She punched him in the shoulder.

He feigned injury. "Alright, I promise."

"Also, the name Suza is available."

"So is Jade," the queen said, stepping next to them.

"So is Sacora." Imanna came to her husband's side.

His eyes widened like a cornered rabbit as he looked over the three women.

"Problem solved. We'll have a boy." He smiled.

Suza was really going to miss him. Her heart pinched, and she wondered again if she should go with them. They were her family, and Ferth might never come back. He'd made it clear she should stop loving him. She could give Mitera another try.

The gate guard whistled, drawing their attention. "Two travelers coming up the path, and it looks like they're accompanied by a pack of wolves."

Suza's heart nearly shot straight out of her chest.

"*Ferth,*" Xandra said as Suza tore through the gates.

She stopped at the top of the hill, clutching her heaving heart. There he was. How did he have four wolves now? He looked up as if he'd sensed her. It was his little wave, partly nervous, partly eager, partly unsure, that had her sprinting down the path toward him.

Ferth stopped, dropped his pack, and held out his arms. Happiness gave her wings as she leapt into his embrace. He lifted her up, his laughter like the music of dreams. She buried her hands in his hair, now past his ears, dirty and a messy tangle. She tilted his head back, and then they were kissing. Eager lips spoke the truths that words were inadequate to express. His laughter turned to heavy breaths. Fire and want burned through her veins. His hands slid up her back as he set her on her feet, only to draw her waist tight against his. He wrapped a calloused palm around the back of her neck. Sparks danced over her skin at his touch.

"I'm dreaming," he whispered against her mouth.

"Even dreams aren't this good." Pleasure warmed through her.

"You taste so good."

He was heaven on her tongue. She pulled back as she heard footsteps approaching. "And you stink."

His grin melted her to the core.

She pulled her gaze away from his tempting mouth and golden eyes. She chewed on her lip.

Ferth. Her Ferth was here. And with a greeting like that…

The others had joined them at the base of the hill. Jade had a slightly injured look on her face when Suza first turned, but the young queen covered it quickly. Jade turned her attention to the travel-worn young man standing with an arm slung around her shoulders.

"That was going to my opening move," Tobin said to the queen. "But now I don't want to be a copycat." Blue eyes danced.

Jade looked up at him with a sly grin that seemed to promise he'd have plenty of time to make it up to her later. He winked at her.

"You must be Tobin," Suza said.

"And you must be Suzaena. If not, you might want to watch out for a beautiful, fearsome warrior coming after you."

She cast a sidelong look at Ferth. "Is that how you described me?"

Tobin held up a hand. "Don't get him started."

Suza tilted her face to the man at her side. She was going to explode from all this happiness. "You missed me."

Ferth kissed her temple. "I nearly died without you."

"That's true," Tobin said. "Like half a dozen times."

Ferth gave Tobin a look that could only mean *stop talking or else.*

Suza's heart gave a flutter of alarm.

"I've had my share of *hunting* trips with Ferth for a while," Tobin said.

"You could stay here with me," Jade said, her voice quieter than usual. "I'll keep you safe."

Tobin faced Jade. No one spoke as his soft gaze soaked

her up. Finally, he brought a hand up and ran nimble fingers over her lush hair. "Last time I saw you, wasn't this fur?"

"Do you like the new look?"

"Yes." Tobin's voice came out husky and low, and Jade's cheeks pinked. His fingers trace her jaw. "Even more beautiful than before, if that's even possible."

"You don't have the guts to eat raw meat, but you can pull off a move like that," Ferth said, pride in his voice.

Tobin ignored him, his focus wholly on Jade.

Uriah looked up from where he'd been talking to Lyko. He shook Ferth's hand. "Will you come with us to Mitera?"

Ferth looked at the woman pressed to his side. "I'm going wherever Suza's going, if she'll allow me."

Suza's stomach swirled with delight. "I want to stay here. For now."

Uriah sighed in defeat. "Well, at least I feel a lot better about leaving Suza here knowing that you'll watch out for her." His voice went soft as he studied Ferth. "You look so much like Cal."

Ferth dropped his gaze to the ground. "I'm sorry."

"Don't be. It's a compliment."

After a heavy silence. Imanna stepped up.

"You no longer wear the scarf," Ferth said.

"No. It's past time for the truth."

"Meet Sacora Imanna Regium," Jade said, ending her private conversation with Tobin and facing the group. "My older sister."

"You've conquered the dragon." Ferth managed a bewildered smile. "I've missed a lot."

"You've been busy," Jade said.

"How was your hunt?" Imanna asked.

Tobin pulled a linen from his pack, unwrapped it, and revealed a massive tooth. The group stared in silence.

"You found the dragon?" Jade's voice was awed.

"And killed him," Tobin said, puffing out his narrow chest.

Suza rubbed at her sternum. "That's why the pull is gone."

Ferth nodded. "It was Nogard. He was poisoning this place. Tainting the Draco Sang with his every breath."

"I want to hear everything," Suza said. "About Laconius and Gristlecove. You went there for me. You almost died…" She swallowed. All her fear these past weeks raced through her mind. She wrenched out of his touch and punched him hard in the belly. His muscles tensed beneath her knuckles, and he folded over with a grunt.

"What if you had died avenging me? What if you had never come back to me?" Her voice was like thunder. She jabbed his shoulder. "Your letter was garbage. I hated it."

Instead of standing, Ferth dropped to his knees in the frozen dirt. He looked up, his face bright despite the dirt and scruff on his jaw. "I'll never write another goodbye."

"Good."

He was more beautiful than she remembered, with his eyes clear and his wide mouth flushed from the crush of her lips. He was her whole world. She brushed wild hair off his brow and cupped the base of his head.

His hands gripped the back of her thighs, sending fire shooting through her center. "Forgive me?"

"I already have, you dolt. Past crimes only, though. No more running off to foolish heroics."

"I promise." His grin was more glorious than the sunrise. He rose to a stand, his palms sliding up her body as he drew her against his chest. "I love you."

She clung tight to his waist but turned away when he leaned down for a kiss. Not now, not in front of the group. Rom came up and nuzzled her thigh.

"Rom is wondering when you're going to fawn over him."

She bent down and rubbed the narrow skull, careful of the scarred ear. "Hello, beautiful."

He purred.

"I see you found some lady friends in your travels."

Rom growled in Lyko's direction.

Ferth laughed. "That's Amber, Lyko's mate. Aisha is still a pup."

Suza gave Rom a look of chagrin. "I see."

A familiar raven flew down and landed on Tobin's shoulder.

"Now that we're all here," Tobin looked to Jade, "when's the part where you offer us a feast and treat us like heroes? I'm not one for eating Ferth's trail food."

"He's probably on the verge of starvation by now," Ferth said.

"Will you stay for the feast?" Jade asked her sister.

Uriah and Imanna shared a look. Uriah shook his head. "We will leave now. We want to get to the plateau before dark."

Tobin held out the dragon tooth wrapped in cloth. "Give this to my mother, would you? Tell her I'm staying to court the queen of Skotar, so depending on how that goes I won't be back to visit her for a while. Or ever, if I can help it."

Jade chewed her lips and ducked her chin, but she couldn't hide the pleasure brimming in her eyes.

"We'll miss you in Mitera." Imanna kissed Tobin's cheek.

"Feel free to name your son, Tobin."

Uriah rolled his eyes.

Tobin sighed dramatically. "Does no one care that I've only been offered questionable meats for *weeks* now?"

"I can remedy that," Jade said. "And you're going to love the mineral pools."

"Are you suggesting I need a bath?" Tobin put his arm back over her shoulders and leaned in close.

She wrinkled her delicate nose. "It's an order from the queen."

As they turned and headed back toward Shi Castle, Suza heard Tobin say, "Are you planning to get in the habit of ordering me around?"

Suza chuckled as she turned back to face Uriah. She handed him a letter for Mira and Titus. "Tell them about Ferth. They have been worried, and tell them he will write to them." She speared Ferth with a serious glance. He pulled a face but nodded.

After another round of goodbyes, Imanna and Uriah went south with their traveling party and Ferth, Suza, and the wolves padded slowly up the hill.

FIFTY-FIVE - SWEET JOY

FERTH

Suza.

Suza was here at Shi Castle. She'd braved Skotar to find him. She *loved* him. His heart jumped up and down like an overexcited squirrel. After he'd promised to be at lunch in an hour, he'd split off from the group, heading straight for the hot pools. The wolves left to do some exploring on their own. Rom knew Shi Castle as well as Ferth, but the other three had never been through the gates.

Excitement sped Ferth's steps up the path to the mineral pools. He tore off his clothes and jumped in so fast he hissed at the burn. Out of habit, he looked around for a slave to bring him a scrubber, belatedly correcting himself. Jade had really done it. She'd freed them all. A boy with a shaved head approached and held out a hard-bristled brush.

"I'll leave you a towel here." He set it on a rock bench.

"Thanks," Ferth said. "Aren't you an underling?"

"I work here in the mornings. I'm saving up for a Dracosteel hammer and chisel."

"For what?"

"Sculpture. Since Queen Jade cut back the battle training

requirements for underlings, I have more time to work on my craft."

Ferth's jaw had gone slack. "What kind of pieces?"

He looked down. "I'm not sure."

Or more likely he didn't want to tell.

"I look forward to seeing what you create." Ferth slipped under the water, tensing against the heat as he scrubbed at his hair. Emerging, he handed back the brush. "Would you please bring a razor and mirror?"

After shaving, Ferth climbed out. As he walked back to his barrack, he saw changes everywhere. Little things that together gave the entire stronghold a vibrant lightness. Clean windows in the slave quarters. Humans walking with their backs straight. A Draco repairing part of a stone wall.

He walked into a low building and padded down the hall. His room was as he'd left it. The single bed was neatly made. The razor and brush hadn't been moved from the table. But when he opened the trunk and put on a pair of pants and tunic, he felt like a thief, taking what belonged to another life.

"It's weird, isn't it?"

He whirled at the voice. Jade leaned against the doorframe with her characteristic sly grin. She looked older around the eyes, and her shoulders drooped under an invisible weight. He wondered how he looked to her. They'd both been through the inferno. They'd come out of it, but not without burns. He scanned his room. "It feels like I've been gone a long time. I'm not the Ferth that left here."

"Battle changed me too." Her spine compressed further as she looked down at her hands, as if she could still see the blood there.

"No. You're the same. You're just not hiding anymore. Now everyone knows you are kind-hearted and brave."

Her eyes went watery. "Thank you."

"I'm proud of you, Jade." His voice was deep with genuine truth. "You make a great queen. The leader Skotar needs."

She looked like she wanted to speak, but her lips wobbled. She inhaled and pinched her eyes. When she opened them, they were clear and cunning again. "The thing I hate most about being human is the emotions. It was so much easier not feeling all the things."

Ferth chuckled as he walked forward. "Come on, little softy."

She punched him, getting a sharp knuckle in his ribs.

He grunted out a complaint before striding through the door. "There's got to be a jackal roaming around eager to meet me."

They walked out of the barracks and stopped in the courtyard. Four wolves circled an angry jackal. She had her fur and ears up, her lips peeled back. Every time she darted for an opening, the wolves would block her exit with a snap of jaws or flash of claws.

"Looks like we found her," Ferth said.

"Looks like your wolves are big bullies."

"We were just walking through, minding our own business. She came out in attack mode," Rom said. *"She kicked Aisha."*

Rom was very protective of the little pup.

"Such terrible manners," Lyko said.

"Call off your brutes," Jade said. "Tell them to stop harassing Jack."

"Jack?"

"It suits her," Jade said, tone defensive.

"I've no doubt." Ferth grinned.

Jade scowled at him and stormed up to the hewans. She marched through the circling wolves and stood at Jack's side. "We have rules here," she said to the wolves.

Lyko let out a deep, grating laugh.

Jade's jaw rippled, but before she could keep lecturing, a tiger Draco strode toward them from the citadel.

"Marko!" Ferth smiled as he made a circle with his fist and punched Marko in his brand in greeting. Marko did the same. It hurt.

"Welcome back, brother. Tobin told me some of the hunt, but I'm going to need more details if I'm to write a proper ballad. Come. We'll talk while we eat." He turned to Jade. "The feast is ready."

Ferth looked around, disappointed when Suza didn't appear. As he and his wolves followed Marko and Jade into the citadel, he wallowed in his novel feelings of contentment. He stopped at the threshold and looked up at the familiar murals, so at odds with his current state of mind.

On the north wall, Draco warriors stood over their human kills. It was not long ago that Ferth had aspired to that hollow victory. He nodded in greeting to the giant painting of Prince Nogard streaking across the sky. He didn't focus on the display of perverse pleasure on the south wall, but instead turned to the west, to the fifteen-foot-tall portrait of Queen Mavras with a crown of flame. Her regime had ended. As had his father's. As surely as every reign ends.

"She did not look like that," Rom said, nose turned toward the glamourized painting.

Ferth turned to Jade. "When are you going to replace that with a giant version of yourself?"

"The past is important. I don't want anyone to forget what we've been through or what we've learned, but I'm sick of looking at these every day. I'm setting up a competition." She looked at the murals. "Whoever comes to me with the best idea, can paint the walls. But there will be no giant pictures of me." She scowled. "There's already an underling around here threatening to make a statue of me."

Ferth stopped listening when he saw Suza come through

a side door. He glided up, his demeanor calm but his insides a swirling dance. "You are beautiful."

She'd changed out of her coat and now wore fitted brown pants with a simple white tunic, tied at the waist with a weapons belt. Lush brown hair hung to her shoulders, and brilliant emerald eyes smiled at him above a wide mouth. "You're clean."

"Enjoy it while it lasts."

She stepped closer. "I intend to."

His pulse skittered as he took her hand and together they joined the head table. Ferth shoveled food in with one hand, keeping his other holding onto Suza, afraid if he let go, she would disappear, and this wonderful dream would vanish. Under the table, she wrapped her palm over his thigh. The spark that shot up his core was very real.

Tobin told the story of their travels, only letting Ferth pipe in once or twice. Ferth was glad though. He didn't want to dilute the pleasure of this moment with his words. Besides, Tobin did a good job painting Ferth a hero. No one mentioned Jade's trip to Mitera where she didn't kill Ferth but did end many others. No one mentioned the battles they fought from opposing sides of the war.

The wolves stalked the halls, intimidating people and looking for scraps. Keturah came in, and after hugging and kissing and wiping her tears, Ferth ate until he couldn't move. Tobin kept talking until Ferth stood, unable to sit any longer.

"Thank you for a wonderful meal and a warm welcome, Your Majesty."

Jade held up her chalice and nodded. "You will always have a room here. Er…. Do you want a nicer room? I just had to kill an officer with a grand suite. It's yours if you want it."

"As appealing as you make that sound, I'll keep my barrack room."

Suza in hand, they stepped down from the high table. Ferth passed many familiar faces, some hostile like Dara, some friendly like Beto. All conversations for another day. Tonight was for Suza.

He told his wolves to get lost then picked up his blanket from his room and took Suza to the roof, his hiding place as an underling. Together they sat under the moon and stars. He wrapped an arm around her as she rested her head against his chest.

"I thought you were going to stay in Elysium," Ferth said.

"And I thought you weren't going to leave me." Hurt made her voice soft.

He held her tighter. "I don't deserve you."

"Something for you to work toward then."

He laughed, his body relaxing. He brought a hand up to the head leaned against his chest. He buried his fingers in her silky hair. Her curves pressed with warm weight against him. "I promise to never stop endeavoring to be worthy of you, but best to keep your expectation low."

"Too late."

She tilted her head back to welcome his kiss. She tasted of hope and heat. Her tongue was thick and sweet, and her body melted against his. When he pulled back, starlight turned her eyes to glittering gems. She shifted her gaze to look over Shi Castle.

"Did you ever imagine we'd end up here like this? That we could make our home here together?" she asked.

His wide lips curved up into a sly crescent. "I've got something for you to see."

"Tell me."

"I'd rather show you."

FIFTY-SIX - HOME HAS A HEARTBEAT

SUZA

A castle.

The surprise Ferth had been teasing her with all winter was a hidden castle.

Suza laughed, letting stunned amusement bubble through her chest as they stood in the center of the high mountain pass. Four wolves sprinted across the marble road, racing to the crystal pools beckoning at the north end of the valley, below a breathtaking waterfall. Xandra flew through the tall pines and whispering aspens in a state of ecstasy. Spring coated the valley floor in wildflowers. Before them, the white castle glittered in the morning sun.

"I cannot believe someone as cruel as Nogard could create such beauty."

"There is good in everyone," Ferth said. "He just chose to hide his behind a wall of stone and scales." He held out his hand and bowed. "Your humble home awaits, my queen."

She snorted but took his hand.

"I hope you like it."

She did. Skies, did she ever. When she got over her fear that someone or something was going to jump out at her from every corner, she relaxed enough to take in the simple splendor. The halls were airy and light with massive fireplaces and solid pine furniture. They walked through a dining hall that was far too big for the lone table. Dust covered the cutting block in the kitchen. A blade lay across it, the wooden handle dry and splintering, but the Dracosteel still sharp.

Hand in hand, Ferth and Suza walked down a marble hallway, tall windows giving ample light. Each door led to a bedroom, and each bedroom had a separate personality.

"Twelve bedrooms," Suza said as they entered the one at the end with a view of the waterfall. "Why would the Dragon make this place if he could never use it?" She ran her hand over the fur blankets that weighed down a wide feather bed.

Ferth picked up coarse homemade paper and a bone pen from the table. "The Dragon I killed could not have done this delicate work."

"Are we not alone?" Her hand drifted to her short sword.

He ran a finger through thick dust, revealing a polished table underneath. "No one has been here for years."

"But who lived here before? Who created all this beauty?"

They found their answer when they came upon a massive boulder behind the remains of an unattended vegetable garden to the southeast. Chiseled into the rock they read the words:

Herein lies Saxon, Aaron, Hibor, Shade, Mickel, Rod, Ethan, Choal, Kitt, Petey, and Nallon.
My brothers in life and in death.
Let this castle stand as a monument to our lives. We dedicate this valley to the wives and children we will never see again in this world. And to our first and greatest queen, Ima. Though the Dragon imprisoned us, kept us as unwilling subjects, he could not destroy our minds or cage our spirits. We built this dream in the

hopes that someday the Dragon will be defeated, and those worthy souls would see our work, remember us, and honor us by carrying on in our place. Bring fire to the hearths and happy children to the halls. This valley was born of blood and pain. May it end with peace and love.

Nogard's greatest desire was to be king. He viewed this valley as his kingdom, and in his broken way, tried to rule well. Never forget that Nogard brought the stones and felled the trees. He laid the foundation and paved the road. This beautiful monument bears his mark too.

Live with honor.
I am Urick, the last to die.
Year of the Dragon 198

Below that was an embellishment in the shape of a plum-loch blossom and lastly the words:

All must conquer the darkness to discover the light.

Ferth and Suza leaned against each other as they read and reread the passage. Suza didn't bother to wipe the tears that fell.

He ran a finger over the names of the soldiers. Little more than a hundred years since they'd been imprisoned here but a world away from the freedom Ferth now enjoyed. "Can you imagining knowing you were trapped here forever and then choosing to spend your life creating a paradise that might never be found?"

"But we found it. You found it," Suza said. "And I want to stay. I want to chase the shadows away and fill the vases with flowers." She looked up at the man who held her heart. "Stay with me?"

"Forever."

She looked over his shoulder at the incredible castle, built by these unconquerable men.

"Do you think the others will come looking for us?" They'd spent the winter at Shi Castle, happy in their reunion and helping Jade build the foundations for a new Skotar. They'd snuck out three days ago, not telling anyone where they'd gone.

"They'll be our first visitors," Ferth said. "But I hope they don't come too soon." He leaned down and kissed her. His lips promising a future full of love.

She sank into him, realizing that it didn't matter where they lived. He was hers. She was his. She pressed her mouth to the pulse below his jaw.

Home had a heartbeat.

And she'd found hers.

*V*isitors did come, and many did stay. Among the jagged cliffs and frozen steeps, the city in the mountain grew into a paradise of peace and prosperity.

Marko and Allie built a home at the base of the cliffs. They lived there for three years before Allie and Marko both gave birth on the same day, Allie to a screaming baby girl and Marko to a howling tiger hewan.

Keturah stayed with her daughter, Jade, in Shi Castle, until she felt the deep pains settle in her belly. She made her final trip up to the mountains and breathed her last breath while looking into Ferth's golden eyes and human face.

Jade and Tobin and their children had travelled up with the weary Keturah. They stayed as long as Jade felt she could be away from the country that was a constant struggle to keep control of. Jack sometimes wandered up alone and would stay for days, tagging along with the wolf packs, before returning to her master at Shi Castle.

Ipsum died that first autumn, his soul returning to his first love, Pelussa. Tobin commissioned a raven statue in his honor and often watched the sky with longing.

Jade established a steady trade with Elysium, selling timber, Dracosteel, and stone for all manner of fine goods. She looked forward to her annual meeting with King Darius in Kiptos every spring. It was a never-ending battle to keep the lawless Dracos from poaching humans and attacking her loyal subjects. Many Dracos worked hard to overcome their blood, but many more refused to surrender their traditions of pride and violence.

Queen Jade never gave up, and Tobin was there to tend to her after every fight. As the decades passed, lasting change settled over her country. And in Elysium too, where Draco humans were welcomed, and hewans could walk freely through the streets.

It was many years before Mira and Titus came north with Uriah and Imanna and their four children. All but their youngest, Zemira, was accompanied by a hewan.

Shem brought his daughter, Callie Poe, now grown, to see the land of her heritage. They did not stay long.

Uriah's family stayed two summers, at the end of which, they all welcomed Zemira's new hewan, a black cat. She named the hewan Opal, in honor of the hero she'd grown up hearing about. Reluctantly, Imanna and Uriah and their boisterous herd returned to Elysium, where King Darius succeeded in convincing Uriah to serve as his premier raja and heir to the throne.

Mira and Titus, silver-haired and serene, stayed and made their home in the mountain sanctuary. When Ferth returned Eio's canine to him, the lion laughed in disgust at the offering. No sane creature wanted their old, gross teeth. Ferth hung it on a nail in the dining room, but it spent the most time as a toy in the children's nursery. Another thing Eio never understood.

Ferth and Suza had twin boys named Callidon and Uriah, but they probably should have switched their names because

Cal's hewan was a bear and Uriah's hewan was a coyote. Their daughter, Miralee, brought Ferth endless joy. She was the treasure of his life, although her falcon hewan was a little tyrant.

That first summer Ferth and Suza had moved into their sparkling city, Rom mated Aisha. She birthed her litter of pups a week before Amber gave birth to hers, a point of pride for Rom that never faded. The wolf packs grew and spread over the northern mountains. Rom and Lyko grumbled about the amount of time they spent managing *illiterate idiots*, as Lyko liked to put it, but Ferth knew they took as much pleasure in their packs as he did in his children and thriving home.

The tributes in the southeast corner of the garden grew. Next to Urick's final words, they chiseled in the many names of those who'd sacrificed all in the battle for freedom and justice. Their lives had not been given in vain.

Ferth never let any who dwelled in the valley forget.

Callidon.

Poe.

Zemira.

Opal.

Guap.

Pelussa.

The list grew longer with time. After Mira died, Ferth put her name next to Keturah and Suza's mother.

Each spring, when the long winter released its icy grip, Lyko and Rom would bring in a magu. While the valley feasted, hearts full of gratitude and bellies full of health, Marko would tell stories. His deep, penetrating voice wove tapestries of perseverance, courage, humanity, forgiveness, and love.

These heroes have passed on to higher spheres, but their stories remain.

Guides for every brave soul to follow.

Let us carry the sacrifice on. Carry it on.
Grant us their mantel of honor that we might carry it ever onward.
Ever forever onward.

ACKNOWLEDGMENTS

Thank you to Monster Ivy Publishing, to Amy Carpenter for taking over this project with energy and optimism. Thank you, Rich Storrs, for doing a fantastic job editing this entire trilogy. And to my critique partner, Tiffany Blanchard, for her edits. Thank you to Cammie Larsen for another fantastic cover and Adam Gray for the map. Thank you to my family for being there for all the bits, good and bad, and championing me all the way. My baby brother, Daniel, deserves the credit for naming Nogard. Which is, after all, dragon spelled backwards.

As always, I thank God for every good thing in my life. And a million thanks to you. Thank you for following this far. Thank you for reading *Dragon Blood* and *Wolf Pack* and coming back for more.

ABOUT THE AUTHOR

Mary is a Whitney Award Nominee and received a Crowned Heart of Excellence Review and a 5-star Readers Favorite Award. She loves exploring our magnificent planet and finding all the best places to eat around the world. She's been a daydreamer since childhood, but after having profound difficulty learning to read, she couldn't be more surprised to have fallen in love with books. If she's not in her writing chair, you'll probably find her painting or hiking in the Utah mountains with her husband and four children.

Connect with Mary at her website www.mary-beesley.com and on Instagram or Twitter.

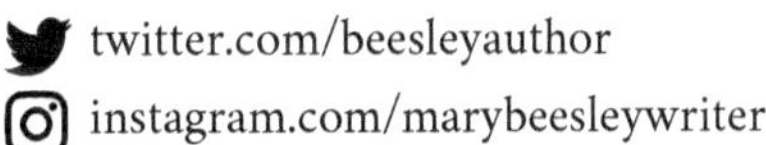

twitter.com/beesleyauthor

instagram.com/marybeesleywriter